Flaw in the Tapestry

by

Joyce S. Anderson

PublishAmerica
Baltimore

ISBN: 1-4137-6487-8
PUBLISHED BY PUBLISHAMERICA, LLLP
www.publishamerica.com
Baltimore

Printed in the United States of America

To my mother, Miriam M. Sloan
and
To all the mothers, daughters and grandmothers who weave
the daily tapestry of our lives.

Part I

Chapter 1 〜❧ *Annie*

"What do you mean, you've been practicing the blue tongue syndrome?" Annie was in the midst of her weekly catch-up talk with her friend Sarah in Florida. With the new long distance rate of five cents a minute, it only cost about a dollar. And although they loved email, it would never supplant the human voice. "Blue tongue means that instead of saying exactly what you want to say, you bite your tongue until it turns blue! I do it all the time with the kids."

Of course, Sarah's kids were not really kids. Her youngest, a son of 28, was single. Her daughter, 33, was divorced. And her oldest at 40 was married with one son. Sarah remarked, "I have one of each kind of young adult available. And no one has come back home to live. Yet!" She had a somewhat ironic view of life and Annie loved talking to her each week.

Annie had the twins when she and David had been married only a year. They were now 36, beautiful Tessa of the long dark hair and Saul, her protector by virtue of his four minute seniority. They had been inseparable through childhood and even though each was married with children, Annie often thought the bond between the brother and sister was the strongest bond they felt.

Grandchildren were the topic of the day. Sarah's grandson, Andrew, in particular. "They use the damn 'time out' when it makes no sense," she complained. "I'm dying to just tell them that. But whenever I share what we did in similar situations, they switch to the long suffering mode and tell me that times have changed. Well, I have news for them, times may have changed, but children haven't! Any way, I practiced the blue tongue yesterday when Andrew's mother told me what Andrew said to her. He's twelve years old and should know by now that he can't talk to his mother that way."

"What way? What did he say?"

"They were arguing about his homework for a change. She was nagging him. It's a constant struggle. He apparently, told her it was his homework and she should leave him the "f---" alone!"

"He used the ' F' word? Oh, my. Poor kid. I bet that he and his friends use it. But to use it with his mother was not a good idea. So what did she do?"

"She gave him a time-out. He had to sit in the time-out chair for an hour and not do or say anything. Supposedly a time of contemplation and repentance. Probably just exacerbated the situation, since he had an hour less for his homework."

"Well, what did we do when that happened? It's certainly not a rare occurrence. That word has been around for a long time."

"I can't remember that happening. But if it had, I think I would have told him we would talk about the 'F' word, later when we both calmed down. And while he was doing his homework, I would have thought up a punishment to fit the crime. Like having him find out the derivation of the word — For Unlawful Carnal Knowledge. Then we would have talked about the Fifth Commandment, once more with feeling, and how one honors thy father and mother. And dishonors them with such language."

"Sounds good to me. The time-out just made the kid angrier and more resentful. Sitting for an hour and seething. And he had less time to do his homework."

Annie and Sarah had been around this subject before. Comparing notes on child rearing and how the methods had changed but the ways of children had remained amazingly the same. Kids were very smart at manipulating their parents, sensing indecision and moving in for the advantage from the time when they were toddlers. Even infants. It took a wise parent to stay in charge and mold character and temperament. " A never ending endeavor," Annie liked to say.

Some days Annie felt that she worried about her children and their offspring too much. She and David had raised the twins during the 60's and 70's , a completely different era, before the microwave oven and the two paycheck family were the norm. She started her freelance writing when the twins were four. She often said that she needed to talk to people who were over three feet tall. Her writing was her form of talking about subjects other than the daily concerns of diapers, croup and temper tantrums.

Annie had gone to the Columbia School of Journalism after college. There was never any doubt in her mind about becoming a serious writer. Her first job was in New York with one of the big women's magazines as a copy editor. The offices, on 57th Street, were glamorous and her job title sounded wonderful when she talked with her friends. But she soon learned that creativity was less valued than correct grammar and punctuation. Her desk was in a small cubicle , sandwiched in between the copy machines and the water fountain. Constant traffic to both destinations made concentration almost impossible.

Annie left after a year and found a job with one of the small literary magazines. It paid less and she was still in a cubicle. But she had the chance not only to edit copy, but also to review submissions that came in and recommend them for further review. She felt part of the creative process. Most important, she sat in on the monthly editorial meetings with the senior staff. The emphasis was always on the writing. She worked there for two years before she met David.

Their meeting, she liked to tell the twins, was 'kismet'! As was the fact of their birth one year after the wedding. In those days, there were no sonograms to picture the babies in advance, their size and their sex. When Saul and Tessa entered the world, it was a double miracle. Two tiny newborns with their perfect fingernails and their different dispositions. From the first, Saul was quiet and composed, looking around the nursery with an inquisitive eye. Tessa, in contrast, was constantly moving, kicking her feet in time to some inner rhythm. And making herself heard as well. They would mature as they first presented themselves to the waiting world. Saul, calm and sure of himself. Tessa, always in motion, asking questions and searching for the answers. They complemented each other as children and as teenagers. And they were always there for each other. Annie and David felt blessed about that.

After the phone call was over, Annie poured another cup of coffee and sat at the kitchen table looking out through the glass doors to the yard and the autumn landscape. The oriental grasses waved their wheat and mauve colored plumes. She loved the way they lasted until the first snow. The ground was covered with a thick blanket of oak leaves that needed raking and bagging. They had bought the house because of the nineteen towering trees and she didn't mind the work each Fall when the leaves came down. She would never move to Florida where the seasonal changes never came, and the grasses and the palms remained ever verdant.

She thought about her friendship with Sarah, their closeness in highschool and how they had drifted apart when they went off to college. When they attended their 25th Class Reunion, they had been completely out of touch for almost three decades. They fell into each other's arms and talked for four hours straight. Sarah had been divorced when she was still in her 20's. When she remarried, she already had Peter. The two younger children were from her second marriage. Her life had been far more tumultuous in that regard. And she had moved over ten times, living in different parts of the country.

In contrast, Annie and David had moved only three times, from their first apartments to the house they bought when the children were toddlers. Northern New Jersey gave them suburban living with New York City just across the George Washington Bridge. The schools were good and they were two hours from either the seashore or the mountains for vacations. David had done his residency at Mt. Sinai in New York, but they decided against living in the city. Instead, they crossed the Hudson and he joined a practice with two other obstetricians.

Annie learned early in their marriage that being a baby doctor was not a career that lent itself to an ordered lifestyle. The office and the hospital were only a half hour from their home, and David wore his beeper at all times. He was on call on a rotating basis with his partners and slept many nights at the hospital waiting until the baby was ready to arrive. He would come home sometimes at two or three and Annie would get up, warm his dinner and they would sit and talk. Especially if it had been a hard delivery with complications. They did plan vacations when the partners covered for him. All in all, he loved his work even with the HMO hassles. And she learned to live with a schedule that was constantly in flux.

Her writing was her anchor. When the twins were small and went to pre-school, she grabbed the quiet hours in the morning. They were always when she did her best thinking. The dishes waited in the sink. The beds were unmade. She did not answer the phone. She had two glorious hours to write. In those days, she used a portable electric typewriter. She wrote short pieces for children's and women's magazines. Stories and features. Gradually, she sold a few. The pay was minimal. $50. Maybe $75. But having her work in print made her writing legitimate.

Once Saul and Tessa entered high school, the hours from 8 to 4 were hers. She could sit undisturbed and work. Or she could play hooky, take the day off and cook, shop and catch up on talks with her mother. Annie and her mother were close in many ways. She disagreed with the popular notion that growing up to become one's mother was something to be avoided at all costs. Her mother had been a role model, having a career as a teacher in an era when women were supposed to be full time homemakers. She had raised Annie and her brother with the help of a part-time housekeeper. When they were in grade school, they missed her at lunch times and after school when the other mothers were home. It was not until they were adults that they understood she worked because the family needed the income. She enjoyed teaching and one salary was not enough to send two children to college. Annie's parents had been determined to do that.

The phone rang twice and interrupted her reverie. It was David. His voice was tense.

"Annie dear, I'm afraid there's some bad news. I've just had a call from Diane. There's been an automobile accident. Saul is in the hospital. He's pretty well banged up. Broken leg, broken nose and several ribs. They're watching him to make sure there are no internal injuries. Diane has only minor bruises. And the kids are fine, thank God! They were sleeping with their seat belts on. Diane was driving. They were coming home from Connecticut late last night and were sideswiped by another car. The other driver failed the sobriety test. Lucky it wasn't worse."

Annie processed the words. The facts told clearly and neatly as David always did. She felt her body stiffen. Saul's face. His clean profile. Possible internal injuries. Her stomach felt queasy.

"What hospital is he in? Can we see him?"

"He's at Columbia Presbyterian. We can see him whenever we get there. I can pick you up in fifteen minutes."

"I'll be ready."

As she hung up the phone, Annie said the 'F' word. Twice. Whenever people asked the twins when they were little, "Where did you learn that word?" , they always answered , "We learned it from our mother."

Before she left the house, Annie called Mark on his cell phone. She had to tell him what had happened and that she would not be at the gym. And she wanted to hear his voice.

Chapter 2 ✤ *Ruth*

"It's all right, Annie. Mommy's here. Tell me what happened."

Ruth Shaeffer had come home from teaching to find Annie huddled on her bed, heaving great sobs into a sodden pillow. Sonia, the housekeeper preparing dinner in the kitchen, could not explain what had happened. All she knew was that Annie had come home over an hour late and had run crying up to her room.

Ruth gathered her seven year old into her arms and rocked her gently. "Tell me what happened, Annie, so we can make it better."

"You can't make it better, Mommy. I told a bad lie and everyone found out."

"What was the lie, Annie? You can tell me. I won't be angry. I promise."

"There was a birthday party for Susan. I forgot to tell you and get a present. So, I asked Wendy if we could say her present was from both of us. She said okay. Then at the party, when Susan opened her presents, the card just said 'Wendy'. Everyone was looking at me in a funny way. And Susan's mother asked me if the present was from me too. I didn't know what to do. So, I said it was. I felt sick to my stomach. I didn't want any cake or ice cream. When I left, I ran all the way home."

After that recital, Annie started to wail anew. This time interspersed with hiccups.

"Don't cry anymore, Annie. We'll buy Susan a beautiful present and I'll call her mother and explain. We'll take it over together. You'll see. It will be all right."

Ruth found that her teaching job in Ridgewood meant that she had to leave in the mornings by seven. She didn't return until nearly five. She knew Annie missed her more than Jack. The two years made a difference. She had gone back to work in 1941 when Annie was only three. Money was very

12

tight. She and Michael wanted so much for the children. His job as a pharmacist was steady, but his salary barely covered necessities. And they were determined to save for college for Jack and Annie. She was not happy leaving the children, but when she heard of the position at Ridgewood High School, she applied for it and was hired.

The first year back had been very hard. Every morning, Annie would cry and beg her not to go. "Please, Mommy. Don't go now. I want you to help me get dressed. I want you to make me breakfast. I don't want Daddy to do it. I want you to do it."

Ruth would listen outside the front door to hear if Annie's crying had stopped. Usually, when she had to leave, Annie was still crying.

That was four years ago. Now Annie seemed to be a happy second grader most of the time. She liked school and had girlfriends to play with. And she loved tagging after Jack when he would let her. Sometimes, if they needed an extra outfielder for the ball game in the empty lot down the street, he would even let her play. Annie was pretty good at catching and throwing. Not so good when she came to bat.

Ruth had very few friends in Pompton Lakes, the small community where they lived outside of Paterson. Michael had seized the opportunity of working in the local pharmacy when jobs were scarce in 1930. He had worked his way all through school and the twelve hour shifts at work now were taken in stride. The nine to nine schedule left little time to see the children, except in the early morning hours. When Ruth went to work, he would take care of Jack and Annie and see them off to school. He might be home before they were asleep. Ruth did most of the story telling at bedtime.

Ruth had grown up in New York City. She had gone to Hunter College when it was tuition free and earned a Master's degree while teaching as a substitute. She always thought of herself as a New York City girl. She never really got used to living out in the country, or 'the sticks' as her city friends called Pompton Lakes. The house she and Michael could afford was wood shingled with a a porch in front and a big yard in back. It was about thirty years old and needed constant upkeep. Michael loved to mow the grass and trim the bushes. Ruth liked best to come home on hot days, take off her shoes and sit with her bare feet in the cool grass in the back yard. There were lilac bushes, forsythia and a big pear tree that Annie and Jack liked to climb.

One year, Michael planted two hybrid rose bushes. They were called American Beauty. After that, every June, when the first rose appeared, he would present it to Ruth. It was a ritual between them. Annie and Jack thought it was sweet, as in the movies. They didn't see much display of affection between their parents.

The Shaeffers were the only Jewish family in town. That meant Jack and Annie were the only Jewish kids in the small elementary school. They had never come home crying that the other kids had called them names. There was no overt anti-Semitism. One family is rarely a threat to a community. They were more of an oddity. The only house without a Christmas tree. The only kids who did not make their first Communion when they were seven.

"Please, Mommy." Annie had begged. " I want a beautiful white dress and veil like Gerry and Alice will be wearing on Sunday. Gerry's is all floaty and has a satin sash. And Alice's dress is called dotted Swiss. It has puffed sleeves and tiny buttons down the front. Please, Mommy!"

Most of Annie's friends were Catholic and their first Communion was a time of excitement before the big Sunday event. For the children, especially the girls, the highlight was shopping for the dress and the veil. The gossamer veil was attached to a matching headband. Annie was bereft!

"Why can't we be Catholic!" she declared angrily to her mother. "I don't want to be Jewish. I want to go with Gerry and Alice and the other girls to church this Sunday. Why am I the only one without one of those dresses? And they will all have parties too afterwards. I'm invited to the party. But I don't want to go!"

The 'First Communion Crisis', as Ruth and Michael called it, had passed. Annie had gone to the parties after all. And they had made the most of Chanukah that year with presents for eight nights in a row. The children lit the beautiful Menorah with an extra candle for each night. They sang "Rock of Ages" together and told the story of the Maccabee brothers and the Miracle of the Lights. Ruth made each Jewish holiday a special time for Jack and Annie. Passover was the highlight of the year with the Seder and retelling the story of the Exodus of the Israelites from Egypt. When Jack was only three, he had bellowed, "Let my people go!" across the table as they reached the description of slavery and beatings. All the adults were convulsed with laughter. Jack was very proud that he had gotten everyone's attention. And last year, when he was eight, he had posed a a profound question that Ruth would remember for years to come. He asked, "Where were the good Egyptians?"

It was 1945. The issue of Good versus Evil had been brought home by the Japanese attack on Pearl Harbor. It was no longer a matter of looking across the Atlantic as Great Britain stood alone against the Nazis in Europe. World

War II had been raging in both the Pacific and Europe. Michael and Ruth listened to the radio reports each night on the news broadcasts. They had distant relatives in Poland . They had no idea of what had become of them when the Nazis overran the country.

Everyone had a ration book. Jack and Annie liked tearing out the little stamps. No one in the family drank coffee and Ruth would trade their coffee stamps with Shirley Burton, next door for extra meat stamps. The Burtons called coffee, 'the elixir of the gods'! Ruth thought they would become vegetarians in order to have a big pot always brewing on the stove. Ruth and Michael loved tea and kept those stamps for themselves.

During late summer, Ruth would put up pears in glass jars for dessert. Annie and Jack would pick them right from the tree. He always climbed higher than she did, but she did her share of collecting those that had already fallen. Ruth would peel and cook them, adding spare amounts of sugar and cinnamon to taste. She would have liked more sugar, but it was needed for their tea. And the sugar ration was sparse. The glass jars would be boiled and then each jar would be filled to the brim with the soft pears and juices. Then the lid placed carefully over the red rubber liner and screwed on as tightly as possible. Annie was fascinated by the entire process.

The War hadn't touched them directly. Only one of their cousins was in the Armed forces. He had enlisted in the Navy, rather than be drafted into the infantry. He was stationed at the Samson Naval Training Base in upstate New York. Another cousin was doing defense work in the Philadelphia Naval Yard, refitting ships. Everyone was buying as many War Bonds as possible. Ruth and Michael felt it was a patriotic way of saving for college for the children.

Ruth and Michael talked often about Hitler and his fixation on the Jews as the cause of all the ills that had befallen Germany after World War I. They saw the movie newsreels that showed him standing before thousands of cheering soldiers, all with their arms uplifted in the Nazi salute. All shouting "Heil Hitler!" They read the papers each day and listened to President Roosevelt when he gave his radio chats. Hearing his voice was very reassuring. Stirring broadcasts from Prime Minister Churchill in England had convinced them years ago that the Allies would win the War. Now victory in Europe seemed close.

Michael and the children planted a small 'Victory Garden' on the side of the house each summer. Sturdy rows of string beans on poles, carrots, egg plant, rhubarb and best of all, the tomato plants. Watching them grow was a daily ritual for Jack and Annie, as well as weeding in between the rows. When harvest time arrived, Annie thought the best fun was pulling the carrots out of the earth. They weren't very big, but then neither were the tiny purple egg plants.

"They're so little, Dad," Annie said. I thought they would look like the carrots we buy in the store."

"The size doesn't matter," declared Jack. "We grew them. That's what matters. Don't you think so, Dad?"

Michael cast a rueful eye upon their harvest and laughed out loud. "You're absolutely right, son. It's not the size. We grew them. And look at the tomatoes. Three big red ones and the others getting ripe. That's our best crop!"

Ruth cut the rhubarb into short strips and stewed them with sugar. Annie and Jack liked the rhubarb for dessert as a change from the pears every night. And Michael ate the tomatoes with salt and declared them the most delicious he had ever eaten. The Victory Garden each year was a resounding success.

Chapter 3 ❧ Tessa

"It's 2001, Robert. And I'm not your mother making pancakes and fresh squeezed orange juice for breakfast!"

Tessa was in a rush as usual. And now, she had lashed out at Robert. The children had to be dropped off before she went to work. Sally, three, to pre-school and Eric, ten, to his friend Dan's. They would walk to school together later. Every morning was a whirlwind of getting the kids up, washed, dressed, fed and sent off with appropriate papers, books and signed permissions slips.

Robert had made the mistake of commenting that, when he was a kid, mornings had been a family time when everyone ate breakfast together. Tessa had exploded.

"I'm not criticizing you, Tessa. I was just comparing that time with this time."

"Well, times have changed, Robert, in case you haven't noticed. Your mother was a full time homemaker. She had plenty of time to squeeze oranges and bake chocolate chip cookies."

"Give it a rest, Tessa!"

Sally and Eric had their jackets on. They had heard arguments before. Eric, since he was a little boy, when his mother had been married to his father. Big arguments with lots of shouting. That was before the divorce. Now, things had calmed down. He spent every other weekend with his dad. Robert was his step-father and Sally his step-sister. It seemed very complicated to Eric at times. But some of his friends' parents were divorced too. At least, he was not the only one.

Tessa would drop the kids off and then go on to her office . She was an associate with a small law firm in Manhattan. Robert was the sales manager of his family's furniture business. The offices and showroom were downtown. They took the train in from Long Island each weekday, parking their cars at the station. Driving into the city was something they avoided at all costs. At least, on the train, they could do some work. Sometimes, they made the same train. Often, Robert had to be in earlier.

Today, Tessa was just as glad that they would be traveling separately. She would make the later train. She needed time to sit by herself and cool down. To put the pieces back together, as her mother often said. It was the kind of day, when she wondered if she and Robert were going to make it.

Her first marriage to Ivan had been such a disaster that anything would be better by comparison. But that was certainly not the measure to use, she knew. Four years of therapy had helped her see that. Ivan had been the tall, dark and handsome man that every girl, including Tessa, expected to meet. When she did, at twenty three, she fell in love and expected to live happily ever after. It was a fairy tale romance with a big, beautiful wedding and a glamorous honeymoon in Hawaii. The only thing wrong was the ending.

Ivan turned out to be an adolescent inside his six foot frame. He moved from one job to the next, always blaming someone else at work for his own failures. He leaned on Tessa for everything. He was heavy on buying roses for Valentine's Day. But light on sitting down and talking through important problems they were facing. By the time she was pregnant with Eric, Tessa knew the marriage was in serious trouble. She convinced Ivan to go with her to a marriage counselor, but he dropped out after two sessions. She stayed with the therapist and gradually came to recognize her own strengths and weaknesses. Ivan had fulfilled a romantic dream. He had not turned out to be a 'mensch' as her parents put it. By the time Eric was two, Tessa had filed for divorce.

Tessa met Robert in the support group she joined after the divorce. He was the opposite of Ivan in many ways. He talked openly during the sessions. He was not afraid to admit that he had been part of the failure of his marriage. He worked in his family's business and that consumed long hours and intense concentration. He realized now that keeping a marriage alive meant that he had to be there for it to grow. "I just was wiped out when I would come home. I didn't want to talk. I didn't want to go out. She felt lonely and neglected and I know now that she was right to feel that way."

After living with a man who would not talk about problems and who could not make a living, Tessa was drawn to Robert and it appeared to be mutual. They went out for coffee after several of the group sessions. He was very easy to talk to. And to look at as well. Not an Adonis as Ivan had been.

Just as well, she thought. He was about her height with sandy hair, even features and a warm smile. They tried not to talk about their first marriages, as if it were a continuation of the group session. She told him about her job as a new associate at Ryder Simmons. He talked about the furniture business and the world of selling. They knew they were still raw from the trauma of divorce. It was not a good idea to share details of their former mates and what had gone wrong.

Robert had no children and Tessa knew many men didn't want to take on a child from the first marriage. She didn't talk much about Eric, but anyone she dated knew he was a very important part of her life. He spent every other weekend with his father and had midweek dinners as well, but his custodial home was with Tessa. That had been wrenched out of a bitter year long struggle. Weekends with Ivan usually fit the 'Disney World Dad' stereotype. Amusement parks. Sports events. Fun and games. Tessa was responsible for the day-to-day discipline, school conferences and planning for music lessons and summer camp. Compared to some of her divorced friends, she felt her relations with her ex-husband were manageable and fairly harmonious for Eric. That had been her goal. To avoid a divorce war and the bitter aftermath for Eric. She had told him when the divorce was taking place that he would have "two happy homes" instead of one.

On the train into the city, Tessa sorted out the work ahead for the day. As an associate, she reported to both partners, based on the current case loads in the firm. She was working with Tom Simmons on several cases at once, preparing a brief for his court presentation and doing research for another. The morning's hassle over breakfast moved back into her consciousness. She knew Robert didn't expect her to squeeze fresh orange juice. But any reference, obvious or oblique to his mother being a full time homemaker was one of her hot buttons. Her career was important to her.

She had gone back to work three months after Sally was born. They could afford a live in Nanny and were lucky to find Denise, experienced and easy to be around. Tessa had heard horror stories of Nannies who took over your life. Denise was wonderful with Sally when she was an infant and Tessa was able to go to work with a free mind. Once Sally was three, they changed to the pre-school schedule plus after school care. Tessa or Robert would pick her up after work. Eric had his after school activities until 5:00 three days a week and played at Dan's house Tuesday and Thursday. It all seemed to be working.

So, why did she become so angry over his reference to family breakfasts.

Robert did not resent her working. He was interested in her work and appreciative of her income as well. Although he made a good salary plus a share of the profits, their needs and desires continued to escalate. He had cut back his weekday work hours and no longer went in on Saturday mornings. This came after long discussions and negotiations with his father and brother. Tessa learned fast that a family business could be very tense and rancorous.

The father-son relationship and roles carried over from the home to the office. And the sibling rivalry between Robert and his older brother Sam as well. Robert's father had created Design Furniture thirty years ago. It was his baby. He was the President and CEO, Sam was VP Finances and Robert, VP Sales. The management style could be described as loose at best, crisis at worst. But, at the end of each year, it provided a good living for the owners and the employees.

Perhaps, Tessa thought, the reference to family breakfasts struck a nerve because she had always loved the closeness in the morning with her mother and sometimes her dad if he wasn't still at the hospital after a night delivery. Her mother did her writing at home after Tessa and Saul left for school. Usually, breakfast was a bagel or pop tarts and cold cereal. There was no fresh squeezed orange juice. The big containers of 'Homestyle' with bits of orange were fine. Although there was hot chocolate in the winter, if they wanted it.

Her mother would sit and drink her coffee as they ate. They would talk about the day ahead and what was planned for after school. It was a warm memory for Tessa. Robert's remark had jolted her. Now, she realized that it had not been fair to lay on him what she herself was missing. She would call him at the office and apologize. If he wasn't there, she would leave a voice message. She didn't want the bad vibes to linger.

Chapter 4

As they drove to New York, Annie and David spoke very little. She was plunged into her fear for Saul and possible internal injuries. She knew what that could mean; pancreas, spleen, liver, kidney. Each could be serious and have lasting effects. And she was torn again by guilt about Mark. Her hands were ice cold and she jammed them into her coat pockets. She had forgotten her gloves.

When she and Mark had met five months ago at the gym, it was casual. She was on the treadmill and he came in one morning and climbed onto the one next to her. Annie had noticed him before. Maybe in his late 50's. Grey hair, muscular body, graceful walk. He apparently had noticed her too. She found out later, it was not accidental that he was on the adjacent treadmill. He had a towel hung around his neck as he adjusted the speed and turned to her and smiled. She didn't usually talk when she was working out. But he said, "Hello, I'm Mark". She smiled back and said, "I'm Annie". And that was how it started.

Seeing Mark twice a week became a new compartment in her life. Annie had always thought of her life as a structure with overlapping compartments. Different people lived in each compartment. She and David in the center. Tessa and Saul and their families in adjacent compartments. Ruth in her own special place. At times they interacted with each other. During holidays and major events, they all came together. And now there was a compartment where she and Mark found themselves. And it was still in an unfinished state.

As they approached the George Washington Bridge, Annie pulled herself back into focus and looked down the Manhattan skyline as she had done ever since September 11. It was only two months since the terrorist attack had destroyed the twin towers. They had been lucky that no one in their family had been killed or physically hurt that terrible day. Saul and Diane lived on the upper West Side but both worked in midtown, he at an architecture firm and she for an ad agency. They still felt the after effects of 9/11, when they had walked north separately through the smoke and the incessant sirens to pick up their two young daughters at preschool.

Annie broke the silence. "David, how long will it take to tell if there are any internal injuries?"

"At least 24 hours, usually. Although they make keep him longer for observation. We'll know better when we get there."

Annie's mind took a jagged leap to Thanksgiving, only two week ahead. It seemed that every year there was some kind of crisis or stress around the holidays. She had almost come to dread the much anticipated dinners and festivities. The enormous preparation and work involved. And the predictable feelings of anti-climax when it was all over.

She thought out loud. "If there are no serious injuries, and Saul is on crutches for his leg, maybe we should just cancel Thanksgiving dinner this year. It will be too hard for them to drive in from the city as they usually do and stay over."

"First things first, Annie. If it's a clean break in his leg, he handles crutches well. Remember how he did when he tore the ligaments in highschool. Twice. And he's in good shape."

David prided himself on his own athletic abilities. And the fact that Saul had followed his lead and taken part in a variety of sports in school. Saul excelled in basketball with his height, agility and endurance. Along with a 3.6 average, he earned a basketball scholarship to the University of Pennsylvania. Tessa joined him with a 4.0 and a total of 1360 on her college boards. She had also been editor of the yearbook, an attendant to the Prom Queen and voted most likely to succeed. On the side, she played a strong game of tennis and swam like a dolphin. The Bertman twins were seen as superstars by their peers.

Columbia Presbyterian Hospital was like the other major New York hospitals, a huge complex of buildings. They parked in the central garage and found their way to the right building and floor. At the central station, David spoke to one of the nurses. "I'm Dr. Bertman. Our son, Saul Bertman was brought in last night. We'd like to see him. Can you tell me his condition?"

Annie noted a slight hesitation as the nurse answered David.

"He's holding his own, Dr. Bertman. His leg is in a temporary splint. The doctor is waiting to set it later today."

"Who is his doctor? I'd like to talk with him. Can you tell me if he has made morning rounds yet?" he asked.

"He made rounds early. I'll give you his name and office phone number."

"Thank you. That will be fine. May we see our son now?"

Annie listened to the back and forth. "Holding his own" did not sound very safe to her.

They walked down the hall. She was familiar with ICU procedures. Her father had been in and out of hospitals for ten years with heart disease before his death in 1988. In his case, the Cardiology ICU floor was where she would sit and wait for the allowed ten minute visits every hour. Intensive Care Units were formidable in the equipment and monitoring systems. They were effective but it was somewhat frightening to observe a patient hooked up to all the devices, IV tubes and oxygen for constant nourishment and support. As they approached his room, Annie braced herself for how Saul would look as a patient.

It still was a shock to see him lying there. His eyes were closed and he looked quite pale and helpless. There were two wide strips of tape across the bridge of his nose.

"Should we wake him, David or let him sleep?

At that, Saul opened his eyes. "Hey, Mom. Dad. Look who the patient is! Would you believe all these contraptions I'm hooked up to? There are even a few under the covers that you can't see."

Annie kissed his forehead and held his hand. David read the chart at the foot of the bed.

"So, Dad, what do you read that they're not telling me?"

David came to kiss him and replied, "Nothing serious, Saul. And they will set your leg this afternoon, the nurse said."

"Then, why do they have me in ICU with all this regalia?"

"It's standard, Saul. They want to make sure there are no internal problems or injuries. I'm sorry I missed your doctor this morning. Did he say anything while he was examining you?"

"Not really. Just that my leg would be set and he would see me late afternoon. Meanwhile, I am getting jumpy as Hell. I want to get out of here as soon as I can. There's a huge project on my desk that my team has been working on."

Saul's architecture firm had four major divisions: residential, commercial, prisons and historical restorations. Saul was part of the restorations unit. The prisons were the busiest and most profitable part of the company. The restorations were the showcase and for Saul the most important. He had been turned on to architecture at Penn when he took the most challenging course of his four years, Fine Arts IV. It dealt with architecture, sculpture, painting and decorative arts. He was mesmerized by the slides projected in the dark lecture hall. The buildings in Egypt, Greece and Rome. Years later, when he traveled to Athens and mounted the Acropolis to the Parthenon, he could still hear the words of his professor describing the North porch and the caryatids, the maidens who were the columns supporting the roof. By that time, the originals were in a museum to protect them from erosion and duplicates were in their place. But, he still felt the thrill of actually being there.

Saul had come home from Penn that semester all fired up with his goal to be an architect. He had shared his excitement with Annie and David. He was in love with the concepts of space and form and function. The beauty and the order of designing buildings for people to live and work in. It was an idealistic view but they thought it was a fine choice to pursue and encouraged him to enter the five year architecture program. He would have a solid base of liberal arts and sciences as well as his major course load. He always felt it had been the right decision for him. Architecture, especially the research and restoration of buildings with what he called "inherent character", was a career he both enjoyed and appeared to excel at.

"I'm going out to see if I can reach your doctor. I'll ask him when he thinks you can be discharged."

"Thanks, Dad. I just spoke to Diane. She's home with Emily and her strep throat. The fever went down, but there's no way she could take her anywhere. And Beth wanted to stay home from pre-school too. Diane will come up later when Amelia comes in to do the cleaning. She'll keep an eye on the girls for a few hours. "

"How's Diane? Is she okay?" Annie asked.

"She's pretty shaken up. Feels it was partly her fault even though the other driver was drunk. She has always said that she drives as if all the other drivers are crazy. Well, there was no way she could have foreseen this guy. He just swerved into us as he was passing. I'm very thankful it wasn't worse. Emily and Beth were fast asleep with their seat belts on."

"Thank God for seat belts! Have you or Diane spoken to Tessa?"

"I haven't yet. Diane said she was going to call her this morning."

"How about if I go out and call in case Diane hasn't reached her. She should be in her office by now."

But Annie did not go to the phone bank when she left Saul's room. Instead, she found the visitors waiting room and sat in a chair away from the couches and the television set that was tuned into one of the morning talk shows. Several other people were watching and she had to shut herself off in an artificial cocoon to avoid the sound of raucous laughter from the studio audience. She closed her eyes and turned inward, trying to find her center. The technique usually worked.

Annie saw the compartments of her life again as a graphic. The center with David was clearly etched. The one with Saul had become outlined in red — for danger. And the unfinished compartment with Mark was defined only by a wavy dotted line. The picture in her head told the story. Mark had receded in importance. She knew the urgency of the moment had done that. As to whether it would remain that way, she was not sure. Mark had become close to her over the past months in ways she could never have imagined could happen. They were not having a love affair in the conventional sense of the term. *Not yet* — Annie thought.

She opened her eyes, stood up, went to the phone bank and dialed Tessa's number. She would call her mother later when she was home. That call could wait.

Chapter 5

Ruth Shaeffer, at 87, led a remarkably independent life. She had been a widow since 1988 when her husband, Michael, had succumbed to a long struggle with heart disease. He suffered three massive heart attacks in ten years and fought his way back from the first two with a determination to live, the care of fine physicians and a wife who would not let him give up hope.

Each time they sped to the hospital in an ambulance with the siren gong full blast, Ruth would grip Michael's hand and say, over and over, "You're going to be all right, Michael. I'm here with you. I love you, dearest. Don't let go."

Michael had not been a candidate for open heart surgery. He lived those ten years on a fine line of moderate exercise, strict diet and a multitude of medicines. He and Ruth found their pleasures in quiet pursuits; watching favorite movies from their huge collection of tapes, playing the New York version of Monopoly and taking leisurely walks when the weather was right. They both were avid readers. He especially loved mysteries and detective stories. A book about breaking the Enigma code during World War II was his all time favorite. Ruth preferred biographies. Eleanor and Franklin Roosevelt forever intrigued her. Having lived through that era, the revelations of their private lives interwoven with the public were fascinating to her.

Ruth was 74 when Michael died. She still lived in the same garden apartment in Teaneck where they had moved after Michael had sold the pharmacy and they both retired. Between their savings, mostly invested in government bonds, her pension and their social security, they felt they lived a good satisfying life. They had no desire to move to Florida even though the cold winters were not a good time for Michael.

"What would I do in Florida?" he would exclaim. "And we would be so far away from Jack and Annie. I would hate that!"

Michael had always been a strong family man. When Ruth first met him, she discovered that they had been brought up only a few blocks away from each other on the Lower East Side of New York. Michael's parents had emigrated from Russia before the turn of the century and he and his four sisters were all born in the United States. Michael was the baby in the family and quite spoiled Ruth came to learn by his older sisters. His father, Aaron Shaeffer, started as a peddler of women's clothing from a pushcart on Henry Street. He later built his business into a small store where the four girls worked as salesgirls when they graduated from high school. Michael was the only one bound for college. It was a given that he would enter City College since the tuition was free. His mother, Molly, had a dream that one day her son might become a doctor. Instead, he chose pharmacy. The years of preparation were fewer and the goal far more attainable.

Ruth also grew up on the Lower East Side. Her parents were born in Poland, near Cracow. They fled the pogroms and entered Ellis Island in New York harbor in 1908. Ruth's mother, Leah Alpers, always told of the thrill it was to see The Statue of Liberty from the deck of the boat. They knew they had arrived, but they did not know what awaited them ashore. Relatives who had already settled in New York had written and had arranged temporary lodging for them. Benjamin Alpers was skilled as a carpenter and found work on construction nearby. Ruth was born in 1914; her sister Tamar followed in 1916. Their mother maintained a very observant Jewish home. Since all their neighbors were also Jewish, this was the expected thing to do.

In later years, Ruth and Michael compared notes on their respective childhood. How they must have seen each other in the red brick elementary school they both attended. And about the branch library nearby, where they went to borrow books. Reading was important to both of them and speaking English at home was also what they wanted to happen. They found out that they each had objected when their parents spoke Yiddish.

"We're in America, now, Papa!" Michael would say. " We have to speak English. Our teachers tell us that we need to speak English at home. Not just in school!"

He would argue with his father about this. Ruth was less direct, but equally insistent.

"You really speak English, very well, Mama. What you have learned at night school is very good. And the more we speak English together, the easier it will be for you. Besides, when you go for your citizenship test, you have to speak English. And you do want to be a citizen as soon as possible, don't you?"

By the time, Ruth met Michael, they were college graduates. She had been a stellar student and had been 'skipped' through many classes in elementary and high school. She was graduated from college when she was only nineteen. She was teaching on a temporary license when she met Michael at a dance. Once they found out that they had practically grown up together, there was instant rapport. And attraction too. She, petite with dark eyes and dark brown curly hair; he slim, medium height with hazel eyes and blond hair. And a moustache. Ruth found that very dashing. That made up for the fact that he really didn't know how to dance. In later years, she would tease him about that. Especially since she loved dancing so.

Their courtship lasted only six months. The wedding was traditional, in the small synagogue with the wedding canopy, the seven blessings and a reception for family and friends after the service. They went to Atlantic City for a three day honeymoon. Ruth loved Michael's gentle nature. She felt they belonged together from the first night she had met him.

Moving from New York to Pompton Lakes, where he had found a position in 1930, was very hard for Ruth. She missed her life in New York with a passion. And she felt lonely being away from her family and friends. Michael had to adjust as well, but his work was completely engrossing and the hours were long. He had little time to miss New York. Ruth's life became centered on her children, Jack born in 1936 and Annie in 1938. And once she returned to teaching, there was little time for anything or anyone else. On the weekends, she was happy to be home with Annie and Jack. Friday night was always special, when they lit the Sabbath candles and had a traditional dinner, usually roast chicken or brisket. Saturday would be a day for catching up on her personal needs.

On Saturday night, she and Michael often went to the movies. It was the era of the super stars, Clark Gable, Lana Turner, Spencer Tracy, Gary Cooper, and Bette Davis. They both loved the movies. Sunday, they might take the children on a jaunt. When the weather was warm, Ruth would prepare a lunch and Michael would drive to one of the nearby lakes with picnic tables. By Sunday night, Ruth would be preparing psychologically for her return to work Monday morning.

Some Sundays, they would drive into New York to visit Ruth's or Michael's family. These were times that Jack and Annie adored. The trip took about two hours since both families had relocated to Brooklyn. They lived in the Borough Park section in the big apartment buildings on Ocean Parkway. There would be non stop food and much admiration from their grandparents. The long trip back to Pompton Lakes in the evening found both children sound asleep in the back of the car.

The first ten days in August, Michael would entrust the pharmacy to his assistant and the family would take a motor trip. They ventured north to Boston and south to Washington, D.C.. One year they visited Williamsburg and Monticello. Another memorable trip was to the Shenandoah Valley. They wanted the children to see some of the beauty of the country as well as some of the historic sights. Jack was entranced by the Gettysburg National Park and Valley Forge. Annie's favorite was Salem, Massachusetts and the House of The Seven Gables.

When Ruth looked back at that time of her life, she wondered how she and Michael ever found the time or privacy for intimacy in their bedroom. Today, physical intimacy was called flat out — sex. She was never comfortable using that word. It was too brash a noun for her speaking vocabulary. She loved movies ,like *Now, Voyager* when intimacy was hinted at between Bette Davis and Paul Henreid. He lit the two cigarettes and offered her one. It was subtle and nuanced. Not blatant as many current films depicted. There was no need in those films for naked writhing bodies under the camera's all seeing eye. When Gary Cooper rumpled Ingrid Bergman's cropped hair in the sleeping bag in *For Whom The Bell Tolls*, their physical attraction transcended the screen and warmed women, including Ruth, across America.

After the hard years of World War II, their lives returned to a more normal routine. Jack and Annie went on to high school and college. The money they had saved made it possible for Jack to attend Rutgers University and live on campus. Two years later, Annie joined him in New Brunswick at New Jersey College for Women. She had won a partial scholarship based on her grades and a state wide essay competition. Jack's best subject in school was science. His all time favorite birthday present had been a starter chemistry set. Ruth bought it with some reluctance, but Michael promised to oversee any experiments that would be forthcoming. Annie loved to write. She started making up stories with imaginary friends when she was about five, in kindergarten.. Once she was in second grade, her stories took on a life of their own. There would be a set of characters, a plot, usually some dramatic twist and finally the denouement and climax.

Ruth liked to think that Jack had followed his father into the sciences and

Annie had drawn her love of language from her. It might have been reversed, but in those days it was the rare woman who aspired to become a doctor. Jack was encouraged to pursue a degree in medicine, even though it meant four more years tuition beyond Rutgers. Annie's interest in writing remained steadfast throughout college. She had loved words and language from her youngest years. Ruth would regale her with the stories and poems of *Winnie The Pooh*. And Ruth, who had studied Greek and Latin at Hunter , found a kindred soul in Annie. Words were magic to both of them. Annie devoured the English novelists during her teen years. Dickens, Thackeray, George Eliot. *The Mill on the Floss, Jane Eyre, Wuthering Heights,* were books that Ruth gave her. They opened Annie's mind to the richness of the novel and the deep human emotions that coursed through the pages. Later, in college, she read Hemingway, Fitzgerald, Edith Wharton and Evelyn Waugh. She memorized certain lines from *The Great Gatsby* and talked to Ruth about them during one holiday break.

"You know, mama, there are some lines in *The Great Gatsby* that sound as if they could be written about me."

"And what are they, Annie, dear?"

"When Daisy turns to Gatsby after he demands that she say she never loved Tom, her husband, she says, 'You want too much!' Sometimes when I think how much I want to be a great writer some day, that line runs through my head. Maybe, I want too much."

"I know that line, Annie. But, I don't think you want too much. I think it would be worse if you didn't want enough. Do you know what I mean?

"I think so. When I am working on a story or a paper for one of my literature courses, I feel a certain excitement in the writing. Putting the words together at times reminds me of the diagraming exercises we used to do in English class in eighth grade. Most of the kids hated to do it, but I loved it, drawing all the lines to show where the words and phrases fit in. It was a picture of the parts of the sentence. And it all made sense. There was a sort of kind of beauty to it too when I worked it out.

Annie had gone on to become a freelance writer. Her first efforts were stories for children's magazines. Her imagination took off in many directions, with each story usually carrying a lesson for the readers. She had found that the 'hook' as it was called in the publishing world was the lesson the child could learn from the story. Of course, the famous fairy tales all had their lessons, some of which were quite frightening to children. Annie's children usually solved dilemmas by using their own ideas and methods. And the princess did as much solving as the prince in her stories. Girls climbed trees and swam like fish in competition with boys. Annie was an equal opportunity author — ahead of her time. Ruth loved her stories and Annie's success in selling her work.

Ruth had taught English at Ridgewood High School. She also became the advisor to *The Senior Year Book*, a job she enjoyed thoroughly. It gave her a chance to work with some of the best students outside the classroom. There was a stipend attached to it, as well, and that was always welcome. Her regular course load varied through the years. Freshman English was probably the most difficult. The students came in from different elementary schools, with different skills and levels of achievement. She would give an initial assignment the first day of class, to write a paragraph about their summer vacation. From this basic exercise, she could learn immediately who could write a sentence and who could not. As for composing a paragraph with a topic sentence, some exposition and a close — that was a rare treat to find.

The upper level classes were another matter, where essays were based on the literature they were assigned. She had to follow the department syllabus, but she had some freedom in recommending extra credit books reports. Word of Mrs. Shaeffer's Reading List spread to students outside her classes: *Hiroshima, Darkness at Noon, Ship of Fools, Catch 22, Exodus.* Over the years, there were repercussions from certain unhappy parents. Telephone calls to the head of the English Department. A few letters to the Principal.

"Unsuitable subject matter for my daughter to be exposed to!"

"Shocking, vulgar language!"

"There'll be plenty of time for my son to learn about war when he's older!"

Ruth defended her list successfully with the department head and the principal. Their backing was essential and gave her the support she needed. Finally, in the late 50's, as fallout from the McCarthy hearings and 'thought police' atmosphere, a group of parents demanded that Mrs. Shaeffer's Reading List be on the agenda at an open PTA meeting. Ruth looked back on that meeting in 1958 as her finest hour at the school. Of course, Michael was there for moral support, sitting in the first row. And she had carefully prepared her presentation.

When her turn on the agenda, or the grill as she called it later, came, Ruth rose and took her slim copy of *Hiroshima* to the lectern. She began to read from the first chapter, "A Noiseless Flash". She only read for a few minutes. Then she closed the book, and looked around the audience before she spoke. "I believe this book, *Hiroshima*, and the other books on my reading list are not only examples of great literature, but they also mirror the age we live in. All the books are novels, based on the World War II and post-War era, the watershed event of this century. I know your sons and daughters are eager to understand what happened then and what has happened since in this country and in the world. They have told me so. These books are pathways into that understanding."

There was silence. And then the applause started. Some parents were standing. Any disgruntled members were either overwhelmed by the mood of the entire audience or came to see the logic and wisdom of Ruth's presentation. That was the end of formal objection to Mrs. Shaeffer's Reading List. Eventually, many of the books became a standard part of the English syllabus. Of course, Jack and Annie read every book on her list when they were in highschool.

Ruth and Michael planned for their retirement as for other events in their lives. Ruth resigned from her tenured teaching position in 1975. She was 61 and had been at Ridgewood for thirty four years. There was the traditional retirement dinner and presentation of a beautiful Waterford crystal vase. Her colleagues knew she loved gardening and flowers. Michael's plan to sell the pharmacy took until 1980 to accomplish. Annie and Jack wanted to throw a big party to celebrate but neither Ruth nor Michael enjoyed those affairs.

"Everyone feels obligated to bring expensive gifts. And the cost can be exorbitant. It's all over in one night. We'd rather celebrate with a week's trip to Paris!"

"That's fine, Dad. Annie and I want to give you both something special. Let us give you the trip to Paris!"

And so they went to Paris. They had flown to California, Florida and Mexico, but never to Europe. Their week in Paris was memorable, exploring the winding streets on the Left Bank, visiting the museums and famous landmarks. Most of all, Ruth recalled the romance of dinner on the Seine one night, gliding through the City of Light. It was truly magical and they drank a champagne toast to the future.

After their return, there was one more important part of their retirement plan to put into effect. To sell the house in Pompton Lakes and find an apartment in either Paramus or Teaneck. They wanted to live near one of their children. Since Jack and his family lived in Chicago, it was to be North Jersey, near Annie and David and the twins. The apartment complex in

Teaneck gave them exactly what they were looking for. There was plenty of space, light and a balcony as well. Two bedrooms and two baths. And the dining room was big enough to hold family dinners on Thanksgiving and Passover. Most important, to Ruth especially, was being only twenty five minutes away from New York. She had been waiting years for the chance to go to the theater, and ballet at Lincoln Center on a regular basis. Just to walk around Soho or Central Park would be a treat.

Ruth made more friends in Teaneck than she had in all the years in Pompton Lakes. They joined a synagogue and she also became a leader of a Brandeis Women's Study Group. It was a natural segue from her teaching and she loved the subjects and the women who attended. Their ages ranged upward from the early thirties. Most were in their 50's and 60's. One of the sharpest members was 83. The syllabus arrived yearly from Brandeis University. Ruth had always enjoyed leading meaningful discussions based on readings and these women did their homework! Several became close personal friends as well. That proved to be a bonus. And especially important, she knew, in the thirteen years since Michael had died.

Her health was holding with the help of a beta blocker to stop the palpitations, and Fosomax for the bone density loss. And Ruth still took a half hour walk every day when the weather was good. She was alone. That had been an enormous adjustment. But she was only fifteen minutes from Annie and David. This gave Ruth great comfort. She talked with Annie every day.

"Hi, Mama. How's the day going?"

Just hearing Annie's voice brought happiness to Ruth. It was her life line.

Chapter 6

"Tessa Bertman"

Tessa had taken her name back after her divorce from Ivan. And she did not take Robert's last name, Silvers, when they married. He said he understood. She always felt good saying 'Tessa Bertman' when she answered her office phone.

"Tessa, it's Mom. There's some upsetting news. It's Saul. There was an automobile accident and he's in the hospital. But he's doing okay."

"Where are you? What happened?"

"I'm at Columbia Presbyterian with Dad. They have Saul in ICU just to make sure there are no internal injuries. He does have a broken leg and nose. But everyone else is fine. They were coming home late last night. Diane was driving. The kids were asleep in the back seat, strapped in. The other driver sideswiped their car. He was drunk. "

It took Tessa only seconds to absorb all that Annie had told her.

"I'm coming to the hospital."

"Tessa, there's no need. He's doing okay. They have to set the fracture in his leg, probably this afternoon. He may be home by tomorrow."

"I'm coming. Now!"

Tessa felt her body stiffen. Her hands had turned icy. Saul had been hospitalized only once, when they were ten and he had to be there overnight for a hernia operation. She had been in with appendicitis in college. To say they felt each other's pain was not a cliche to Tessa.

"What floor are you on? What building?

After her mother gave her the answers, Tessa grabbed her coat and bag, and notified the receptionist that she had an emergency.

"I'll be in touch, Jenny."

She walked quickly to the elevators. It was easy to find a cab and she was at the hospital in fifteen minutes. She found her parents in the waiting room. After they embraced, Tessa asked,

"How is he? Can I see him?"

"The nurses are doing some routine stuff right now. They should be done soon."

"Have you talked with his doctor, Dad?"

"He hasn't called back yet. I left my cell phone number so he can reach me here."

"Are you sure he's okay? The phrase 'internal injuries' is scary."

"They didn't say he had them, Tessa. They have him here for observation."

"Well, this ICU unit gives me the creeps! It reminds me of Grandpa Michael, when he was in the ICU before he died."

"Tessa, you need to calm down. You'll upset Saul if you take that mood in with you."

"I won't upset him, Mom. I don't have to tell you how close we are. I just want to make sure he will be fine."

They sat without talking for about five minutes. Then, David's cell phone rang.

"Hello, this is Dr. Bertman."

"Dr. Bertman, this is Dr. Desmond. I saw your son this morning."

"Thank you for getting back to me, Dr. Desmond. Can you tell me his condition? I know the fracture in his leg has to be set. I am concerned about any signs of internal injuries."

"Up to now, I can tell you, his vital signs are good. He sustained a hard blow to his head when the crash occurred. As you know, his nose was broken. But, he was conscious when he was admitted. And they kept waking him through the night to make sure there was no skull fracture. There appeared to be a mild concussion. But he seemed alert this morning when I checked him. I'm sorry to add that the X-rays of his leg show a complete fracture with two definite breaks."

"It sounds as if he may not be playing any Sunday morning basketball for a long time."

"We can't really predict that at this point as you know. He's still young and if there are no complications, his leg could be stronger than before when it heals."

"I appreciate your sharing this with me, Dr. Desmond. Thank you, again. Good bye."

David filled Annie and Tessa in on what Dr. Desmond had told him. They both absorbed the news about Saul's leg and possible long term effects.

"I'm going down the hall to see him," Tessa said. "I won't say anything about his leg."

"You go ahead,"Annie replied. "We'll be in here or getting some coffee. There's a machine at the end of the corridor."

As Tessa approached Saul's room, she heard someone yell, "Stat!" and saw two men in uniform running with a huge machine down the hall. They pushed open the door to the room next to Saul's and she breathed an enormous sigh of relief.

Tessa had hated hospitals ever since Grandpa Michael had died. Her own experience with the emergency appendicitis had not been traumatic. Her father and mother had come to see her late on a Saturday night, when she called and complained of "a strange stomach ache." Her father had asked her to describe it and then said, "We're coming to see you." She had been studying for a final exam and was sitting cross legged on the bed when they arrived at midnight. Her father examined her and she was at the hospital in an hour and operated on by two a.m. When she awoke, her parents were at her bedside and the next day there were flowers from Saul. Her greatest regret was that she would miss the exam and forget all the facts and dates she had memorized!

With Grandpa Michael, it had been very different. He spent weeks in the cardiology ICU. They were only allowed to see him for ten minutes at a time. Tessa remembered the tissue paper feel of his hand when he would reach out to touch her face. The blue veins were so clear through the skin on the back of his hand. He would smile when she came in the room. She had been his favorite, she knew. He loved Saul, but Tessa with her dark eyes and quick movements had endeared herself to him from childhood. She could do no wrong as far as he was concerned. She knew he would take her side in any argument with Saul.

When he died, she was bereft. And any time she had entered a hospital since then, the very odor of disinfectant in the halls made her queasy.

Saul's door was ajar. She knocked as she said, "May I come in? Are you decent?"

"Tessa! I knew you'd be here. Come on in. The nurses are gone."

She moved swiftly to the bed, bent down to be embraced in his strong arms. She kissed him on the cheek.

" Oh, your nose, Saul.! And your leg. Do they hurt?"

"Not too bad. They've given me pain pills. The leg should feel better when it's set."

"Where's Diane? Mom told me they're all fine. Thank God!"

"She's home with the kids. Emily still has the strep throat and a fever. She'll be here in a few hours when Amelia comes in."

Tessa and Diane were not particularly close as sisters-in-law. Perhaps it was that Tessa would never have been satisfied with any woman Saul married. She had been super critical of most of the girls he dated when they were in highschool and college. She knew he had to have a life of his own. And fall in love with someone some day. But she really had trouble letting go of him to any other woman. Saul had been hers for so many years. And only hers.

Grandma Ruth had pointed out an article in *The New York Times* to Tessa about research that showed there was far less friction with mothers-in law than with sisters-in-law. It refuted all the old mother-in-law jokes and showed that in today's families, mothers-in-law often gave considerable baby sitting time as well as contributed financial help when needed. By contrast, sisters-in-law often felt they were in competition for status and recognition. Tessa had no problems with Robert's mother. They had become truly fond of each other over the years of the marriage. They respected each other and Tessa felt Robert's mother really understood why she wanted to pursue her career in the law. She never said anything disparaging about the children having a Nanny or going to pre-school. She was supportive in any way she could be. Based on what some of her friends reported, Tessa felt blessed.

When Tessa was going through her divorce, Diane was far from empathetic. Saul, of course, was there for her in any way he could help. But Tessa felt a certain aloofness from Diane just when she most needed warmth and comfort. Perhaps, Diane sensed the special bond between Saul and Tessa and resented it. Diane might see her as a rival for Saul's feelings and attention. Tessa had made some small attempts to reach out to her, for Saul's sake, but they were met half-heartedly. Their relationship could best be described as civil and polite.

Tessa and her Grandma Ruth, on the other hand, were close in many ways. As children, Saul and Tessa had loved visiting the house in Pompton Lakes. It was almost out in the country and they had fun climbing the same pear tree their mother had climbed as a little girl. Grandma Ruth would tell them stories of when their mother and Uncle Jack were children. About the Victory Garden during World War II. And how she was a highschool English teacher and would bring home books for them to read. Sometimes they stayed overnight as a special treat. Grandma Ruth would play cards with them. All the games they liked. And she played fair, not letting them win all the time.

Now Tessa and her grandmother shared a passion for *The New York Times* Crossword Puzzles. Each day, they would exchange tips if one of them became stuck on a clue. The puzzles became progressively harder from Monday on. And Saturday was even more difficult than the big Sunday puzzle. Tessa did the puzzles in pencil. Grandma Ruth never used anything but a pen! She said research showed that doing puzzles kept one's brain active and involved. She was definitely better at them than Tessa.

When Grandma Ruth and Grandpa Michael moved to Teaneck, they started receiving *The Times* every day. Grandma Ruth wondered how she had ever lived without it. Of course, in the years when she was teaching, she would never have had time to read it. Now, it was, as she said, "The staff of life!" It was another bond between her and Tessa.

Tessa learned after her divorce that the ties she had to her family were both a strength and at times a crutch. During therapy, she came to see her closeness to Saul, in particular, as a barrier to giving herself completely to any other man. Being a twin had forged a unique bond. She had told Saul all her secrets since they were children. Even when they were adolescents, they had confided their inner most thoughts, fears and dreams. Some were tied to their sexual development. Tessa was very self conscious when her body changed and her breasts rounded. She couldn't bear being teased when she started to wear a bra. And Saul made sure his friends made no joking comments about his sister. He was her protector in many ways.

Tessa needed a man in her life. After her divorce, she had felt a deep emptiness. There was the shared custody for Eric and the nights and weekends he was with Ivan were very hard for her. She did a lot of crying. Her mother and Grandma Ruth both tried to help with comfort and advice. But it was Saul, who helped her accept what her therapist was telling her.

" You didn't make a bad decision, Tessa, when you fell in love with Ivan and married him. At the time, it seemed right. We all liked him and his family. Maybe that was the problem. We couldn't see him in his own light. When you found out he was just a great big handsome kid, you made the hard decision to leave him and take Eric with you."

"But, it hurts, Saul. It is so hard to be alone. And Eric is very confused with the going back and forth. Even though I told him that he would have 'two happy houses', he knows something is very wrong. He has been crying a lot. And having tantrums."

"Little sister, it does not sound easy. But I know you can do it. And it will get better. You'll see."

When Saul called her, 'little sister', it was his sweetest form of endearment. And his confidence in her helped her in large measure to face the present and deal with it. Which she did.

Her life now with Robert was good — most of the time. They had their arguments, usually she knew due to her own thin skin. As this morning, when she had jumped on him during breakfast. She often felt the pressures of being a working mother. She had taken a maternity leave when Sally was born and returned after three months. She felt she was on the infamous 'Mommy Track' and would have made junior partner if she were a man. But, she would not leave the firm. There were certain advantages and flex-time was available if she needed it. Her aim was to be made a full partner, but that seemed a long way off.

Tessa sat in the one arm chair as Saul seemed to become sleepy. Having his leg set later could be quite an ordeal. She shuddered to think about it.

"Take a fast nap," she said softly. "I'm going down the hall to find Mom and Dad."

Chapter 7

Cafeterias near noon in hospitals were very much the same. Big and busy. The doctors, nurses and orderlies in their uniforms, usually talking animatedly. Surgical staff, still wearing the shower caps. Other personnel in street clothes with official badges. The visitors, easily distinguished by their dress and their demeanor. They often just sat, without talking, and nursed their coffee as David and Annie were doing.

"So, do you think he's going to be okay, David?"

"I do. But the double break in his leg will take plenty of time to heal."

"And how do you think Diane will cope with that? She is at her wit's end with the baby home with strep throat. She relies on Saul to do so much with the children and in the house. It's a good thing she has Amelia."

"She will just have to cope, that's all! I get sick of her prima dona routine at times. I know she came from a family with all that money and all those maids, but that was then. And this is now."

"David, she's caught in the same bind that Tessa and other working mothers are at times. Their children get sick and they are supposed to be at work. I never had that, working at home. I don't envy them that pressure."

"Well, she doesn't have to work. Saul makes a good salary. A lot of her income goes to pay Amelia."

"David, that is the classic uninformed argument against working mothers. I really hate it!"

Annie and David had been around the bend on this before. She would quote the statistics and the reasons mothers with pre-school children work. But he really wasn't interested in argument on that basis. He had come from a traditional home and that had given him his life view on the subject. As far as he was concerned, Tessa and Diane had made their choice and they had to deal with crises when they occurred. He resented any time Annie was called upon to help by babysitting a sick grandchild. He, of course, was always on call and was not expected to lend a hand.

Annie knew there was no point carrying the argument on the subject of working mothers any further. She and David always ended up at the same place. Stalemate. Tessa and Saul would tease him and call him their 'chauvinist Dad'. And sometimes it wasn't teasing.

"Let's get lunch, David. I'm getting hungry."

"Fine. I haven't eaten since five this morning when I finished the delivery."

As they picked up their trays and started down the line, his beeper went off.

"Dr. Bertman. Yes." He listened and then responded.

" How close are the contractions? How much has she dilated?"

"Okay. This is her first and just the beginning. Keep in touch. I'll be there in about an hour."

Annie was very familiar with these conversations. She knew David was always there for his patients when they needed him. There were many times when he had left a dinner party and driven to the hospital over the speed limit. Today, he would have time to eat his lunch first.

They told Tessa they were going home and stopped in Saul's room before they left. He was fast asleep. Tessa went down in the elevator with them.

"We'll be in touch, dear. Talk to you later. He seems to be doing fine."

On the ride back to New Jersey, David turned on the Joplin tape and they spoke very little. He dropped Annie off and went on to the hospital. Once inside, she hung up her coat, moved the clothes from the washer to the dryer and went up to her desk. It was the place where she felt most herself. She sat in the swivel chair and pulled her center back together. She would call Mark, but not until her mind and feelings settled down.

First, she thought about David. When she had met him, it was 'kismet', she told the twins. She felt as if she already knew him. Perhaps, because he had the physical qualities that had always attracted her. He was tall, just under six feet, loose and lanky. His features were uneven; nose a little too big, craggy eyebrows. Soft dark eyes. They met at a party given by one her friends in the city. They started to talk and 38 years later were still talking. She had never slept with anyone until she met David. In those years, sex was seen in a very different light. For girls like Annie, it was off limits until marriage. Her mother had drummed that into her as soon as she started dating.

Annie was thin, pretty and popular with the boys in highschool. She knew how to make conversation and put them at ease. And she loved to dance. The fact that she was also very smart did not scare off the boys she was interested in. Later, in college, she had several love affairs that never quite went "all the way". She often thought now that it would have been better than the heavy necking and petting that ended up with sweaty frustration for both of them.

When she met David, she was 25 and ready to find the right man to marry. She felt she had dated enough men to recognize him when he came along. She and David fit together so naturally when they talked. And danced. And went to bed in his apartment after their third date. She told him it was the first time, and he was very gentle with her. He would always prove to be a considerate lover in the years to come. He came to understand about all the years of holding back. Her inhibitions about nudity and having sex with the lights on were still factors in their love life. She had never slept with anyone else. And she was pretty sure David hadn't either. Even when he went away to medical conventions in Chicago or San Francisco or New Orleans.

David was not a complicated man. He had married for love and forever. He was sure of himself and completely committed to Annie and Saul and Tessa. His life was centered on his family and his work which he loved. If temptation had come his way on the trips, Annie was pretty sure that he would have not succumbed. At home, he simply had no time in his life for any extracurricular activities. Sex was important to him, but not an obsession. It was ironic, Annie, often thought that as an obgyn, every day would really be concerned with sex in one way or another.

And now, Annie's thoughts segued to Mark. He was four years younger than she, but it didn't seem to matter to him or to her. When they had first met at the gym, and started to talk on the treadmills, it was the second time in her life that she felt she already knew a man. After their workout at the gym, he asked her if she wanted to go for a cup of coffee. It seemed completely natural to say, "Sure." They showered, dressed in the locker rooms, and drove in their separate cars to a nearby Deli. When she slid into the booth, she realized that if one of her friends came in, she wouldn't know how to introduce him. That didn't happen and they talked for two hours.

Mark worked at a design firm, where he was a commercial artist. That paid the rent and the alimony. He had been married and divorced twice. He had no children. To some extent, he was a free spirit compared to Annie. He told her his first love had always been painting, but his works had never been recognized. He exhibited oils and water colors at art shows and sold a few. Won a few prizes too. But he had never been asked to present a show by a gallery owner. He had hoped for such a breakthrough for many years. He was still painting. And still hoping.

Two days a week, he did his design work at home in his studio. Those mornings, he also spent several hours at the gym. He was paid on results, not clocked by the hour.

Annie told him about her writing. How she had moved from the world of children's stories and features to articles on a wide range of subjects. She did write some short stories, but the markets were very tight and the returns were regular. Usually with printed rejects. Once in a while, an editor made an encouraging comment before writing that it was not quite right for them.

She confided something to Mark that first morning that she hadn't even told David. She was thinking of writing a novel.

They had met on a Thursday. Annie remembered that as they left the Deli, Mark said, "Will you be at the gym on Tuesday?" "Yes," she answered, without even thinking about her calendar. Over the weekend, he entered her mind more than once. And on Tuesday, she saw he was already there, when she came in. They found adjacent treadmills.

"So, how was your weekend?"

"Nothing spectacular. I'm working on an article about parents and adolescent children. How to improve communication between them."

"Sounds challenging. From what I've heard from some friends, their teenagers are into a lot more than just pot."

"That's an understatement. The latest research shows that teenagers are engaging in oral sex because of Aids. Does that blow you away? Oops! No pun intended."

He just smiled at her response. Annie found she could say anything she wanted to Mark. He was not shocked easily. His full name was Mark Trianos. He was from a Greek Orthodox family with two younger sisters. His father, Christos, had started out as a baker and later owned two large successful diners in Newark. Mark had learned to cook and bake from both his father and his mother. He told Annie that he made a delicious baklava as well as a "memorable moussaka". Annie, who adored Greek food, was impressed.

Going out after their workout became a given, but Annie wanted to avoid the neighborhood places. She told Mark why, and he smiled an enigmatic smile.

"Why are you smiling? How would I introduce you to my friends?" she

43

said.

"You would say, "This is Mark Trianos.""

"And then?"

"What do you mean, and then?"

"Then, they would call me up as soon as they got home and ask me, 'Who is Mark Trianos?' And what would I say?"

"Whatever made sense. Like. He's my treadmill friend. Or he's an artist and I'm interviewing him for an article. Or, he's this sexy guy I see twice a week and mind your own business!"

Annie laughed. "Oh, that's great. Very helpful!"

The solution came one Thursday, when Mark said, "I made baklava last night. Do you want to come to my place? I make marvelous coffee too."

He lived in a townhouse about half an hour from Annie's home. The walls, as she expected, were hung with his pictures. Mark took her coat and gestured around.

"I'll make the coffee. You take an unguided tour."

Large abstract oils with clashing brilliant colors dominated the living room. Pen and ink with water colors were hung in the dining room and up the stair well. Many were nudes; others were profiles of women. One set of nudes were ten poses in positions that Annie found very erotic. She felt as if she were intruding just to be looking at them. She and David had several original paintings that they had bought at art shows over the years. Most were portraits that had attracted them for the subject matter as well as for the medium. The largest was an oil of a young girl, seated with birds and cats. The artist called her "The Fortune Teller". She reminded Annie of Rima, the bird girl in *Green Mansions.*

"So, what do you think?"

"I'm not sure what to say, Mark. I have never understood abstract art. When we go to the MOMA, my favorite place is the curved wall with Monet's 'Water Lilies'. They touch me with their serenity and limpid beauty. We visited his home once in France and I saw the Japanese bridge, the water lilies, the weeping willows. Seeing his paintings, the dreamy greens and blues, brings it all back. I just sit there and feel at peace."

"Peace is not what my oils are about, of course. When I worked on most of them, I was in a state of anger, fury or deep frustration. I painted most of them during the fifteen years of my discontent with two failed marriages and a job that bored me to distraction. The slathering of reds and purples and blacks makes that pretty evident, doesn't it. If you're looking for peace, it's no wonder they are not for you. And I've sold very few of them. The water colors with pen and ink have sold better. They're not as hard to live with."

Annie took a chance with her next comment.

"Was one of your wives the model for the series of ten nudes? They've very powerful."

"Yes. Elena and I were highschool sweethearts. We practically grew up together. Two Greek families. It was taken for granted that we would marry some day and we did."

"What happened?"

"The storybook ending fell apart when we could not have children. She blamed herself even though tests showed she was fertile. She was a traditional girl, patterning her life on that of her mother. When no babies arrived, she became withdrawn and angry at the world. And at me. That was before some of the anti-depression drugs we have today. We stayed together for twelve years. Then, she discovered I had found female companionship elsewhere. Her family urged her to divorce me. The fallout was that the two families still feel the bitterness of the divorce."

"I'm sorry, Mark."

"Those pictures of Elena were also a focal point during the divorce. Her lawyer charged me with exploiting her. He called the pictures, 'filth'!"

Annie didn't know what to say. She had gone over to Mark, and kissed him on the mouth. She still remembered how that had felt. He looked at her, sighed and said, "Let's have the baklava."

Since that day, Annie and Mark had gone back to his town house more than once. There had never been any other physical contact. Annie wondered at times, what he saw in her. She knew what she saw in him. She loved the fact that he was younger and an artist. That, and his being Greek, were new worlds to her. He apparently was as interested in her stories of growing up in a traditional Jewish home. And he wanted to learn more about writing, where the inspiration came from. As far as physical attraction, Annie knew she was still a "looker" as Saul put it. Her hair, although no longer blond, was cut short and frosted with ivory streaks. She still kept to her 110 pound weight and it was in the right places. She dressed in the same sport clothes as Tessa. David always complimented her on her looks and her clothes.

David. Annie was brought up short in her reflections. Did she feel guilty about her relationship with Mark? At times, yes. But, she would quickly rationalize that they had not crossed the line. They were not having an affair. They were not going to bed upstairs in his town house or anywhere else. She could not deny that she often thought about doing just that. She had never been unfaithful before. But then, the temptation had never been as great. And the opportunity as well.

She called Mark on his cell phone. He picked up on the first ring.

"Hello."

"Mark, it's me. We just got back from the hospital."

"Is Saul okay?"

"He's doing pretty well. No internal injuries, thank God. But his leg is broken in two places. Not good. They're going to set it this afternoon."

"How are you doing, Annie?"

"I'm okay. But seeing him like that shook me up some. His nose is broken too. I'm just sitting here and trying to sort out my life for a change. David has a delivery and left for the hospital."

"Do you want to come over? I have some spanikopita left from last night. I'll give you a taste with a cup of chamomile tea to lift your spirits."

"Maybe. I have to call my mother first, Mark. Talk to you in a while."

"I'll wait for your call."

Part II

Chapter 8

Ruth Shaeffer was in her living room when the telephone rang. It was 2:30 and almost time for a nap that she took most days, sitting on the couch in the sun. She would just put her head back on the curved cushion and doze for about an hour. It was a delicious feeling. She still rose at 7:00 every morning and by mid afternoon, the day often caught up with her.

"Hello."

"Hi, Mama. Did I interrupt your nap?"

"No, dear. I'm awake. How are you?"

"I'm fine, but I have some unpleasant news. Not serious, though. Not to worry. Saul was in an automobile accident and is in the hospital. He has a broken leg, but he should be home tomorrow. Diane and the children are fine."

Annie was always concerned when she had to convey bad news to her mother. She tried to put it in the least upsetting terms. She heard the pause, as if Ruth were catching her breath.

"Are you alright, Mama?"

"Yes, dear. I'm alright."

"David and I went to the hospital. He's at Columbia Presbyterian. David spoke with his doctor and we feel he's in good hands. Tessa was there too."

Ruth knew Columbia Presbyterian well. On Washington Heights, it was the hospital where Michael had been twice. She would not want to visit anyone there. It brought back too many memories of hours, sitting and waiting for the doctor to tell her how Michael was doing. Ruth hated being in limbo more than bad news. She could deal with bad news. But, when she had to wait for anything, it raised the anxieties she had felt all those years in the hospitals.

Now, her thoughts jumped ahead two weeks to Thanksgiving.

"Do you think you will still have the big Thanksgiving dinner, Annie?

"Sure, Mama. Saul knows how to handle crutches and Diane will drive. She was driving, by the way, when they had the accident. It was not her fault. The other driver was drunk and side-swiped their car. Emily and Beth were strapped in and asleep when it happened. They're fine."

"Thank God!"

Ruth had stopped driving when she was 83, after her cataract operations. Her vision was 20/30 afterwards, but she was not comfortable behind the wheel. She had given up driving at night years before. It was not an easy decision to lose the freedom and independence her car gave her. She did not want to call upon Annie or friends to take her places. She used buses whenever possible. There was excellent service to New York and to the nearby malls. Annie did take her once a week to the supermarket and that was welcome. There was also a local taxi service that was fairly reasonable to use. It was a major adjustment in Ruth's life, but she dealt with it.

She sold the car and used the money to splurge on a trip to Florida with Rachel, one of her close friends. They spent a delightful two weeks in Sarasota with the opera, the theater and warm balmy weather. It was February, the bleakest of months to Ruth. She disagreed with T.S. Eliot about April being the "cruelest month." She had always been restless in mid-winter, eager for Spring and the first daffodil tips in her garden.

When she and Michael lived in Pompton Lakes, Thanksgiving was the time when the family gathered in their home for the traditional holiday feast. After they moved to the apartment in Teaneck, the setting shifted and Annie and David became the hostess and host. Ruth would bring one or two of her signature dishes, like the cornbread and apricot stuffing. She would cut the apricots up and soak them overnight in apple juice until they plumped up. Everyone loved her stuffing and she loved making it. She was not much of a baker and had always relied on guests or the local bakery for apple and pumpkin pies. One year, Michael bought a mince pie which proved to be a flop. He was the only one who ate it and liked it.

After she hung up the telephone, Ruth knew she would skip her nap. Instead she reached for her needlepoint. She had learned to knit and crochet in high school when there were Home Economics classes for girls and Shop for the boys. She envied the girls today who knew how to wield a hand saw as well as a needle. When her great grandchildren were born, she had crocheted carriage blankets in a shell pattern and matching tiny hats with satin ribbons and a pompom. She gave Tessa the yellow set and Saul the aqua. Tessa was thrilled and Diane had seemed pleased as well. Although she also used a pink cashmere carriage blanket her mother had found in one of the Madison Avenue boutiques.

Ruth had started doing needlepoint after her retirement. She began with a relatively small project, a pillow for their living room. It was a floral and the colors were creams and blues. A large iris, it reminded her of the clump of bearded iris next to the house in Pompton Lakes. She was pleased with the results and ventured to make seat covers for the dining room chairs. This turned out to be a major endeavor, since the pattern was more intricate and far more demanding. After completing two, she decided to use them just for the armchairs. The other four chairs would remain with the solid seats. She rationalized that it looked as if it had been planned that way.

Now, she was working on a wall hanging. If it turned out well, and Tessa admired it, she was planning to give it to her as an anniversary gift. It was a copy of the Unicorn Tapestry that she knew Tessa loved. They had seen the tapestries on a visit to the Cloisters Museum years ago and Tessa had been enchanted with the colors and the intricacies of design. As well as the story.

Ruth spent most of her hours alone. The first years after Michael's death had been the hardest. They had shared half a century of living together and she had felt as if a part of herself was missing. Every morning, she had to realize all over again, that he was gone. She did a lot of crying the first year when she said Kaddish each day. She knew it was a prayer of affirmation of God and life, but she felt her spirit was crushed.

"Oh, Michael", she would say softly. "I need you."

Annie was there as much as a daughter could be to help her during those months. Jack, with his life in Chicago, she saw infrequently. He would call once or twice a week just to keep in touch. When he came with his family for Thanksgiving, it was a huge effort. Sometimes, he would fly East for a conference in New York and then spend an overnight with her before returning home. Those visits were the best. She had him all to herself and they would talk for hours into the night about his work and his life. Jack's schedule as a physician was very different from David's. He was an internist in a joint practice with two other men. They worked regular hours and took time for planned vacations. Ruth was proud of his accomplishments — her son, the doctor.

Jack had married late, when he was 42. Before that, he had been immersed in his work and completely indifferent to any social life. When he did marry, it was impulsive and bound for failure. She was 20 years younger and flattered by his attentions. He was hungry for affection and ready to take it when he found it. She was a nurse and they could talk the same language. That helped ease his comfort level. Jack had never found it easy to make conversation with women.

They were married at City Hall, after knowing each other for six weeks. And no one in the family had a chance to meet her before the wedding. It had been a severe shock to Ruth and Michael when they were told. The marriage lasted a year. Two years later, Jack began dating a woman his own age whom he had met through a friend. She had a child from her first marriage, but that didn't seem to be a deterrent. In fact, Ruth thought it turned out to be a plus. When he and Lois were married, her son, Ted who was eleven, was an usher at the wedding.

Ruth did her best thinking when she was doing her needlepoint. It gave her a chance to let her mind roam freely, while her hands worked. She had always felt that she wanted to do something worthwhile with every day. When she was raising the children and teaching, every hour of every day had been full of activity. There was almost no time for assessment. It was all consuming. But after Jack and Annie left for college, and were 'launched' into their respective careers, she could devote more time to her teaching which she found very rewarding. When they moved to Teaneck after their retirements, leading the Study Groups brought her new friends as well as an intellectual challenge. She had given up being a leader four years ago, but she did join one course each year. She loved the structure of the readings and the discussion sessions.

Ruth also belonged to an informal movie group with Rachel and three other friends. They all enjoyed seeing the latest and most avant garde films. They would choose one in particular and spend two hours doing an analysis and appraisal of its merits. Each would give the film a rating on different factors: plot, characters, script, costumes (if relevant), and direction. She enjoyed the give and take on controversial films like *American Beauty* and *Memento.*

"*Memento* may be playing in New York art theaters for a year, but I think it is the worst picture I ever saw!"

"How can you say that? I gave it the highest rating for script and direction. What a twist, that a man would have no short term memory and have to write all those notes on his body! I found it fascinating."

"The flashbacks, running the scenes over and over almost made me run out of the theater!"

And so they would argue. Ruth found it invigorating when there was a good argument. As long as it was about movies, or books or politics which she adored — but not about family matters. Michael had always avoided family conflicts, often at any cost. Ruth had been the one who had to smooth over hurt feelings. When they made the long trip to Brooklyn to see the Alpers and the the Shaeffers, neither set of parents ever felt the visit was long enough. And there was always a tug back and forth as to where they would have dinner. They usually ended up eating non-stop in both homes. Jack and Annie thought that was perfect.

Ruth had been the disciplinarian with the children, a role she did not enjoy. But if she waited for Michael to come home, it was often too late and the immediacy of the situation had faded. Besides, she knew he was too softhearted to ever be angry or firm with either of the children. He would spend countless hours teaching them how to ice skate on the frozen pond nearby. And he swam with them in the summer at Cold Spring Lake, where the geysers of icy water bubbled up and made the entire jaunt a special treat. He had an assistant at the pharmacy on the weekends so that he could have free hours to be with the children. And he would take them out some nights to see the stars, a favorite interest of his. They went reluctantly, especially if it was cold, but Michael would insist.

"There's such a clear sky. Do you see the Big Dipper? And the Little Dipper? And the North Star? The Constellations are so beautiful tonight!"

"I see them, but I'm freezing, Dad!"

"We'll go inside in a minute. Look up, Jack. And Annie. Can you imagine that the light from those stars left there millions of years ago? And it's reaching us now? Isn't that amazing!"

"Yes, Dad. It's amazing. Now, can we go in?"

Ruth smiled when she thought of those nights when Michael took his children out to see the stars. He loved explaining the concept of light years to them. And a solar or lunar eclipse was a major event in their household. Ruth found astronomy interesting, but for Michael, it was a passion. She wondered if it helped balance the mundane nature of his daily work. It certainly was the antithesis of measuring out pills into bottles. Once a year, they would go to the Planetarium in New York to see the celestial show. Annie and Jack loved that part of their exposure to the stars. Years later, they each would take their own children and pass on the planetarium experience as part of their grandfather's legacy.

Some days, as she did her needlepoint, Ruth's reflections were on the past. At 87, she had many memories. Today, she thought, was one of those days. It was comforting to remember where she had been, as well as to think about where she was going next.

Chapter 9

When Tessa returned to her office, she found ten e-mails, and four voice messages. As well as the urgent remark from Jenny, as she had walked through the glass door.

"He wants to see you as soon as you come in!"

'He' meant Tom Simmons. Tessa was working on two major projects for him. She knew that he was waiting for her draft of the brief. It had been due that morning.

She listened to the voice messages before she went into see her boss. The last message was from Robert. He sounded laid back and sweet. She was glad she had called and apologized.

"Tessa, don't worry about this morning. Forget it. I love you and your orange juice, baby. I'll see you tonight."

She loved his calling her 'baby'. He only did that in private. If he was sending her a signal for sex, she got it. They had no arguments in bed.

Robert had left the message before she called him from the hospital to tell him about Saul.

She walked to Tom Simmons office and found him on the telephone. He motioned for her to sit down. She had the folder in her hands and calculated the time it would take to complete the draft. When he hung up, she jumped in with her explanation.

"Tom, I have two more hours and the draft will be complete. I had planned to do that this morning when I had an emergency call. My brother is in the hospital. He was in an automobile accident."

"I hope he's okay, Tessa. But I need the draft."

Tom Simmons was usually a fair man to work for. But quite lacking in empathy. She had expected this type of reaction. He didn't want any details about Saul.

" Yes, they say he'll be okay. I'm sorry, Tom, about the delay. It's 2:30 now. I'll have this on your desk before I leave."

As soon as she said the phrase, "before I leave", Tessa knew it was a mistake.

"You may just have to stay later tonight, Tessa. I need some information on the housing project assignment as well — before you leave."

"I'll do my best, Tom."

Tessa's hours were flexible, to a degree. At times, and this apparently was going to be one of them, Tom would become rigid in his demands. As an associate, the question was not whether to jump, but how high. Tessa hated that part of the job. Someday, she thought, when she was a partner, she would not treat an associate that coldly. She went back to her desk and ignored the waiting e-mails. The brief was her first priority. She had learned, in a time management course, to set aside whatever is expendable and concentrate on the A list. The B's and the Comfortable C's could wait.

At 5:30, she had completed the draft of the brief and walked it down the hall to Tom's office. He just looked up, nodded, and said, "Thanks." She went back to her desk and called Robert on his cell phone. She thought he would be in the car on his way to pick up Sally at pre-school. He answered on the second ring.

"Hi, Robert. It's me. I'm going to be late. Tom insists he needs some work tonight. I think he's just being nasty since I didn't have the brief done this morning. I should be home before nine. I hope. There's half of the lasagne in the refrigerator. The kids are happy with that. I had planned to add a salad for us."

"We'll be fine, Tessa. Order in a sandwich from the deli. Don't try to work on empty. See you when you get here."

It was times like this that made Tessa question what she was doing with her life. She wanted to be home with her family for dinner at night. The evening work shift didn't happen often, but when it did, she found it very hard. And it made her angry. Everyone else was gone and she was sitting there in her office digging up information on the housing project. *Damn Tom Simmons!*'

At seven thirty, she left, locking the office glass doors on her way out. She wanted to make the eight o'clock train. Traffic was not too heavy, and she made the train with five minutes to spare. Once, settled in, she had time to catch her breath. She thought about Saul and called her mother.

"Mom, it's Tessa. I'm on the train. Had to work late. Did they set Saul's leg? How is he?"

"He's good, dear. And he will be going home tomorrow."

"That's a relief. Did you talk with Diane?"

"Yes. She sounded quite rattled. She is not good at handling life's crises, as we both know."

"Well, she's used to Saul being there. He does so much with the girls. She'll have to carry the load for a while. I'm sure that's upsetting her too."

"He won't be able to do much on crutches, that's for sure."

Tessa and her mother had a similar view of Diane. When Saul first introduced her to the family, he had only known her for two months. But, he told them he had met someone special and wanted them to meet her. He had already met her parents at a restaurant in New York for dinner. Tessa remembered that her mother wanted Saul to bring Diane to their home for dinner. Tessa and Robert, who had just married six months before, were there too.

Her mother set a beautiful table and was most gracious and warm to Diane. They all were very welcoming when they saw that Saul was "smitten" as the twins used to say when they discussed respective dates. Diane was smart, sophisticated and attentive to Saul. She was, Tessa and her mother said later, "Almost too good to be true." Robert added diplomatically, "As a newcomer to the family, I reserve judgement. But she certainly has the private-school look. Very well taken care of."

David Bertman was kinder in his assessment. "I like her. Saul seems head over heels. That's good enough for me."

After the train pulled in at her stop, Tessa had a short ten minute drive home. Robert was in the dining room with Eric. The table was covered with the beginnings of his history project.

"Hi, Mom. We missed you at dinner. The lasagne was still good. We left you a little piece."

Tessa kissed Robert and peered at the charts Eric was assembling.

"Looks like you have your work cut out for you. I could never keep track of the English kings and the wars that went on for hundreds of years. When is this due?"

"I have two weeks. Robert was just helping me sort out the different dynasties. There are really great names. Tudors. And Stuarts. And Henry VIII with 8 wives. Did you know that he had some of their heads cut off?"

"I did. It was no fun being one of his queens!"

At that point, Sally came running down the stairs, to smother Tessa with hugs.

"I wanted to see you before I went to sleep. I was lying in bed trying to stay awake until I heard your voice."

Sally felt warm from the blankets and Tessa held her tightly, smelling the sweetness of her. At three, Sally was a bubbly, affectionate child. She loved playing. She loved pre-school. She loved new adventures. Tessa would often say, "Sally loves life!"

"Mommy, will you come up with me and say Good Night to 'Gorgeous'?"

Gorgeous was Sally's favorite doll. She was an old fashioned doll with a Victorian dress and tiny kid buttoned high shoes. Once, Sally had dropped her by accident on the sidewalk and her china head had cracked. Sally could not be consoled with a replacement. Tessa found a doll hospital in the city and had Gorgeous mended at a formidable cost. Since then, she had been restricted to living inside the house.

Tessa tucked Sally and Gorgeous into bed, went back downstairs and joined Robert in the kitchen.

"Should I warm the lasagne for you?"

"No, I did order a sandwich. I'm not hungry. Maybe a cup of hot tea. I could use that."

She sat at the table while he put the kettle on to boil

"So, did you finish the work Simmons wanted?"

"Well, I made a dent. Enough to put something on his desk in the morning. He was very unhappy that I didn't have the brief ready. And when I told him that Saul had an accident, he was not really interested. I know that's how he is. My personal life is not supposed to interfere with my work. Fine! But sometimes, there are emergencies and this was one of them."

She sighed deeply. Robert poured her tea and sat down.

"Well, today I might have traded jobs with you," he said. "Being in a family business can be pretty tough at times. Today was a doozie! Sometimes I feel as if Sam and I are still kids — Sam bossing me around since he's the older brother. And Dad staying out of it, letting us fight it out the way he did then."

"What happened?"

"We have been preparing our forecast for next year. As VP Sales, I work with the reps to project business. It's number crunching based on current customer sales Then we give the forecasts to Sam since he's in charge of finances. Today, we met with Dad to review the projections and Sam cut the ground out from under me!"

"What do you mean?"

"First, he questioned the validity of the numbers. Said our method of projecting was flawed and we were only guessing. From there, it became personal. He said, I had never been good at facing reality in numbers or anything else! I don't know where that came from, but I went ape!"

"What did your Dad do?"

"He just sat there and listened to us as we deteriorated into some pretty rough name calling."

"How long did it go on?"

"About five minutes. Then, I walked out and slammed the door."

"Oh, my, sounds awful. Was that how it ended?"

"No. Dad came into my office and tried to smooth it over. He wasn't actually picking up for either one of us. He rarely does, as you know. Just said, we needed to cool down and take a look at the projections in a day or two. He said he would review them himself and get back to me."

"His hands off style of management may actually be the right one for you and Sam. You will always be the kid brother to Sam, ten years younger. He will always feel that he knows more than you. Wrong assumption, but its always there, isn't it?"

"Not only is it there, but I am tired of trying to introduce him to new methods in the business. Selling furniture is very different today from what it was when Dad founded the business. Sam is always looking at how we did it "in the beginning". I am so sick of hearing that phrase. The reps are out there competing in a completely new market. It's 2001!"

Eric came in to say he was tired and going to bed.

"Is it okay to leave the papers all over the table? I have them in a certain order."

Although Tessa usually tried to keep the living room and dining room as havens of order, she said, "Sure. Sleep well. Come give me a kiss."

Eric had adjusted well to the dual custody since the divorce in 1994. Tessa said he was very resilient, going back and forth every other weekend and one night during the week as well. Several of his friends lived the same life with two homes and two families. There were problems at times with forgotten homework or books, when Tessa had to drive to Ivan's before work and bring them to Eric. Ivan never seemed to be able to get up in time to do the pickup. Solving problems was always Tessa's responsibility as it had been when they were married.

When Tessa and Robert finally went up to bed, she knew the intimations of sex in his voice message had long since simmered out. She was bone tired herself, and wanted nothing more than a hot shower and a soft pillow. They were both asleep by ten thirty. Sex would have to wait for the weekend.

Chapter 10

Annie had spent most of the afternoon with Mark. It had turned out to be far more than a cup of chamomile tea and tasting the spanikopita.

After she had talked with her mother about Saul, she felt at loose ends. She usually did her writing in the morning. Two to four was her least productive time. And today she felt particularly restless. She called Mark back.

"I'll take you up on the offer of a cup of tea. Are you sure you're not in the middle of something?"

"Of course, I'm in the middle of something. But the offer still stands."

"I'll be there in a little while."

"Good."

She washed her face and put on moisturizer and fresh lipstick. And her gold hoop earrings. She wore the same black turtleneck sweater and camel slacks she had worn to the hospital. It was one of her classic comfort outfits.

When she reached Mark's door, he had seen her coming and opened it before she rang.

"Hi."

"Hi."

And then he opened his arms to her and she came into them as naturally as if she had been doing it for years. He embraced her for about ten seconds and then pulled back, looked into her eyes and said, " I've been wanting to do that for a long time. Maybe, from the first time I saw you walk into the gym."

She looked up at him and smiled.

"I guess that makes two of us."

They had their tea and she raved over the spinach pie. Then, she kissed him for the second time since they had met. And they went upstairs to bed. It happened without any discussion. Or asking on his part. Or reluctance on hers. He just took her hand and led the way.

When Annie thought of it now, sitting alone in her kitchen, she felt a storm of emotions. Wild exhilaration mixed with enormous guilt. They had been wonderful together, swept up in their initial passion. Mark was an experienced lover, gentle, tender and in no hurry. She loved that. The light touch of his exploring fingers had brought groans of pleasure from her. He told her she had a beautiful body. His body felt right when he held her closely to him. For Annie, there was mounting excitement and then sweet joy. Finally, contentment. She had fallen asleep in his arms.

When she woke, he was looking at her.

"I think I may be falling in love with you, Annie Bertman."

"Oh, Mark. I don't know what to say."

"You don't have to say anything. I know you're married. I know you love your husband. I'm just telling you honestly how I feel."

"I can only tell you I feel so alive, Mark. I am filled with happiness."

"I'll settle for that. For now."

They didn't talk as they dressed. He walked her to the front door, gathered her to him and kissed her lightly. He spoke softly.

"Don't be too hard on yourself, Annie. You're human not perfect."

"I'll call you, Mark."

When she arrived home, the house was dark. There was a voice message from David, that the patient in labor was dilating very slowly. He would probably be there all night. She reached Diane at the hospital.

" Diane, it's Mom. How's Saul? Did they do the cast for his leg?"

"He's okay. Had to wait hours til they took him. But once they did, it wasn't too bad. Do you want to talk to him?"

"Sure."

" Saul. How are you dear?"

"I haven't had this much fun since I tore my ligaments in highschool."

"You're doing fine if you're making jokes. We used to call you the Crutches Kid."

"At least then it was for a good cause on the basketball court. Oh, well. Eight weeks in the cast, the doctor said."

"Not easy. For you or Diane."

"We'll manage. Diane will pick me up in the morning. Take a cab home."

"Talk to you then. Love you."

"Me too, Mom."

Annie felt as if the compartments of her life were imploding. The space with Mark, that had been unfinished on the periphery, had suddenly become her center. She just wanted to sit and think about him and how she felt with him in bed. It filled her with excitement to remember his caresses. How he had looked at her. What he had said.

She knew she had violated the real center of her life, the compartment with David. And that she had betrayed his trust in her. But she also knew she had not felt this alive in a long time.

Mark had said that she was human, not perfect. But that was a rationalization, Annie thought. How was she going to feel when David came home? There was only one thing she knew for sure. She was not going to tell him what had happened.

When Tessa called from her train, Annie was still sitting at the kitchen table. She had made a tuna sandwich and eaten only half. Food was the last thing she wanted.

She cleaned up the kitchen and went upstairs to bed about nine. The afternoon kept replaying in her head. Then, she called Mark.

"It's me."

"Hi, Annie."

"I can't stop thinking about this afternoon, and you. And how I felt with you."

"Is that bad?"

"I don't know if it's bad. It's just how it is. How are you?"

"I'm good. But then my life is less complicated than yours. I just have me to worry about."

"I talked with Saul. His leg is set and he's coming home tomorrow. And Tessa checked in too. David's at the hospital with a slow delivery. I'm not sure how I'm going to be able to look at him when he comes home."

"You'll be okay, Annie. Remember what I said, about being human. Just be yourself."

"That's the trouble, Mark. Myself is who I was before this afternoon. Now, I'm someone else. And I'm not sure who that someone is."

"I can tell you, that someone is one hell of a woman!"

Annie smiled. She needed that. It didn't solve anything, but it made her feel better.

"Good night, Mark. Sweet dreams."

"Good Night, Annie."

David came home about three a.m. She stirred when he got into bed, but didn't say anything. Usually she would ask if the delivery had gone well. She was afraid he might want to switch on the light and talk. She knew she wasn't ready to face him. He turned and settled into his side of the bed.

The afternoon flooded back into her mind. *Mark!* She tried to push it away. But she couldn't. She drifted off to sleep thinking of him. She would face what she had done, tomorrow — at Tara, like Scarlett.

Chapter 11

When David's alarm went off at seven, Annie was already downstairs. She had made the coffee and brought in the papers. She was sitting at the kitchen table reading *The New York Times* when he came down. He usually made early rounds at the hospital at eight.

She tried to talk as they usually did. As if everything were the same and yesterday had not happened.

"How did it go last night? I heard you come in but I was out of it."

"First baby. It went well. Over eight pounds and she's not a big woman. She was exhausted with the pushing. And so was I by the time it was over. I had to use the forceps."

"Boy or girl?"

"Girl. They were very happy about that. I think it's a myth that parents want a boy first. They both seemed delighted. And they didn't know in advance either, the way so many parents do. They wanted to be surprised. It was refreshing."

"Sorry I missed your call in the afternoon. I was out at the Mall for a few hours."

The lie was not easy for Annie. And it hurt her to look at David and say what she did. She was reminded of the Native American tale about each of us having a triangle in our heart. When we tell a lie, it turns and the points hurt. After a while, when we tell enough lies and it turns many times, the points of the triangle are worn down. It becomes rounded. And it doesn't hurt anymore to tell a lie. She wondered if that was the road she was starting down with Mark.

David told her he had talked with Saul right after she did. He was, of course, pleased that his leg was set and he would be home today.

"Do you want some toast or cereal?"

"Not really. I ate something at the hospital after the delivery. I'll have an early lunch later."

They leafed through different sections of *The Times* and *The Bergen Record* as they drank their coffee. They liked to compare notes on special stories and columns. If David wasn't home in the morning, Annie would highlight articles in *The Times* and leave it for him on his desk. She tackled the daily crossword puzzle just as her mother and daughter did each day. It was a time for her to lose herself completely in the mental challenge. Today she needed that more than ever. She didn't want to think about Mark while she was sitting across from David.

"I'm going. Call me later and let me know if Saul is home and okay."

He kissed her lightly on her bent head. She looked up at him and saw that he was the same man he was yesterday It was she who was different. She said in as normal a voice as possible,

" Hope your day goes well. See you tonight. Call me if you're going to be late."

When she heard the front door close, she stopped doing the puzzle and sighed deeply. She knew she had to work on the article. She had a deadline to meet and it would be the best thing to become immersed in her writing. It would take her away from the turmoil in her mind and her heart. At least for a few hours, she would not think of Mark Trianos.

When Annie was writing, she didn't answer the telephone. She had realized years ago, that working at home to many people meant they could call her at any time. It was then that she stopped being available. She would check her messages at noon. Her family and close friends knew not to call her before then, or after eight at night. By then, she said, she was all out of words. She would call her mother each day to make sure everything was going well. Usually after lunch. She knew that phone call would also be hard today. Her mother could sense in her voice when anything was troubling Annie. She often said she could tell just by the way Annie said, "Hi, Mama" if there was a problem. So it went with mothers and daughters. Annie felt the same way about Tessa.

She worked for three solid hours, incorporating the interviews she had conducted into the narrative of the article about communication between parents and their teenage children. Using the direct quotes was a time honored technique in such pieces, and she enjoyed bringing their voices to life. It was something like the Japanese movie, *Rashomon*. The parents and the adolescents seeing the same situation from entirely different perspectives.

Their recounting of an incident that had occurred in their homes would have a completely different slant. Their assumptions were different to begin with. And their needs.

Annie enjoyed working on this type of article. She felt there could be valuable insights to present to the readers. In this case, the readers would be primarily the parents. The emphasis in the article was on listening as the most vital part of communication, and the part that most people often overlooked. She drew on research studies to show that most people think of communication as sending rather than receiving. This is of central importance in families and in all forms of human relationships. As she developed this theme, she found she could not divorce herself completely from her own life. And what had happened.

She stopped writing. Looked out the window and thought about what she and Mark had said yesterday. With their words. And with their bodies. When he said he thought he might be falling in love with her, she had no real response. She only knew how she felt. She was drawn to him physically and emotionally. And his mind excited her when they talked. She loved listening to him explain why he painted. And he listened intently when she told him about her writing. They had learned about each other through many months of listening. And they sensed the physical cues as well. There were more than intellectual interests developing between them. That had become evident yesterday

At noon, she called her mother

"Hi, Mama. How are you today?"

"Annie, you sound as if you've been working hard this morning. Is the article going well?"

"Yes, it's going along pretty well. You'll enjoy the quotes from the parents about their unmanageable teenagers."

"Well, I never had too much trouble with you and Jack when you were teenagers. Of course, your father left most of the managing up to me. Do you remember?"

"I remember lots of times when you were the bad cop and he was the good cop."

"Exactly! I would have to be the disciplinarian. And he would listen to all your complaints later, when he came home from the pharmacy."

"It wasn't until I was raising Tessa and Saul that I appreciated what you had to do, mostly on your own. I had much of the same with David having his irregular hours at the hospital. I would have to deal with a situation with them when it was still hot. By the time, he came home, they both were calmed down and he would wonder what all the fuss had been about."

"Did you talk to Saul? Do you think he's home by now?"

"I'll give them a call and let you know what's happening. What time is your movie?"

"Rachel is picking me up at two. We're going to see " A Beautiful Mind" . It's supposed to be very powerful. It will give us a lot to analyze in our discussion next week."

Annie was continually impressed with the range of her mother's activities. She had recently enrolled in a course that took place over the telephone with conference calls. It was called University Without Walls. She would enter discussions with people from all over the country, often led by retired teachers just as she was. She called some of the people she had met through these courses her "telephone friends".

"Enjoy the movie, Mama."

"Bye, dear."

Annie reached Saul, found he was settled at home and Diane was frazzled from the trip to the hospital and taking another day off from her job. She was trying to arrange with Amelia to come in for a full day for the next few weeks. Annie did empathize with her and the dual pressures of home and work, now exacerbated with taking care of Saul's needs as well.

"How can I help, Diane? Maybe do some cooking for you?"

"Thanks, Annie. We can order in for a few days. And then I'll take you up on it."

Diane was not comfortable with calling Annie, 'Mom'. She and most of her friends called their in-laws by their first names. For their part, Annie and David were not comfortable with this, but they had gone along with it to save Saul a conflict with his wife. After five years, Annie was still not really used to it. She felt it lacked respect for her position in the family as well as warmth. She and David had decided to do the 'blue tongue' and let it be.

She called her mother and left the message that Saul was fine. And then, she could not stop her mind from surging back to Mark. She knew she wanted only one thing. To be with him again. Her senses were aroused just thinking about him.

"Mark. It's me."

"Hi, Annie. I've been hoping you would call."

"I want to see you. Is this a good time?"

"Do you think I've been doing anything other than wait for you?"

"I'm on my way."

This time, when she arrived, they stood for about a minute just looking at each other. Then, he took off her coat and slowly undressed her in the living room. The Roman shades were drawn and the light was filtered. He stood behind her, slid off her sweater and unhooked her bra. Then he cupped her breasts in his hands and drew her back close to him. She felt her nipples harden and wanted desperately to turn and face him, but he kept her in that position. Next, he eased her slacks and panties down to her ankles. She couldn't move. And her knees felt weak.

"Mark, I feel as if I'm going to faint."

"You're not going to faint, Annie. I'm going to make love to you as you've never been made love to before."

His hands moved down over her hips and he bent to caress her legs slowly. Then he lifted her in his arms and carried her to the couch where he took off her shoes, socks, slacks and panties.

Annie was completely naked, lying in the half light, and she felt as vulnerable as she ever had in her life. It was frightening and thrilling at the same time. Mark stood and looked at her. He was fully clothed and that excited her even more. He eased one of the pillows under her head.

"Please, Mark. I can't stand it. I want you!"

"I want you to want me, Annie — as much as I want you."

He undressed and came to her. His mouth first on hers for a long sweet kiss. And then he entered her and they were one, as they had been only 24 hours before. Annie felt as if she were drowning in her passion for him. It was far beyond her control. She cried out aloud when she reached her climax. He had waited for her to be there before he joined her.

They lay together for some time before Annie spoke.

"Oh, Mark, I don't even know who I am."

"I know who you are, Annie. You're beautiful. And loving. And the smartest woman I have ever met."

"Flattery will get you everywhere with me," Annie said with a smile. "But, I'm not young anymore, Mark. Do you think that's why we're good together? Because we have all those years of living and loving behind us?"

"Well, my years have been rocky. My marriages going bad. And the women in between only lasting for brief times before they burned out."

"Do you think we're going to burn out?"

"I don't know, Annie. I don't think so. Yesterday and today were explosions

69

waiting to happen. And they have. But we're grownups. I know you have a husband whom you love. And you have built a family with him. Where we will fit in, I just don't know. We will have to work that out."

"We're in uncharted waters, Mark. And I feel as if I have no compass."

"You have a compass, Annie. It's inside you. You've gone off course. That doesn't mean that you should feel guilty."

"Ah, that's easy for you to say, Mark."

"No, not easy, Annie. Just trying to help."

"Just kiss me, Mark. I want to feel and not think."

Chapter 12

Ruth Shaeffer and her friends left the movie, overwhelmed with the intensity of the story and the fact that it was based on truth. *A Beautiful Mind* was about a brilliant mathematician who developed schizophrenia and fought his way back to sanity with the help of his wife. They started talking as soon as they left the theater.

"He should get the Academy Award for that role. Don't you agree?"

"Well, he's won one already. But that doesn't matter. Look at Tom Hanks with three!"

"I don't think I can wait until next week to really get into this movie. Let's go for a very early dinner and talk about it now. How does that sound?"

Ruth, Rachel and one of the other women were free. They were widows and lived according to their own schedules. But two women were still married and begged out of the idea. They all agreed to stay with the original plan, and wait until the following week for their discussion.

Ruth and Rachel couldn't stop sharing their opinions as Rachel drove home.

Rachel commented, "One of my cousins was a schizophrenic. His illness first emerged when he was a teenager. All of a sudden, one day, he started watering everyone with the garden hose. They couldn't control him. It went on for hours, until he was subdued. That was their first experience. It grew gradually worse despite everything his parents tried. Eventually he was stabilized with drugs. But he never resumed a normal life."

"This movie may give the opposite impression."

"Yes, it might. But, this was just one case. And such a dramatic one. No wonder it was made into a movie."

Ruth asked Rachel to come in and stay for dinner. They were very close friends and did not stand on ceremony with each other. Ruth had half a chicken that she warmed with baked sweet potatoes, fresh string beans and cranberry sauce. No bread or butter. They both watched their cholesterol and their weight. Ruth still wore the same size twelve that she had for most of her life.

She believed that her health regimen of never smoking, good diet and keeping active were as important as her mental regimen of reading, taking courses and doing the daily puzzles. And, of course, she had the nurturing of being a part of her family of children and grandchildren. This gave her warmth and consolation when she missed Michael. It was not easy being 87 in a culture that was besotted with youth. She often thought of the traditional lands where the elderly were valued and revered for their wisdom. But then, there was the other extreme, the Eskimo tribes who were known to set the elders out on the ice floes when food was scarce. Perhaps, she concluded, being who she was in the year 2001 in the United States was just fine. Ruth had always been a realist in dealing with life.

She had listened to her answering machine and heard Annie's message that Saul was home and settled. She wanted to hear his voice. She hoped he would pick up — not Diane. She was in luck.

"Hello."

"Saul, it's Grandma Ruth. How are you, dear?"

"I'm doing good, Grandma. Hobbling around on the crutches, but at least it doesn't hurt much. And the kids think it's a hoot!"

"Some hoot! When will you be able to go back to work?"

"I'm going to give it a try tomorrow. Maybe not for the whole day. I need to catch up on some work and it will be quiet in the office. I should be back to my regular schedule by Monday."

"How's Diane coping?"

"She's doing okay."

"Take care of yourself and give Emily and Beth a kiss for me."

"I will. You be good."

"Do I have any other choice?"

"Good night, Grandma. I love you."

"Good night, Saul. I love you too."

Ruth always felt that Diane was not very interested in her. When there were family gatherings, Diane would give her a perfunctory peck and then never seem to find time to sit and catch up on what Ruth had been doing. Her eyes would stray when Ruth talked about the courses she was taking or the books she had been reading. And Diane had no interest in politics, a subject that was almost an obsession for Ruth, Annie and Tessa. Especially during a national election year. They were all fierce Democrats with a big D. They suspected that Diane actually voted Republican although she never took issue with them on the candidates. And she never joined in their political discussions.

Ruth had volunteered as a poll watcher up until ten years ago. She made small contributions to certain candidates. And Annie often teased her that she watched so much CNN and C-Span that she knew the voices of many of the members of the Senate and some members of the House as well.

"Not just their faces, Mama — you actually know their voices!"

"Well, it's hard to miss with some of them, Annie. And I'm happy to say that a few of my least favorite members of Congress are finally retiring this year. I say 'Good Riddance!'"

"You never lose your fire, Mama. You are so loyal. When you believe in something, you never give up. It's amazing!"

"Thanks, dear. I remember what Norman Thomas' daughter said at his funeral, when a reporter said, 'Your father was a fighter for lost causes.' 'Oh, no", she countered. 'My father was not a fighter for lost causes. He was a fighter for causes whose time had not yet come!' I'm happy to say I have lived to see many of the causes I have believed in come to be part of our lives that we now take for granted. Tessa and Saul, and certainly, their children, have no idea what it was like to live in this country before the Civil Rights Movement and the Women's Movement made revolutionary changes. After all, the twins were born in 1965, just as the major laws were passed."

"I remember, Mama, that you wanted to take part in the March on Washington in 1963 and Dad was afraid there might be violence. I had just met David and we watched television together as Martin Luther King gave his 'I Have a Dream' speech on the steps of The Lincoln Memorial. It was a wonderful day!"

After Rachel left, Ruth settled down with her needlepoint and the recording of "La Boheme". She still used her LP records on the machine that she and Michael had bought decades ago. Annie and Jack had wanted to buy her a CD player, but she had her huge collection of beloved albums and she was not ready to discard them. Besides, she knew these singers and their interpretations of the arias so well. This recording of the opera was conducted by Arturo Toscanini. She could almost play it in her head. Michael had loved the Italian operas. They shared that together. And when she listened to one of them now, she felt as if he were there with her.

Her fingers were somewhat stiff tonight. The arthritis was acting up, but she persevered with the needle and the stitches. The threads in the tapestry were a metaphor for the beauty and complexity of life. It was all there in the intricate design. The figures, the rich colors and subtle shadings. Some caught the eye by surprise. *Yes,* she thought, — *an apt metaphor. Life was full of surprises.*

Chapter 13

"Eeeny, meeny, miney, moe. Catch a tiger by the toe. When he hollers, let him go. My mother says to choose this one!"

Sally was using a time honored method to choose which cereal she would have for her breakfast. Eric, looked at his three year old step-sister with a bemused expression.

"That is one silly way to decide!"

"It is not!"

"Is too!"

"Is not!"

"That's enough, children," Tessa intervened. Sally, give me your bowl. Which one did you choose?"

"Sugar Pops."

Eric had the last say, "You eat Sugar Pops every day. What's the point of pretending you want anything else?"

"Please, Eric. She's not bothering you. Just eat your own breakfast."

Sally usually held her own with Eric in a verbal exchange. She would toss her dark pony tail, fix her blue eyes on him and hang on until he gave up. Tessa was sure Sally's persistence came down the maternal line starting with her great grandmother. It was a trait highly prized by all the women who possessed it. Tessa had seen it in her mother and in Grandma Ruth. And now, there it was in Sally. She was sure there was something in the genes!

Tessa felt good. It was a clear sunny day. And it was Friday. The weekend would be especially welcome. She and Robert had their steady sitter for Saturday night. They would go to dinner at one of their favorite French restaurants on Third Avenue, drink a good red wine and enjoy each other later in bed. At least, she hoped it would turn out that way. On Sunday, maybe she would drive into the city to see Saul. Robert would be with Eric at his basketball game, and Sally would go with her. Sally loved to visit her cousins and play with their elaborate toys and dolls. Emily and Beth had a splendid doll house with all the tiny rooms and furniture. Sally was entranced with it.

Robert had left earlier to be in the office before Sam, if possible. He wanted to talk with his father and clarify what had happened the day before. He hated the fights with Sam, just as he had when he was a kid. Now, in the business setting, they were particularly upsetting. Sam knew the money end of the business, but he was essentially, in Robert's mind, a 'bean counter'. He lacked vision, and bucked any of the new ideas Robert brought to the table. It was a constant battle between them to gain their father's ear and support.

Tessa had never known much about the business world. Her father was a doctor and her mother a writer. But, since her marriage, she had a thorough introduction, not only to the business world, but to a family business. And that she soon learned was a world unto itself.

"Eric, are you going to work on your project tomorrow? I would love to have the dining room table back as soon as you can manage it. You do have a desk in your room or we could set up a bridge table if you need more space. What do you think?"

"It's not going to done tomorrow, Mom. And Sunday I have basketball league. But I could move the stuff to my room. I can set up the bridge table myself."

Tessa didn't believe in doing Eric's homework with him. She did keep track of when the big projects were due, but his daily assignments were his responsibility. She had learned that from the way her father and mother had handled homework when she and Saul were in school. It was up to them to have it completed and then they had free time to go outside or watch TV. Sometimes, on beautiful days, they were outside after school and homework was put off until after dinner. The system seemed to work well based on their grades.

Some of Tessa's friends complained bitterly they had to be on top of their kids to get their homework done. Tessa didn't give any advice. She just followed the system she knew with Eric and he was doing very well in school. It was working in the next generation.

She dropped Eric at his friend's house and Sally at pre-school. Then she caught the eight ten into the city. She would put in a full day and hope that Tom Simmons was in a better mood than yesterday. She found out as soon as she opened the outer door, that today was going to be a rerun.

"He's really on the warpath, Tessa!"

"Thanks, Jenny. Any idea why?"

"He just said to tell you he wanted to see you as soon as you got here. And he sounded very unhappy."

She went to her office, hung up her coat and took a fast look at her desk. The brief she had left for Tom was sitting, front and center with a huge question mark in red on the cover of the file. She opened it and found red marks all over the first pages. Question marks. Exclamation marks. A few scribbled notations. It looked like the map of South America. She always had hated teachers using red ink on her papers. This brought the same visceral reaction.

She took it with her when she went down to his office. He was sitting at his desk.

"Good morning, Tom. I gather you are not happy with the brief."

"Sit down, Tessa. We have to talk."

She sat across the desk from him and waited.

"We have been quite satisfied with your work, as you know from your evaluations. I guess that's why this brief threw me. I would never know that you had written it. The reasoning is faulty. The order of the argument is disjointed. And the writing is, how shall I say this — pedestrian."

Tessa knew better than to interject any sort of humor, like Woody Allen's line about the hotel in the Catskills. 'The food was no good and the portions were small.'. She just listened.

"I don't know if your brother's accident got you rattled. But, I need the best from you, when you walk through that door."

"I'm sorry Tom. I thought it was pretty coherent and persuasive. I'll take it back and address the questions and comments you've made."

"And how about the information I needed on the housing project?"

"It is almost complete. Which do you want me to work on first?"

"The brief."

She was not a happy camper as she walked back to her office. If he were a woman, she thought, they would say he was in a snit. Or worse, that he had his period. The stereotypical reactions to someone in a bad mood. And taking it out on his employees. Not good! She wondered what was eating him. Trouble at home? Not enough sex? His wife was something of a 'Dragon Lady', cool and aloof at company parties. Tessa had not been able to make any inroads with her. Maybe she used sex to keep her husband where she wanted him. It was certainly possible.

When she read the brief carefully, she found certain valid questions. She had been distracted when the call came about Saul in the hospital and it showed in the organization of the brief. Other notations and questions seemed far less important, almost petty. Those she addressed as well, but with a skeptical eye. The work took the greater part of the morning. She brought the revised brief into Tom's office.

"I've addressed all your questions and notations, Tom. I think it is much stronger and better organized. I hope this does it."

"Thanks, Tessa. Let me have the housing project material as soon as its complete."

Keeping the pressure on! Not allowing a moment for her to breathe! She wanted to lash out and say, 'This is no way to run a ball game!'. But, of course, she did not. She wanted to keep her job.

She took less than a hour for lunch and worked steadily through the afternoon on the housing project research. It was four thirty when she brought it to Tom's office. He wasn't at his desk and she left it for him in his In basket. She was tempted to put it front and center on his desk, as he had left her brief, with COMPLETE written in red on the cover. But she restrained herself.

She planned to leave by five and make the five thirty train. She didn't really want to see Tom and find out that he had something else for her to work on over the weekend. She went to the ladies room, washed her face and put on fresh lipstick. When she came back to her office, Tom was sitting there and waiting for her. Her heart sank. More trouble?

"Tessa. I took a fast look at the brief and it looks okay. I'm sorry if I came down hard on you. And I'll review the housing research Monday. Have a good weekend."

Slap, lick — slap, lick! Tessa had met that kind of authority figure before. Certain teachers she had studied under. And counselors at camp. Two bosses in previous summer jobs. They kept you unsure and unsteady. Off balance. Alternating their harshness with kindness. She had never liked that kind of teacher or manager. You never knew what to expect.

When she settled into her seat on the train, she started to relax. She would not think about work or Tom Simmons until Monday. The weekend was going to be slow and easy. Doing what she wanted to do, with Robert and the children. Without anyone else pulling the strings!

Chapter 14

Once she opened her own front door, Annie felt as if she were on automatic pilot. As if she were going through the motions and at the same time, watching herself from afar.

She would broil steaks for dinner with baked potatoes. David would be home after rounds and they would eat about seven. And then, she thought, what would she do with tomorrow and the next day?

She had written a long article, "Love and Infatuation", for one of the glossy women's magazines. With a lot of preparatory readings in psychology and literature as well. Poems by Ovid, Rilke and Millay. And Shakespeare's sonnets. It was a complex subject and she had learned much from the research. As she tried to sort out what she was experiencing, she kept coming up with the same answer — infatuation. Wanting to be with Mark more than anything else was at the core. Hearing his voice was thrilling. Even saying his name in her head brought a frisson of pleasure. The sexual intensity of their relationship had overwhelmed everything that led up to it. Love took time. Annie knew that.

When David came home, she was in the living room. She went back on automatic pilot.

"Here I am, David," she called. "Tell me what time you want to eat. I've got steaks."

"I'm just going up to wash and change. I'll be down in ten minutes."

He found her in the kitchen and kissed her as she turned from the stove.

"How was your day?" she asked.

"Just routine for a change. That's okay. All those deliveries in a row. I need to breathe. How about you? Are you making progress with the communications article? And did you talk to Saul?"

"I had a good morning at the computer. And I did talk with Saul. He sounded feisty and eager to be back at work. I thought we might go into the city Sunday and see him."

"Unless someone goes into labor, that sounds fine with me."

So they talked. And ate. And Annie felt as if she were an observer to her own life. Was this how it went? Sharing the news of the day. His and hers. Planning the weekend. Yes, that was how it went on a normal Friday night. But, of course, this was not a normal Friday night. And only she knew that.

David went up to his study to catch up on medical journals and she watched some mindless television, just to stop thinking about Mark.

In the morning, after David left for the hospital to make rounds, she went to her desk and called Mark.

"Hi. It's me."

"How are you?"

She resisted the pull of his voice and spoke somewhat haltingly.

"Mark, I think I — we, need to take a few days off. "

"I understand, Annie."

"I hoped you would. Because the only place I want to be right this minute is with you. I can't really concentrate on anything else. I need to slow down and sort things out as the British say. I think about you and the way I feel with you— constantly! We're on instant replay."

" It's like that for me too. But my life is simpler than yours. I know that."

"I'll see you at the gym next Tuesday. If I last that long."

"I'll be there, Annie. It will be a very long weekend."

After she hung up the phone, she turned on the computer and read the last page of the article she was writing. She had learned of Hemingway's technique in college and found it worked well for her. He always left his work with a paragraph or story line unfinished so that when he returned, it would be natural to pick it up and continue. Today, she read her own writing and it seemed very distant. She had given a quote from an interview with a teenager who felt smothered by his mother. She reread the words and looked back at her notes. She knew that writing today would be a struggle. She began to work. Self discipline was not a stranger. She would have to draw on it to get through the next three days.

She worked through until noon. Finished the tuna salad for lunch. And called her mother.

"Hi Mama. Are you busy?"

"No, dear. I'm having a quiet day. Just staying put. We saw *A Beautiful*

Mind yesterday. And Rachel stayed for dinner. It was a very powerful movie. A must see."

"Maybe David and I will go. I've read a lot about it. We're probably going to drive in and see Saul tomorrow."

Again, Annie felt as if she were a third party listening in on their conversation. There was no one who would be more shocked, she thought, than her mother at what she was doing. Even more than David — if that were possible. Her mother was anchored in her principles that had been formed in another era. You married, for love hopefully, and then you were faithful to each other. There were no exceptions in her belief system. It was in effect, etched in stone. Annie didn't want to think about what it would do to her mother to discover that she was having an affair.

And Tessa and Saul! How would they react? Probably be stunned and incredulous. They certainly knew of stories of infidelity among their friends. But this would be very different. And shocking. Tessa might be more forgiving. But Saul would identify with his father and become angry. He would take the hurt personally. Annie could see all the compartments of her life imploding.

She made it through the afternoon without calling Mark. She reorganized the linen closet and did two loads of wash. Then she went for a three mile walk. The sun was out and the day had warmed. Usually walking helped clear her head and she certainly needed that today. Her usual route took her to the little shopping mall and back. She took time off to go to the children's store and browse in the Girls department. She loved to buy clothes for Sally, Emily and Beth. When each had been born, she had set aside about a dozen outfits in graduated sizes from six months to two years. It was one of the purest pleasures of being a grandmother. One did not have to build their characters, she liked to say. That was their parents' job.

She found matching pants and tops for Emily and Beth. Diane liked to dress them that way. And an adorable pinafore for Sally. She had them set aside and would stop later and pick them up. She never carried money or her credit card with her when she walked. Then she went to the bookstore to see if the new Anita Shreve novel had come in. It hadn't, but she leafed through several others before leaving to resume her walk and the return lap home. On the way in, she picked up the mail. There was a returned manuscript in the familiar big first class envelope. Not what she wanted to find. She wrote most articles on assignment, but still sent out a few on speculation. The envelope was a portent of rejection.

It was a piece she had written spontaneously, entitled "Generation Talk".

It had been sparked by the table servers who always used the term, 'you guys'. It didn't matter how old the customers were, or what sex, they were 'you guys'. In the article, she explored the talk habits of the different generations and how they reflected age, history and values. It was her favorite kind of piece and she was looking for a home for it. When she was not writing on assignment, some of the articles could go out for months or years before they were published. She was thankful for her contacts with certain editors whom she had cultivated over the years. Of course, editors changed and then she had to go back to Go to keep the relationship going with the magazine.

David was home from the hospital. She called up to him.

"The mail's here. Do you want me to bring it up? It looks like junk and catalogues."

"Only if it's good news or money!" David loved that Jason Robards line when he answered the telephone in *A Thousand Clowns*.

"Doesn't look like either."

Annie went upstairs and stuck her head in David's study.

"I'm going to take a hot bath in the Jacuzzi. Long walk . I need to soak a while."

"Any ideas for tonight?"

"Maybe eat at the diner and then see *A Beautiful Mind.* Mama said it was a must see movie. And so do the critics."

"Sounds good to me."

David usually left their social life up to Annie. And she knew most of it had to be last minute with the demands of his schedule. They often took two cars to an event, in case he had to leave for the hospital. She did make plans with friends, but they all were used to his being beeped in the middle of a dinner party — at his own house or at theirs. Sometimes he cut it pretty close, but he had never missed a delivery and his patients seemed to adore him. He treated each mother as if she were important. He gave them time during their appointments to ask questions and to talk. Annie heard through the grapevine that his patients never felt as if they were on an assembly line in his office. He was a kind and considerate man with them, just as he was with his family.

There was a line at the movie, but they found seats where they were comfortable, in the next to the last row. They both found it completely engrossing and just sat in their seats at the end while the credits moved down the screen. When the lights came on, they put on their coats and left.

"I thought it was a stunning movie, David. Didn't you?"

"Amazing! I guess we all find schizophrenia an enigma. And this story was a blockbuster!"

"Such acting. I feel numb."

They talked about the movie on the way home in the car and into the house. It was that kind of film. It was eleven and their usual bedtime.

"Are you sleepy?" David asked.

"Not really. Let's listen to some music and unwind. I could use a glass of Chablis."

Annie knew she was putting off going up to bed. They often had sex after a good movie when they were both relaxed and removed from their work. She didn't want that to happen tonight. She felt enormous guilt about Mark and her lack of desire to be with David. Their sex life was uneven for the past ten years or so. The best times were when they took their vacations to Europe. They both loved the small villages of Provence and her senses would be aroused quite easily when they were there. But, at home, they had fallen into more of a routine with their lovemaking . They gave each other pleasure as they had for years, but the fire was often missing for her. He would be concerned and solicitous when that happened.

"Tell me what to do, Annie. I want you to be happy," he would say.

"I'm fine David. It's okay. I'm happy.," she would reply.

Now, they sat on the couch in the living room, drank wine and listened to a CD of Frank Sinatra classics. Evocative songs of the 40's and 50's. Annie and David had danced to all of them.

"Let's go up to bed," David said.

Annie could think of nothing to say. She rose from the couch and they went up together.

Chapter 15

'After the lovin', as Englebert used to croon, David pulled up the blanket and went to sleep as he was. Annie rose to put on one of her long sleeved nightgowns. She needed the warmth and comfort on her body. She washed her face and smoothed on moisturizer. She did not want to look in the mirror.

Back in bed, she could not fall asleep. What she had done with David, she had done a thousand times. She knew his body so well. Now, she was wracked with a feeling of betrayal for having had sex with him. Her husband! She actually felt as if she had betrayed Mark as well as David. It was a disaster! Mark had said she had an inner compass. If so, it was wildly askew.

She hugged the blankets and thought of how she had lain on Mark's couch. And how he had looked at her. She knew she was betraying David again, lying next to him and bringing that image back into her mind. She tried to push it away — with no success. When she finally fell asleep, it was with Mark Trianos still in her thoughts.

Annie awoke at six with a headache. It was not surprising. She was glad it was getting light and she could get on with the day. She would keep busy. Make a noodle kugel to take to Saul when they went into New York. It was one of his favorites and the children loved it too. She would call and see if coming in about noon would work. Then, they could have it for lunch.

First she took two Advils and a hot shower. Then, she dressed in her walking clothes and went down to start the coffee. David stirred but was in no hurry to get up. It was Sunday and he had no patients on Maternity. He would not have to go into the hospital.

She brought in the papers, *The Times* almost too heavy to carry. While she was having her first cup of coffee, she took out the ingredients for the kugel and put on the pot of water to boil. She made a sweet kugel with fine noodles, cottage cheese, eggs, sugar, lemon juice and raisins. It had been one of her staples when the children were growing up. Saul loved it with sour cream. Noodle kugel was one of the 'comfort' foods, Annie made. It always seemed to be welcome. By the time David came down, it was baking in the oven.

He kissed her on the cheek, poured his coffee and took out Section 4 of *The Times*.

"I'm ready for The Week In Review", he declared. "Let's see what the pundits say."

"I'm going out for an early walk, David. I thought we would go into the city by lunchtime if that's okay with Diane and Saul."

"That's fine with me. Have a good walk."

Once outside in the air, Annie's headache began to ease. Just mixing the kugel had helped. She was programming herself, going through the regular motions of a normal Sunday. She would stop at the children's store to pick up the presents for the girls on the way to New York. They were open on Sunday mornings until noon. And Tessa had said she might be there too with Sally. That would be perfect. She would immerse herself in her family roles. Being a mother and a grandmother — and try to forget about the turbulent emotions of the past three days.

The day was overcast and windy and Annie found herself braced against the gusts. It felt like November, finally. The oak trees were almost completely bare, except for certain stubborn branches that held their dry leaves until the sap rose in the Spring. She thought about Thanksgiving. Maybe Jack and his family would make the trip East. He hadn't been with them for two years. She liked Lois, and her son, Ted, would be good company for Eric. She would call him later and see what their plans were for the holiday. When she spoke with him several weeks ago, they were still undecided.

She walked to the one mile point and then turned back into the wind. By the time, she reached home, her hands were cold despite the woolen gloves. It was a foretaste of winter, and she felt chilled. David was still sitting at the kitchen table, eating oatmeal and reading the paper. She always kept the regular and cinnamon apple oatmeal in the instant envelopes. She often thought they could not live without the microwave oven.

David looked up and told her that Saul had called. Coming about noon would be fine.

"Did you tell him, I was bringing the kugel?"

"I did. And he was delighted. Said it was the best medicine."

"Good. Did he say if Tessa and Sally are coming too?"

"He wasn't sure, but he thought they were."

"I'll be ready by eleven, David. Okay?"

He nodded and went back to *The Times*. He had progressed to the Sports section.

There was very little traffic, driving into the city, and they arrived at the apartment door just before twelve. Diane answered their ring and greeted them each with the air kiss that most New Yorkers bestowed. No hugs there. Beth and Emily came running from the playroom and Annie bent down to embrace each of them. Warm bodies. Joyous faces. David carried the kugel into the kitchen. Saul was stretched out on the couch.

"What's in the big bag, Grandma?"

"A box for you, Beth. And one for Emily. Do you want to open them?"

The question, of course, was rhetorical. While they sat on the floor and pulled off the ribbons and paper, Annie and David sat down to talk with Saul. Diane was setting the table for lunch.

"How are you getting around? Is it very painful?", Annie asked. She reached out for his hand.

"I'm still not comfortable with the crutches. It's been a long time since I used them. But I'm managing. It feels better when I have my leg up like this."

"That should ease in a week or so," David said.

"The girls have been helping. They bring me the paper. And other necessary items like the television remote."

The children had opened their boxes and were holding up the new outfits. Emily ran with hers into the kitchen to show her mother. Beth came to Annie and gave her another hug.

"I love these colors, Grandma. Pink and purple. They're my favorites!"

Diane stuck her head out and voiced approval of Annie's selections. It had been a success all around.

Tessa and Sally were there in the next half hour. She swept in with her hair a dark cloud about her face. Annie thought she looked radiant. Sally pounced on her gift box and held the pinafore up to be admired by everyone. Then she and her cousins disappeared into the playroom.

"It's almost time to eat, girls." Diane called.

Tessa came to Saul, gave him an appraising look and kissed him.

"So, big brother, how are you?"

"I'm not doing dunk shots, but I'll survive. "

86

Annie went to the kitchen to ask Diane if she could help with lunch.

"I'm almost ready, Annie. Nova, sliced tomatoes and onions. Bagels. The usual. Thanks for the kugel. It's always delicious. And for bringing the sour cream too. You are a first rate caterer."

The girls were summoned and everyone came to the table. Saul sat with his leg on an extra chair. It was awkward but the best way for him to eat. David sat at the other end of the table. Tessa was next to Annie. The three girls always wanted to sit together. Diane was across from Annie.

Annie listened to their conversations. She felt like an observer again, sitting with her family as if everything were normal. Spreading cream cheese on a bagel for Emily. Dishing out the kugel. Eating, but not really tasting the food.

"You're very quiet, Mom," ventured Tessa, turning to look at her.

"Just being, dear. I'm fine."

"I love that color on you. Foam green. It's very soft and great with your skin."

"You are a confidence booster, Tessa."

"She's right, Annie." Diane joined in. "You have beautiful skin. As the ads say, you glow."

Annie didn't want to be the center of attention. It was the last place she wanted at that moment. She just needed to sit and absorb her family and feel their warmth. To shore up her center. And put all the compartments back in place from where they had imploded in her mind.

Saul asked for another helping of kugel. Annie noticed that Sally was picking out the raisins from her portion. She had forgotten that raisins were a no-no to Sally. Even golden raisins. But, she was solving the problem herself, making a little pile of the discards and happily eating the rest. Sally was not easily daunted by life's obstacles. It made Annie smile as she watched her. She felt that Tessa was doing a wonderful job as a mother with Eric and Sally. Working full time at the firm and still giving them the attention they each needed. Of course, Robert was with her all the way. He adored his little girl and he was a caring step-father to Eric. Annie felt good about their marriage. So very different from the bad years that Tessa had lived through with Ivan.

Lunch ended with chocolate chip cookies from the bakery for the girls, and any interested adults. Annie adored chocolate and ate two. They were sinful.

Saul made his way back to the couch. "The kugel was perfect, Mom.

Thanks."

David joined him to watch the football game while Annie and Tessa helped Diane clean up. The girls were playing with the doll house. Stereotypical gender roles for all of them, Annie thought.

"How's Grandma Ruth?" Tessa asked her mother.

"She's fine. Busy as usual with all her activities."

"I don't know how she does all she does." Diane commented.

"She's become involved in so many interests since she retired. I think she has more energy than I do!" Annie often looked at her mother and found it hard to realize that she was 87.

At four, Tessa coaxed Sally away from her cousins and David and Annie went down with them in the elevator.

"Have a good week, Tessa. Sally, give me one of your super hugs!"

"Bye, Grandma. And Grandpa. Love you!"

Annie and David reached their driveway by five. As they walked in, she remembered that she was going to call Jack and find out if they were coming East for Thanksgiving. That gave her a jolt. She imagined what he would think if he knew that she was sleeping with another man than David. Jack had always been both protective and judgmental when it came to Annie's behavior. That's all she would need!

Chapter 16

Ruth awoke Monday morning to the sound of heavy rain on her bedroom window. She snuggled under the down comforter and thought of all the Monday mornings when she had to get up and go to work. A rainy Monday was always the worst. It was more than twenty years ago, but she still remembered exactly what it felt like to leave home and turn herself into Mrs. Shaeffer, the English teacher. Now, she could luxuriate in the freedom of lying in bed and thinking about the day ahead. It was all hers to do with what she would. It was a sweet feeling.

The weekend had been quiet. She had stayed in the apartment except for a brief ten minute walk on Saturday. Yesterday, the weather had turned cold and very windy and Ruth avoided going out on days like that. She found her breath shortened and she would have pressure on her chest at times. Even if her checkup showed no change in the cardiogram, she was alert to any warning signs. After eight decades, she felt she knew her body better than her doctor. When her arthritis flared and getting out of bed was a struggle, she would think of what her friend Rachel often said, and smile.

"When you hurt all over in the morning, at least you know that you're alive!"

Yes, she was alive and she was determined to make the most of it. Today was her telephone conference for the course she was taking from University Without Walls. It was called "You're Getting On My Nerves" and she had met a very different group of people, most of whom were very opinionated and outspoken. Perhaps the title of the course had attracted them as it did her. The readings were in psychology and several provocative short stories. There were seven other participants from all over the country, most of them seniors. Ruth found it great fun to listen to them, and to argue when she felt it was worth the effort. She had nick names in her head for the others: "Big

Shot", the retired executive. "Mrs. Miniver", the stalwart. "Clark Gable", the silver haired Lothario.(He had referred to his wavy hair often.) "Fats", he related everything to food and diets. "Mae West", sex dripped from her every sentence. "Baby", she needed to be loved. And "William Jennings Bryan", he would give brief lectures until the leader cut him off. She wondered what name the others would give her.

The sessions were set for three o'clock Eastern time to accommodate those in the Western states. She had some final preparation to do on the readings. She always liked to underline particular sentences to refer to when she took part. Some of the others spoke as if they hadn't read the material. Ruth always did her homework. She considered it insulting to the leader just to wing it. He seemed to give her as much time as she wanted when she made contributions. It was good for her ego. And it reminded her of her classes, with the students who were prepared and offered valuable insights on the readings. She was now in the reverse role of student, but it didn't bother her. It was a new experience and that always made her feel alive.

After breakfast, she caught up on the news and finished off *The Times* puzzle rapidly. Monday's puzzle was the easiest by far. Not really a challenge. The same small words; aloe, anil, oboe, tor, ibis, tau... et al. The editor had his favorites and any puzzle addict knew them by heart.

Her housekeeping chores were minimal. She made the bed, washed the dishes and settled into her favorite chair to work on the tapestry. The rain was steady and she was very happy to be inside, warm and comfortable. As she did her needlepoint, her mind shifted to Tessa, who would be in New York already, at her law firm. Tessa, who was doing what Ruth had done for years, balancing home and work. In her case, she and Robert were in a far better financial position than Ruth and Michael had been in the 30's. Tessa's generation of women had been raised and schooled to pursue a career, just as the men. For most of the women in Ruth's generation, being a full time mother was a given. For Tessa, and her friends, the pendulum had swung 180 degrees. They were expected to be lawyers, and doctors and college professors. And mothers. And to fulfill both of their roles well. Ruth knew what a tough road that was. She had been there.

The last time she and Tessa were together, they had a long talk that Ruth found very revealing.

"You know, Grandma, sometimes I just want to get off the merry-go-round. To give my boss two weeks notice and quit!"

"I thought you loved your work, Tessa."

"I do, Grandma. I enjoy the law. And I prepared for it for so long. But, most of the work I'm doing is fairly routine. Digging out research. Writing drafts of briefs is more interesting. I rarely, if ever, get into court."

"Isn't that what it means to be an associate?"

"Yes. I know that, but I get restless. And some days, I really resent being at the beck and call of two bosses. I want to be in charge of my own life. And I hate leaving Sally in the morning."

"Ah, how well I know what that feeling is. Every day, I left your mother, when she was about Sally's age, she would cry and beg me not to leave. It was horrible!"

"I remember your telling me that. Mom was three. But, in an ironic way, you had no choice. You had to work to bring in the second income. I really don't have the same reason. Robert's income is considerable."

"How does Robert really feel about your working?"

"He's a liberated guy. He wants me to be happy and fulfilled. And Sally, of course, has thrived in pre-school. She's not the one who seems to feel the pull in the mornings. She's raring to go each day."

"So, your dilemma is with yourself, dear. And those are always the hardest to resolve."

"You're very wise, Grandma. My aim is to become a partner at the firm. Right now, I'm going to stick it out with my eye on that goal. But, I'm not going to continue if it is only a means to an end. I have to feel good about my life right now as well."

"That makes good sense to me, Tessa. You have Robert and Eric and Sally at the center of your life. You're a wife and a mother. And a lawyer. As well as a daughter, sister ,granddaughter and aunt! When one thinks of all the roles we play in life, it's mind boggling!"

"I'm concentrating on wife, mother and lawyer these days."

"That's a full plate, Tessa."

"I know, Grandma. It's good to talk to you. You understand."

That talk with Tessa had been very important to Ruth. It kept her close to her granddaughter who was very dear. The Unicorn Tapestry she was stitching would be a lovely surprise for Tessa. Today, she would work the flaw into the dense pattern of colors.

Ruth loved metaphors. She appreciated them in her reading and she used them often in life. The flaw in the tapestry would be similar to the deliberate flaws created by the weavers of Oriental carpets. Ruth had learned that years ago, when she and Michael were shopping for one for their living room. The owner of the store, pointed out a flaw or error in a blue background Sarouk. One of figures appeared to be facing in the wrong direction.

"The weavers believe that each carpet must have a mistake or flaw woven into the design. The carpet cannot be perfect. Only God can be perfect!"

She and Michael could not afford to buy the rug, but Ruth loved the concept of the flaw. Now that she was doing the needlepoint for Tessa, she saw it as a metaphor for life in its beauty and complex design. *But life — like God,* she thought, *is not perfect.* She would stitch a deliberate error or flaw into the tapestry. It would symbolize the unexpected events, the surprises in life. Some good and some bad. The twists and turns. The choices we face. The mistakes we make. She loved the whole idea!

She would not make the flaw obvious. She reversed the threads she was using and created a reverse pattern of greens and blues in the lower lefthand corner of the border. She would explain it all to Tessa when she gave it to her. Tessa would appreciate the imagery.

Ruth thought that she might even write about it in a separate letter. She often did that on important occasions. This would be one of them. She smiled as she worked the colors. It was a labor of love.

Chapter 17

Tessa was not in her office as her grandmother imagined. She was home with Sally who had thrown up during the night and was running a l02 degree fever.

Tessa had called into Jenny to give the message to Tom Simmons that she would not be in.

"Please tell him my little girl is sick. I hope to be in tomorrow."

" I'll tell him. I hope she's better fast, Tessa."

They both knew that Tom made some allowances for women with sick children, but only up to a point. Robert would check his schedule and see if he could take over tomorrow if Sally was still sick, One of the advantages of a family business, Tessa thought. When the boss was also the grandfather of the sick child.

Sally was asleep, with a dose of children's Tylenol working on the fever. Tessa looked out the window at the sheets of rain, and was thankful to be home. The weekend had been slow and easy, just as she had hoped it would be. Robert took care of household errands on Saturday and she helped Eric with his project when he said he was stuck. It was almost finished and she felt a little help over the finish line was acceptable. Eric had a sleep-over at Danny's and their sitter came at six to take care of Sally. Tessa and Robert went to a Country French restaurant, had a relaxed dinner, a bottle of good Bordeaux and came home to find Sally sound asleep. After the sitter left, they turned to look at each other and Robert said, "Are we there yet?" She smiled and they went upstairs.

Tessa loved the way Robert made love to her. The years with Ivan had not been good. In bed or anywhere else. She and Robert enjoyed sex from their first time together. And since then, their sex life had deepened and had become more fulfilling to Tessa. The years she had spent in therapy dealt with her sexual feelings as well as the other parts of her failed marriage to Ivan. She had to learn how to be open and give herself again to a man. When she met and married Robert, it seemed very natural.

Sometimes he called her 'Tessa Baby'. He adored her long dark hair and would run his fingers through it when they lay in bed. Blue eyes and black hair, the same startling combination she had passed on to Sally.

"You are so very beautiful. Sometimes, I can't believe you married me."

"We both were lucky, Robert."

"When you were in high school, the boys must have been stacked ten deep!"

"They were. Saul used to have to beat them off with a stick." She laughed up at him.

"When I first saw you at the support group, do you know what I thought?"

"No. Tell me. It's good for my ego."

"I thought, what idiot let her get away!"

She reached up, closed her eyes and pulled him down so that his mouth covered hers. She loved his long, slow kisses, as if time had stopped for them. His hands moved down her body and she felt both arousal and safety with him. She did not feel vulnerable as she had for years with Ivan. She could allow herself to become excited because she knew there would be a slow, steady climb to a climax. Robert always wanted her to experience her pleasure before he sought his.

They never discussed their sex life with their former spouses. It was tacitly agreed that there was nothing to be gained by sharing that part of their first marriages. Tessa only knew that Robert came with scars that affected his confidence in bed. She made sure he felt her happiness. She showed him with her body as well as her words that he was a wonderful lover. Saturday night, she had told him again how she felt and how good they were together.

"I love how you hold me — and love me, Robert."

"That's not hard to do, Tessa. I am one lucky man."

Robert had driven Eric over to pick up Danny, and then dropped them off at school before he went into the city. If it was still pouring, Danny's mother would pick them up at 3:30. Tessa felt the day stretching ahead of her. She was so used to being at work that she didn't really know what to do with the free hours. It was like having the bends, coming up for air too fast. Especially knowing that Tom Simmons would have work waiting for her on her desk.

"Mommy!" She heard Sally calling from upstairs.

"Here I come, Sally."

Sally was sitting up in bed, looking almost like her happy self again.

"Did I throw up last night? I hate that when it happens!"

"It's okay, Sally. We all do that sometimes. It means that something we ate didn't want to stay down."

"Yuck!"

Sally's forehead felt cool to the touch and Tessa was relieved.

"Let's get you up. Wash your face and hands and pick out a pretty outfit. Do you want to wear the pinafore that Grandma got you yesterday? You could put it over tights and a shirt and be nice and warm that way."

"Am I going to school?"

"Not today. You need one day to catch up from feeling sick last night. You'll probably be able to go back tomorrow."

"I like it when you're home with me when I'm sick, Mommy."

Tessa let that statement sink in as she helped Sally wash her face and hands in the bathroom. Tessa had changed the bed linens during the night and thrown them into the washer. All traces of the episode were gone. They went downstairs to the kitchen.

"I'm not hungry, Mommy."

"That's okay, Sally. When you're hungry, I'll make you something good. Why don't you play with your dolls. Gorgeous looks lonely. Maybe she didn't feel well during the night either."

Tessa called Robert to give him the good report.

"Sally feels and looks normal. No fever. She's happily taking care of Gorgeous who apparently had the same thing happen to her last night."

"Good news. I'm jammed up here with delivery problems from North Carolina. They had an early ice storm and the tractor trailers are delayed."

"Well, unless her fever returns this afternoon, she'll be back in preschool tomorrow. I hope."

"Call me later."

She considered calling Tom Simmons and decided that would be a no-win. Instead, she dialed her mother.

"Hi, Mom, it's me."

"Tessa, is everything okay? Are you at work?"

"I'm home with Sally. She's okay now, but she threw up during the night and had a fever. She just woke up her cheery self, I'm happy to report."

"She seemed fine yesterday. And had such fun with Beth and Emily. I love to see them play together. Usually three is not a good number, as we all

95

know, but it seems to work with them. Maybe because Sally and Beth are almost the same age and Emily just goes along with their lead."

"She's wearing the pinafore. She loves it. Over navy tights and a shirt."

"Well, at least you didn't have to go out in this horrible rain."

"To tell you the truth, I wouldn't mind being at the office. I know there'll be work waiting for me. I'm not used to a day off."

"Isn't there anything you can work on at home?"

"Not really. When I left on Friday, I could hardly wait to get home. It was not a good week. Tom Simmons goes back and forth, being Atilla The Hun and Mr. Nice Guy!"

"It does not sound pleasant! I know the Atilla feeling with some editors. The ones who are never satisfied and need endless rewrites. I try to avoid them. You have no choice but to deal with your boss. Of course, you do have the choice, if it gets too bad, to leave."

"You know, I just realized you picked up the phone. You don't usually answer before noontime. What's up?"

"I thought it might be Sarah. She often calls on Monday mornings from Florida."

"I'll let you go. Sally just came in. She may be ready for sustenance."

Sally not only wanted her beloved Sugar Pops, she asked if they could make muffins.

"That is a great idea, Sally! We will make muffins and have them for Eric and Daddy when they come home. Then we could watch one of your favorite tapes. "Mary Poppins" or "Peter Pan". You get to pick."

"I'll do eeny, meeny, miney, moe to pick. I love to do that!"

Chapter 18

Of course, Annie did not pick up the phone expecting it to be Sarah. She hoped it might be Mark. She hadn't talked with him since Friday and it seemed like forever. One more day to get through before she would see him at the gym. The pouring rain added to her anxious mood.

She usually enjoyed a rainy day. It would enclose her from the outside world and make concentration on her writing easier. Not today. She needed to hear his voice.

"Mark. It's me."

"How was the weekend, Annie?"

"It's hard to answer that. Part of me was with David, and Saul and Tessa and the children. And part of me was still with you."

"I don't have all those distractions, Annie. All of me was with you."

"I may not last until tomorrow, Mark."

"I'm here."

Annie sat at her desk. She knew very well what would happen if she drove over to Mark's townhouse. Especially in the rain. She loved having sex while it rained. There had always been something magical about that for her. Pulling the blinds. Hearing the rain on the roof of the bedroom. She let her mind play with the fantasies. Then, she steeled herself and blotted them out. She would make it through until tomorrow.

If she couldn't write, she would plan for Thanksgiving. When she had reached Jack, last night, he said they would probably stay in Chicago, but might decide to come at the last minute. She told him that would be okay. He sounded as if something were wrong, but she didn't want to probe. He said Lois and Ted were fine, when she asked. Perhaps, she had gotten him at a bad time.

She counted the definite number at the Thanksgiving table as eleven. She and David, Ruth, Tessa and Robert, Eric and Sally, Saul and Diane, Beth and Emily. She could accommodate twelve easily with the two leaves in the table. If Jack did come, they could squeeze three more. She would cook a big bird, over twenty pounds, and ask her mother to make the apricot corn bread stuffing. The kids loved sweet potato pie with marshmallows on top. Whole cranberry with orange slices. Green beans with mushrooms. It was not a complicated meal to prepare. Tessa and Diane would help serve. Saul would need extra room for his leg. He would sit on a corner. They would manage.

Annie had a special cloth for Thanksgiving. It was really an Indian bedspread, wine colored heavy cotton, with stylized turkeys woven in the border. She loved setting it with a centerpiece of red Delicious apples in a rustic pedestal bowl. David would take out the chest of sterling and she would use her Waterford crystal for the adults. Special party glasses for the children. It was always a festive table. Sometimes she added wine colored candles in the brass candlesticks that Ruth had given her. They had belonged to her mother, Leah Alpers. She had brought them with her from Poland when she came to America.

She called the supermarket to order the turkey.

"Hello. This is Mrs. Bertman. Would you put me down for a fresh killed turkey for Thanksgiving. About 20, 22 pounds."

"Okay, Mrs. Bertman. When do you want to pick it up?"

"Wednesday morning sounds right."

"I'll have it for you. Thanks for the order."

Next, she dialed her mother.

"Good morning Mama. How are you, this rainy Monday?"

"Annie. You're not working?"

"I just couldn't get into it this morning. So I took a break."

"Did you go into see Saul yesterday?"

"Yes, we did and he's doing fine. The girls had a great time as usual and Diane made a nice lunch. I brought my noodle kugel. Saul loves it."

"Sounds like a good visit."

"Tessa asked for you. She looked so beautiful, Mama. She was wearing a red cashmere sweater and matching lipstick. You'll see her in two weeks for Thanksgiving."

"I'm just working on the Unicorn tapestry. It's about three quarters done. The center part is really complicated, but I am persevering. I want it to be finished for her anniversary."

Annie knew that Ruth was doing the needlepoint as a surprise for Tessa.

She had introduced her to the Unicorn tapestries at the Cloisters years ago. It was indeed a labor of love.

The rain was steady, but Annie decided she had to get out of the house. She put on a weather proof jacket and drove first to the supermarket where she bought a large eggplant and a pound of chopped sirloin. Then to the gym. She would work off some of her angst on the treadmill. Her body in motion helped her to calm down. And sort out what was whirling around in her head.

If she were to continue seeing Mark, it had to be more than the heated sexual encounters they had experienced last week. Even though that was all she really wanted at the moment, she knew in the recesses of her mind that sexual passion would burn out. And what if it burnt out for him and not for her? Then, where would she be? It would be devastating to her.

And then, her mind turned to David. Could she continue an affair with Mark and continue to sleep with David? Friday night had been terrible. A double betrayal. What kind of person had she become? Where was the faithful wife, who was shocked by tales of adultery that surfaced among their friends and acquaintances? She had not really been judgmental in the past. She just found some of the situations hard to understand.

Now, she understood how that could happen. How a wife of 37 years could become involved with another man. *Involved was not the right word,* she thought. *Infatuated with another man, that was the right word. Infatuated!* At age 62, it seemed absurd, but it was true.

She knew she still was an attractive woman, but he could have many women much younger than she. It flattered her that Mark wanted her. That he said her body was beautiful. It was far from the firm body she had once had. But he said she was lush and her skin was soft as silk. Annie knew that was true. David had always loved to caress her skin. *David!*

She sighed. She had gotten nowhere in sorting out her dilemma.

She drove home through the rain feeling somewhat less anxious. Some of the afternoon would be spent preparing the stuffed eggplant. It was one of her favorite dishes and it took an hour or more to put together. That was her plan. Keep busy. Fill up the hours. And then it would be Tuesday.

Tuesday she would see Mark!

Chapter 19

Mark was already at the gym when Annie arrived on Tuesday. He was the only one on the treadmills. She climbed onto the one next to his.

"Mark, we have to talk."

"That sounds ominous, Annie."

"No. We just have to talk. Later."

"Okay."

When they were in the parking lot, he asked, "Where do you want to go, Annie?" He had not touched her on the way out. She felt the space between them. It felt cold.

"It's not where I want to go, Mark. I want to go to your house. Yesterday, it took all my will power not to call you."

"And, now?"

She looked at him. And sighed.

"I'll follow you home, Mark."

As Annie drove, she knew her desire for him had dispelled her firm resolutions. She wanted to be in his arms again. She wanted to feel what she had felt last week. Nothing else seemed to matter.

When he opened the door, Mark turned and smiled.

"We will talk. I promise. But— later."

They went upstairs to the bedroom and he undressed her very slowly. She had deliberately put on sports underwear. He didn't seem to notice or care. She found herself responding to his touch as she had before. It was as if the sensations she felt had lain dormant or had never been awakened. Somewhere in the recesses of her mind, she realized she had often held David back. Now, she was letting go of her inhibitions. It was exhilarating! When he entered her, she felt complete happiness.

Much later, when they were lying in bed, they did talk.

"I'd like to paint you, Annie. But, not with the sheet and blanket wrapped around you."

She looked at him and laughed.

"I'm not exactly Olympia, Mark."

"That's fine. I'm not Manet."

"I don't think that would be a good idea. Remember what happened when I was downstairs on the couch. I couldn't just pose without any clothes on. It would be much too erotic for me."

"This would be different. I would be painting you."

"Ah, but for me, I'd still be lying there completely naked. I couldn't stand it."

"You have a lovely body, Annie. The color of your skin is exceptional."

Annie remembered vividly the pictures of his wife downstairs.

"How did your wife react when you painted those pictures of her? "

"She didn't seem to mind. She posed for hours. And in different positions, as you saw."

"She was young and seems very confident of her beauty in the pictures."

"Yes, she was confident when I painted her. Years later, she came apart, as I shared with you."

"Mark, let's talk about what has happened between us. I feel as if my life is almost out of my control."

"You're here because you want to be, Annie."

"I know. That's what I mean. What we began last Thursday is all I think about."

" Is that bad?"

"You're not helping me, Mark."

"I can only answer you honestly, Annie. I've been married and divorced twice. I'm a single man with a normal appetite for sex. But that is not what this is all about for me. We spent a lot of time together, talking and sharing and finding out about each other, before we went to bed last week. It became an important part of my life to see you twice a week at the gym. And to go out for coffee afterwards. To learn about your writing and about living in a Jewish family. About the twins and your grandchildren. I feel as if I know Tessa and Saul. I learned what matters to you in politics and in life. And I have found that we share the same values in many ways. Being Greek makes me something of a philosopher, you know. As well as a great cook."

He smiled and drew her to him.

"I was serious when I said, I think I'm falling in love with you, Annie. You're a magnificent woman."

She couldn't use the same words to respond. She couldn't say she was falling in love. She cared for him. He was a warm compassionate man. He had many interests. She had learned his likes and dislikes in life. A lot of them matched hers. And she felt this intense physical attraction. She wanted to be with him. He was in her thoughts constantly. She called it infatuation. Could it become love? Perhaps. If she let it.

"Falling in love? Where would that lead, Mark?"

"Does it have to lead somewhere, Annie?"

"I think it does. Human relationships are always in movement, I have found. They grow and deepen, or they start to die. If we continue as we are, something will change. Maybe, I don't want to care too much for you, Mark. There's so much at stake."

"I know, Annie. It's not simple for you. But, do we have to decide the future, today?"

She lifted her hand to touch his face. Her fingers outlined his mouth.

"No, Mark. We don't have to decide the future today."

"Good! Let's take a shower and go downstairs. I have moussaka and a Greek salad. The least I can do is feed you properly."

"Sounds delicious. But, let's not go just yet."

"Annie — you're incorrigible!"

She smiled and kissed him lightly.

"Yes. I guess I am."

Chapter 20

In the ten days before Thanksgiving, Annie saw Mark twice. At the gym and later at his house. Each time she tried to resist going. And each time she went. He did not press her. She went because she wanted to.

She saw her mother once, taking her to the supermarket on Saturday. Her mother had remarked on how well Annie looked.

"What have you been doing, dear? New makeup? Haircut? You look wonderful."

"Thanks, Mama. Nothing special. Working out at the gym. Must agree with me."

And so, she had lied to her mother. It didn't feel good.

David had been swamped with deliveries and spent long days at the hospital. When he called and missed her in the afternoon, he never questioned where she had been. It was really all too easy, she thought. Except the night when David had wanted sex. That had been very hard. That was when the guilt had been heaviest.

Since then, he had been coming home exhausted at all hours during the night and day. He would snatch a few hours sleep and his beeper would summon him back to the hospital. Being a solo practitioner had its rewards, but it also meant he was always on call.

Sunday, after lunch, Sarah had called her from Florida.

"Hi. I thought this would be a good time to call. We haven't talked in a while. Are you getting ready for a big dinner on Thursday?"

Annie's heart sunk. She had talked to Sarah the day Saul was in the hospital. The day she had gone to Mark's house for the first time. It seemed years ago.

"Hi, Sarah. We're going to be twelve. Not too big a crowd. Jack and his family won't be coming East. How about you? How many of the clan are gathering?"

Annie knew she was stalling for time. She and Sarah had been roommates in college. They had always been open with each other. And there for each other through the hard times. For over 40 years. There were no secrets between them. She couldn't lie to Sarah.

"The usual mob. I'm going to make two turkeys. I can't pick up a 30 pound bird anymore!"

"Sarah, I need to talk with someone. And you're the only one I can talk to."

"Annie, what's wrong? Are you sick? Or David? Or the twins? Not your mother!"

"Well, it's not that something is wrong. No one is sick. Something has happened."

" What do you mean, something has happened?"

"I don't know how to say this — so, I'll just say it. I'm having an affair."

"Having an affair! You're kidding!"

"I'm not kidding, Sarah. I walk around feeling like someone I don't even know."

There was a long pause and Annie could imagine the look on Sarah's face. And how her mind would be racing to understand what she had been told

"I'm having trouble believing this. Who is he, Annie? How long has this been going on?"

"He's a man I met at the gym months ago. And the affair has only been going on for about three weeks."

"You met him at the gym! Does he work there?"

"No. No. He's not the trainer. He's an artist and he goes there to work out. We started to talk one day when we were on the treadmills. Then we went out for coffee afterwards. It got to be a routine. Twice a week. We would talk for hours."

"I'm still in shock, Annie."

"Me too, Sarah. It just happened. Saul had been in an accident. He's okay. But we had just come back from the hospital and I was very jumpy. David had gone back to work. I called Mark, that's his name, Mark Trianos, to tell him how Saul was. It was a day we usually saw each other at the gym and I had called him earlier to tell him I wouldn't be there."

"You were that close, that you called him about Saul?"

"Yes. We had become that close over the months. I would look forward to seeing him. He's very attractive, Sarah. And a little younger than I am, 58. And interesting. Different from anyone I have ever known."

"Go on."

"I called him. He invited me over for a cup of tea and some of the Greek food he cooks. And I went. The rest just happened."

"I don't know what to say. I'm having trouble with this. It's your life, but— are you crazy?"

"Yes, 'crazy' may be the right word. I know what I'm doing is wrong. And risky. But, I can only tell you, I feel more alive than I have in decades! When I'm with him, I'm in heaven!"

"But what about David? Are you telling me you're not in love with David?"

"Sarah, I've tried to sort this out. Of course, I'm still in love with David. But, I'm infatuated with Mark. I can't stop seeing him."

"So, it's sex!"

"Yes, it's sex , but more than that. For the first time in my life, I've let go of my inhibitions. I feel a sense of freedom with him that I have never felt with David. That must sound awful, but it's the truth. I feel like another woman when I'm in bed with him. It's not only that he's a wonderful lover — which he is. It's me. I'm different."

"Annie, you've got a big problem."

"I know."

"What if David finds out?"

"Don't you think I am aware of that? He has been so busy with deliveries for the past month that he has hardly been home. But, yes, what if he were to find out? I know it would be a disaster! We have always trusted each other. When he is away at conferences, I never worry that there is some woman in his room. And to him, it is a given, that I am faithful. I know that, Sarah."

"So how can you be doing what you're doing? I don't understand you."

"I can't seem to stop. I keep telling myself that I won't go there again. And then I go."

"You're not some kid, Annie. You're 62 years old! You know what it would do to David. And how about your children, if they found out? And your mother!"

Annie just listened. Sarah was not telling her anything she didn't already know. And the questions she raised were not new.

"I can't argue with you, Sarah. I knew when you called, I would tell you.

You're the only person I couldn't lie to."

"What can I do to help, Annie?"

"Be there if I need to talk to you."

"I'm here for you Annie. You know that."

"I know, Sarah. I'm doing the best I can do, right now. Bye."

That was Sunday. She had not seen Mark on Tuesday and now it was Wednesday, the day before everyone would be coming for Thanksgiving dinner. Annie was keeping busy with preparations. She had picked up the turkey and it was fine. Twenty two pounds. Now, she was peeling the sweet potatoes for the pie that the children loved. She would use canned whole cranberry sauce. It was just as good or better than the from-scratch recipe she had once tried. She served it in a crystal bowl with orange slices fanning out. David would pick up the stuffing from her mother in the morning. She knew some people baked the stuffing separately, but she always liked it better inside the turkey. More flavorful and moist.

Setting the table gave her a sense of continuity and helped quiet the anxiety she had been feeling all day. Just spreading the special cloth and placing the plates and the sterling helped restore a sense of order to her mind. It was like programming, she thought, that people go through when they are being brought back to normal after a stroke. Going through the motions. Helping the body remember what it used do automatically. In this case, it was not her muscles that needed to come back to normal. It was her head. And her heart.

Sarah had been shocked when she told her about Mark. She had asked, "Are you crazy?" *It was a fair question,* Annie thought.

She knew that Thursday with everyone coming would have a surreal quality to it. She would be submerged in her family. The children would all be running around. David would enjoy his pater familias role. Ruth would be very happy to be with everyone once more at another holiday table. And she ,Annie, would absorb the warmth and beauty of the day. She would enjoy having Tessa and Saul near her again. Another Thanksgiving to add to the many they all had shared together.

And yet — she knew a part of her would be somewhere else. She would meet Mark next Tuesday. And that thought suffused her with warmth.

Chapter 21

Ruth was up very early on Thanksgiving morning. When there was a busy day ahead, she never slept late. She dressed and made herself a pot of tea instead of coffee. She would mix up the stuffing to be ready when David came over to pick it up at ten thirty. She agreed with Annie that it tasted best when it was cooked inside the bird.

It would be a wonderful day, seeing everyone. Tessa and Saul. And her great grandchildren. She enjoyed talking with Eric about his school work. He was just beginning to appreciate that she had been a teacher. She had helped him with an important English composition last year and he now saw her not only as his Great Grandma but as someone who belonged to that significant group in his life — teachers.

"Was it real long ago when you were a teacher?" he had asked her.

"I guess to you, Eric, it was very long ago. Would you believe fifty years?"

"Wow! That was long ago!"

Ruth had laughed and hugged him. He was her oldest great grandchild and very special to her.

Today she would also delight in the three little girls, Sally, Beth and Emily. They usually threw themselves upon her for kisses and possible treats she had secreted in her pocketbook for them. Wrapped candies would appear and she knew it was the fun of the ritual that mattered most. Children loved games and expectation.

The Unicorn tapestry was nearing completion and she was very pleased with how it was going. The flaw she had worked into the needlepoint was just right. It did not jump out at the viewer, but the weaver knew it was there and that was the key to the concept and the imagery. Ruth smiled when she thought of Tessa's surprise when she would present it to her. Yes, it was the perfect gift for their anniversary.

As she mixed the apricot pieces into the crumbled cornbread, Ruth found herself thinking of Annie. When they had gone to the supermarket on Saturday, she had noticed how wonderful Annie looked. She thought she might have just had her hair cut and styled. Or changed her make up. But when she asked her, Annie had said she had been working out at the gym and that must account for it. Ruth remembered what it was like to be in one's mid sixties. Each morning in the mirror, new unwelcome lines seemed to blossom overnight. No amount of rejuvenating cream could stave them off. And it always drove her to distraction that the models in the ads hawking anti-aging creams looked like twenty five! How stupid did the advertisers think American women could be! Annie was very lucky. She still had beautiful skin and very few wrinkles. She had never used much makeup.

Ruth also remembered the first time she felt arthritis in her fingers, in her early sixties. Her hands were stiff when she awoke in the morning and a knob gradually appeared on the last joint of her little finger. The orthopedist had looked at her hands and the offensive knob and told her it was an arthritic cyst. If it didn't hurt her, one usually left it alone. Ruth had thought of the poignant scene in the movie classic, *East of Eden*, when Cal who was played by James Dean bursts into his mother's office. She always wore gloves but in this scene her hands are bare and exposed. The fingers were completely swollen and knobby, disfigured by arthritis! That shocking picture was etched in Ruth's mind. She had always been proud of her hands and long slim fingers. Now, they were no longer going to be pretty. That had hurt her deeply at the time — her vanity and the sign of age that she had to accept. But, her fingers had not become distorted over the years. She was very thankful. They were stiff on most mornings and she had learned to live with it.

Her thoughts went back to Annie again. She was smart to take her long walks every day and go to the gym to keep her body in good shape. She had once shared that she still weighed the same as when she and David were married. And Annie wore the same kind of clothes that Tessa did. Sports clothes and dresses in the stores were ageless. Women had so many choices today, Ruth thought, and not only in what they wore.

She had chosen her lovely plum wool dress for Thanksgiving dinner, with a fashionable to-the- knee length. Tessa always said, "Grandma still has the best legs in the family!" Ruth loved to hear her say that. It made her feel young again when Michael had always admired her legs and slim ankles.

Chapter 22

Tessa had no time to think about what she was going to wear to dinner. First, she had to get Sally dressed and that turned out to be something of a battle of the wills.

"I want to wear the pinafore that Grandma got me."

"I'm sorry, Sally. The pinafore is in the wash pail. You wore it three times to school and it's dirty."

The chin was determined as Sally countered with, "But Grandma won't care about that. It will make her happy to see me wearing it. I want to wear it!"

"No. I don't think it will make her happy. Today is a party. It's Thanksgiving. Why don't you wear one of your party dresses? The navy blue velvet or the flower print with the long skirt. You love to wear that."

There was a long pause, as Sally assessed her chances. "Okay, the flower print."

As Queen Victoria would have said, the look on her face was, "We are not amused!"

As Tessa buttoned up the back of the dress and brushed Sally's hair, she reviewed the past week and a half in her mind. It had been very hectic, a whirlwind at work, plus conferences for Eric at school and Sally at pre-school. She was able to schedule the last one of the day for each of the children. The teachers were very cooperative about that. And the reports she heard were good. Eric was doing well in his subjects and the euphemisms about his "social behavior" were positive. She remembered when he was in pre-school and the comments were not good. "Eric needs to learn to play more democratically." In short, he was something of a bully with the other kids. It was during the divorce and he was letting out his anger at school. Tessa had worked hard on that, without much help from Ivan. Eric had settled down and learned how to make friends and get along better.

Sally, her teacher said, was a delight. She loved school. She loved to be with the other children. She was the first to volunteer to help clean up after the morning snack. And she especially enjoyed painting and all kind of arts and crafts. Sally had produced a picture made of tiny beads glued to the heavy oaktag paper. It was displayed on a small easel. Tessa was impressed. At home, Tessa never wanted Eric and Sally to receive birthday presents that turned out to be water color sets or packets of beads to be strung — with one's mother's help. She loved presents that the children would enjoy, on their own. And did not mean messy sessions on the kitchen table. *So, I'm not the perfect mother,* she thought. *Tough!* There were limits to what she could deal with.

The demands at the firm during the past week had been huge. She was doing two jobs for both bosses at once. It was a pressure cooker. They each would walk by her office to see how she was progressing. Unless there were a client sitting in her office, which had never occurred to this point, her door remained open. She could hear the office manager and the receptionist talking. Phones ringing. It drove her crazy. She had finally closed her door on Thursday and Tom Simmons had knocked and peered in to ask if she was okay. They were supposed to be an open firm and the door was symbolic. She didn't explain that she worked best without all the outside distractions. She just opened the door again.

And Robert had been fighting with Sam all week about the yearly projections. It was an ongoing struggle between them. On Sunday, it had spilled over from the business to the family when they had visited his parents. Robert's mother had planned a lovely dinner and the afternoon had passed without any upsets. The three generations of men watched the football game, with Eric sprawled flat on his stomach in front of the television set. Tessa and Sally were in the kitchen most of the time, helping with the preparations. Sally loved to watch the ingredients being put together in the salad. And she was given the final important task of holding the large wooden fork and spoon and doing the tossing.

Tessa found it easy to talk with her mother-in-law. She had always been a full time homemaker but she had also been active in social service organizations that expanded her interests beyond her house and her family. She organized yearly fund raising drives that culminated in dinner dances at the local country club. She was not stranger to the world of finance. But she rarely took sides with one of her sons when they argued about the business.

And the arguments did erupt at times in her home. Last Sunday, as they were eating the salad that Sally was so proud of, there was a major explosion.

Sam looked up from his food and asked Robert pointedly, "So, when are we going to get the final, final figures? By Christmas?"

Perhaps it was the inherent sarcasm of his wording. Or perhaps, Robert was feeling pressured because he knew he was behind schedule. Whatever the reason, he put down his fork, fixed his glare upon his brother and answered.

"When they are fucking ready! That's when!"

Everyone froze. That word was never used in front of Robert's mother. Or in front of the children. There was a pained silence. Robert turned to his mother and apologized.

"I'm sorry, Mom. That just flew out of my mouth."

"I know that word, Robert. I wasn't born yesterday. But to use it here, and in front of the children, was inexcusable." She rose and added, "I'm going to check on the roast."

Eric looked embarrassed and Sally piped up with, "Why is Grandma upset?"

Tessa answered her, "She's okay, Sally. Eat your bread and butter. I'm going to help her in the kitchen." Before she left, she surveyed the faces at the table. And she could hear what they were saying from the other room.

Sam had an ironic smile on his face as he commented, "The women retreat to the kitchen and the warriors remain in the center of the arena."

His father rebuked him at that point. "This is not an arena, Sam. It's my home and we were going to have a peaceful dinner that your mother has been working on all afternoon. What are you trying to do here?"

"Just asked him a simple question. Don't see what all the commotion is about."

Robert made no additional remarks. Tessa knew he had to be seething. And angry at himself for allowing Sam to catch him off guard. And bait him.

When the roast was brought to the table, there was very little conversation. Tessa complimented her mother-in-law on how delicious everything was. And Eric and Sally were enchanted with the dessert, apple pie ala mode. One of their favorites. The tension at the table was palpable. Only the children seemed unaffected.

"Can I take the ice cream out of the container?" Eric asked.

"Sure, Eric", said Tessa. " Just put one scoop next to each piece of pie."

On the surface, they were proceeding through the meal as planned. In reality, except for the children, the dinner and the visit had been ruined.

Later in the car, Tessa had waited until Robert raised the subject. The children were playing a word game in the back seat.

"So, why do I let him do that to me?", he said.

"It's a built in reflex, Robert. He's had your number since you were kids. And he knows how to get under your skin."

"But why did he do that when we were having a good family time together. When my mother had worked so hard to make a nice dinner? What is his problem?"

"His problem is that he always has to assert that he is the big brother. In the office. At the dinner table. Whenever and wherever the two of you are together."

"But, he never lets up!"

"Right. And you have to accept that. And try to deal with it other ways than head-on. We've talked about this before. Probably the best way would be to ignore him. It would drive him crazy, but he's a little crazy with all this, anyway. And this way isn't working."

"My father doesn't do much about it when we're in the office. Tonight was an exception because we were in his home. And he was angry that Sam had ruined Mom's dinner."

"And tomorrow, when you see him, he may ask you the same question. What will you say then?"

"Maybe, I'll try to ignore him. I won't say anything! I'll just walk away."

"Good!"

At which point, Sally chimed in from the back seat, raising the classic children's question, "Are we there yet?"

Chapter 23

By three o'clock on Thursday, Annie was ready for the family to arrive. The turkey had gone in at noon at 325 degrees. She had sauteed the mushrooms to mix in with the green beans later. The sweet potato pie was ready to go in the oven. Oranges were sliced. She had done everything ahead of time as she liked to do to take the pressure off at the last minute. David had picked up the desserts yesterday afternoon, a chocolate layer cake and a deep dish peach cobbler. She had arrayed them on her best crystal pedestal stands on the sideboard.

The dining room looked very festive with the long table, the candles and the centerpiece of shiny apples and nuts spilling about them. The day was crisp and clear and Annie was thankful for that. She had squeezed in a half hour walk early to maintain her equilibrium and pace herself for the big day ahead. David was home and in a relaxed holiday mood. He had no one in labor or on the verge.

"Annie, the table looks magnificent! This is going to be a wonderful day!"

Annie smiled. She was determined to enjoy the day. And to shut Mark away from her thoughts.

The doorbell rang to announce Tessa, Robert and the children.

Sally burst into the room and ran to hug Annie.

"Grandma, I wanted to wear the pinafore you gave me, but Mommy wouldn't let me!"

Tessa kissed Annie and said, "It was in the wash, Mom, from non-stop wearing. She loves it."

Annie hugged Sally and helped her out of her ski jacket.

"I'm happy you like the pinafore, Sally. But this dress is so pretty with all the flowers in the material And with a long skirt too! Let me see you. Turn around. You look just right for a holiday dinner."

Tessa rolled her eyes upward and mouthed, "Thanks."

"Eric, come give Grandma a hug. Do you smell the turkey roasting? There are big drumsticks and one of them has your name on it."

Eric and his uncle Saul usually chose the drumsticks. Today, they would have their work cut out for them.

Robert kissed Annie on the cheek and joined David in the den. There was, as always, a football game to watch and they enjoyed the camaraderie as much as the sporting event. Eric assumed his position on the floor. The teams were evenly matched and the game was tied at 14 all.

Ruth arrived next. Her friend Rachel had dropped her off on the way to her own family dinner.

"Mama, you look lovely in that color," Annie said as she helped her off with her coat. "And your stuffing is cooking merrily away inside the bird. Do you smell the aroma?"

"I do. And thank you for the compliment. You always make me feel good, Annie."

Tessa kissed Ruth warmly and Sally hugged her great grandmother.

"Do you like my flower dress, Great Grandma?"

"I think it's beautiful. It makes you look like a flower, Sally!"

That left Sally at a loss for words and just in time. The doorbell rang and Saul, Diane and the girls joined everyone. *The usual suspects had been rounded up,* Annie thought happily.

Saul made his way on his crutches to the den. Diane hung up the girls coats and asked if she could help. Sally, Beth and Emily found their games and toys in the den closet and staked out the corner farthest from the television set.

Annie led Ruth, Tessa and Diane to the living room.

"Let's sit peacefully and have a glass of wine. There's nothing to do in the kitchen. Later, I'll take you up on helping with the serving and washing up. Mama, you sit in the armchair. You always find that most comfortable. How about white Zinfandel, or Chardonnay?"

"Chardonnay for me", Tessa replied.

"That's fine for me too," said Diane.

"Just half a glass, Annie." Ruth smiled. "Why not? It's supposed to be good for you."

Annie poured the glasses and then raised her own.

"Here's to everything we have to be thankful for!"

And as she made the toast, she knew that a part of it was about Mark. She couldn't shut him out of her heart and mind. Not even today, surrounded by her family.

Their conversation ranged through Tessa and Diane's jobs, Annie's writing and Ruth's many interests. Tessa spoke of her frustrations the past several weeks. Feeling as if she were a marionette with two bosses pulling the strings. Diane had more control of the work she was doing, writing ad copy for a new campaign. But she too felt very pressured, with Saul on crutches, and Emily having strep throat and being home from school. Annie, who had done very little productive writing during the past three weeks, just said her work on the article was going well. And Ruth told them about the course she was taking in the University Without Walls.

"It's called, 'You're Getting On My Nerves!' We've been reading articles written by psychologists. And several great short stories. There are seven other people in the course, from all over the country. There's a group leader and we're all on a conference call together."

"It sounds very interesting, Grandma", Tessa interjected.

"It's really a lot of fun, Tessa. I have nicknames for the other seven. I try to imagine what they look like."

"What are some of the nicknames, Mama?" Annie asked.

Ruth laughed. "Are you ready? 'Big Shot', 'Mae West', 'Fats', 'Clark Gable', 'Mrs. Miniver', 'William Jennings Bryan' and, whom did I leave out? Oh, yes, 'Baby'"

Diane was looking at Ruth with newly found admiration. "Those are such fabulous names. We need you at the agency. I am intrigued by the imagery. Let me guess. 'Baby' needs everyone's love and attention. 'Mae West' has only sex on her mind. But 'Mrs. Miniver', I'm pulling a blank on her."

"I think she's before your time, Diane," Ruth answered. "Mrs. Miniver, Greer Garson in the film, was a stalwart. Nothing fazed her during the Blitz in World War II. This woman reminds me of her."

"Well, I think the whole course sounds fabulous, Grandma," Tessa added. "And you will never stop impressing me with your intellect."

Ruth was pleased with their responses. She usually felt somewhat on the periphery and it was nice to be center stage for a change. Annie rose and came over to kiss her on the cheek.

"No wonder you do the crossword puzzles in ink, Mama. And so fast. What a brain you are!"

JOYCE S. ANDERSON

Loud cheers emanated periodically from the football fans in the den.
"That a way to go!", yelled Eric.

The roar of the stadium crowd rose and fell like waves in the background.
David, Robert and Saul took turns adding whoops of delight when their team
was winning. Long, audible groans followed an intercepted pass and a failed
field goal. Watching the game together, Annie knew, was as important to the
men as the turkey dinner. Her mother called these rituals, strands in the tapestry
of life. It was an apt metaphor.

By five, the timer in the turkey had popped up and Annie turned the oven
down to Warm. It was plump and browned — looked perfect. She started the
green beans, kept stirring the gravy and heated the sauteed mushrooms in the
Microwave. But the marshmallow crust had melted on the sweet potato pie!
The kids wouldn't mind, Annie thought. Ruth arranged the orange slices around
the rim of the cranberry sauce dish. A basket of small dinner rolls was on the
table. Diane and Tessa filled the water glasses and two bottles of wine were
open. White and red. The children would have soda for a treat. When David
took the turkey out, she would put the peach cobbler in to warm. They were
almost ready to sit down at the table.

Annie lit the candles. It was time to call everyone in. She hesitated for a
moment and Tessa, who was by her side, looked at her and asked, "Are you
okay, Mom? You're all flushed."

"I'm fine, Tessa. Call in the troops!"

And they came, they ate — and they conquered everything in sight.

"This is one huge drumstick, Grandpop!", declared Eric.

"I want extra marshmallows with the sweet potatoes, Grandma. Please!"
implored Sally.

"The stuffing is delicious, as always, Mama."

In between requests and compliments, the dinner proceeded. Saul was
the trencherman, far outdoing his father and brother-in-law with second
helpings. He decimated his drumstick, leaving Eric in awe. David served the
wine and made a toast to "Annie, our hostess par excellence!" Annie found
she had little appetite. She took something of everything and left most of it
on her plate. Tessa noticed.

"Mom. You're not eating much. Are you sure you're okay?"

"I guess I nibbled in the kitchen while I was serving. I'm fine dear."

When the table was cleared, she brought the peach cobbler from the oven
to the table. Diane carried the chocolate cake to the opposite end. There were
appropriate oohs and aahs.

116

"Now, who wants what?" Annie asked.

The children all opted for the cake. It was a success every time. The adults chose the peach cobbler. Annie had expected that. There was uniformity in the generations.

"Just a small piece for me, dear." Ruth said.

"And a man-sized piece for me!" added Robert.

"Same for me, Mom". Saul was still hungry apparently. "And a sliver of the cake too."

"How many regular coffees? How many Decafs?" Annie had brewed a pot of each.

The children were excused once they had finished their cake. The adults sat, lingering over their coffee. Annie sat back in her arm chair and couldn't stop her thoughts from going where they shouldn't go. To Mark. He would be at his parents house, he had said. The entire clan. Greek specialties as well as the centerpiece turkey. She imagined their table. The dark heads. The vivacious conversation. The arguments Mark had told her usually dominated their coming together. Robust and noisy. She wondered what it would be like to be with him in that setting. She couldn't imagine it.

"Mom, why don't you go with Grandma into the living room. We're going to clean up." Tessa and Diane usually took over and Annie was grateful. David and Robert would take turns washing and stacking the dishwasher. Tessa and Diane would clear and put away the left over food. It would not be exactly as she would do it, but it would be done. All of a sudden, Annie felt very tired.

David came to her and put his hand on her shoulder.

"Are you alright, dear? You've been so quiet."

"Just a little frazzled. I'm fine."

"It was a wonderful dinner, Annie. Everyone loved it."

"I know, David."

He kissed her on the cheek and went to his post at the kitchen sink. Annie joined her mother in the living room. Saul hobbled off on his crutches to the den to supervise the kids.

Thanksgiving, 2001 was over.

Chapter 24

Friday morning, David left early for the hospital and Annie felt as if she were in slow motion. She knew everyone had enjoyed the dinner. And had fun as well. Diane had seemed closer than usual, more at ease and that was good. The little girls were well behaved at the table and her mother was so happy to be with the entire family. David took particular pleasure sitting at the head of the long holiday table, surveying his offspring— and their offspring. He said that it gave him a deep sense of fulfillment to have them all there together.

Annie knew that she should be feeling a similar sense of well being. But she did not. Tessa and David had both noticed that something was bothering her. They were very astute at picking up clues. And, of course, they were right. She had felt somewhat removed the entire afternoon and evening. It was a sharp stab whenever she thought of Mark. The need was palpable, for her. Now, she wanted to be with him. To see him. To talk with him. To go to bed with him. She could not lie to herself about that. She felt as if she were being consumed by her passion for him.

She called Sarah.

"Sarah, it's me."

"Yes, Annie. I thought it might be you. How was the dinner?"

"The dinner was fine. But, I'm not. And David and Tessa noticed that something was wrong."

"What happened?"

"They each asked if I were alright. I didn't eat much and I must have seemed distracted."

"Not good, Annie."

"I know. I just said I was tired. And that I was fine. It gets easier to lie the more I do it."

"What are you doing to do about this?"

"Do? All I can think of is that I want to be with him. I may call him when we hang up."

"You are in big trouble, Annie. I don't know what to say to help you."

" I have to get over this intense need I have for him, Sarah. And I don't know how to do it."

"If David and Tessa sensed something was wrong, it's getting dangerous, Annie."

"I know that too. I'm taking it one day at a time, like the drug addicts and the alcoholics."

" I think that's a fair comparison. You are hooked on him. And you need to break the habit."

"Easy for you to say. And besides, I'm not ready to break the habit, yet. That's the truth! "

"Oh, Annie. I'm worried that everything may go up in flames. What if David finds out?"

Annie sighed deeply. She knew that Sarah would have no answers. And would raise the hard questions all over again. She was sorry she had called.

" I never even asked you how your dinner was. How was it?"

"It was good. Hectic, but good." She paused. "Be careful, Annie."

"I will be, Sarah. Talk to you in a few days."

As soon as she hung up, the phone rang. It was Tessa.

"Mom, it's me. I was just thinking of you. You didn't seem like yourself, yesterday."

"I'm fine, dear. I was busy with all the preparations. Sometimes it gets to me a little.

There's a lot to do."

"I know. It just seemed as if you had something on your mind."

"No. Nothing unusual." Annie wanted to change the subject. Fast.

"Are you at work? Or is there a four day holiday for the firm?"

"No. I'm at work. Even though there is almost no one else out there to do business with. Tom Simmons doesn't believe in too many long holiday weekends. We probably will all leave early. I was not in the mood to come in today. That's for sure!"

"Is Robert home?"

"Yes, he is. With the kids. His firm is closed. A most civilized business, I want to tell you."

"Well, have a good rest of the weekend, when you get home. The kids were wonderful, as usual. I love to watch Eric tackle the drumstick!"

"Take it easy, today, Mom. You earned it."

"Bye, dear."

Annie thought of the Indian legend again, of the triangle turning in one's heart. With each lie, the points would be worn down a little — until it didn't hurt anymore. It was true. The more she lied to David and Tessa, the easier it became. And the less and less it hurt.

Annie called Mark's number and waited. He did not answer. She listened to the recording just to hear his voice. She did not leave a message.

She drove to the gym on the chance that he might be there since yesterday was a holiday. His car was not outside and she didn't even go in. Instead, she drove back and took a three mile walk. That was always the best way to find her center and she needed to do that desperately today.

When she returned home, she took a hot jacuzzi, ate some of the leftover turkey and worked on the article until David came home at five. She had managed to avoid calling Mark again and considered that something of a victory of will power.

Over the weekend, she called Mark several more times without reaching him. She did not leave messages. She was on edge, not knowing where he was. It left her with an empty feeling. Perhaps he had gone away for the long weekend. Without telling her? It didn't make sense. She began to worry if he were alright.

David noticed her mood. "Annie, you seem very restless. Are you okay?"

"I'm just feeling the pressure of this deadline with the article. It's taking much longer to do than I thought it would."

"Can't you ask for an extension? You know that editor pretty well."

"Editors don't want extensions, David. No matter how well you know them. They want it when they want it!"

"It sounds like an expectant mother who's a week past her due date. She wants the baby now!"

"That's exactly how it is."

Annie worked long hours both Saturday and Sunday. She forced herself to concentrate on the article. It was almost finished. Monday morning, she arose with free floating anxiety swirling about her before she even remembered what the problem was. At nine, she tried Mark's number and there was still no answer. *This is going to be one hell of a long day,* she thought. It was. She finished the article on communications between generations and mailed it off to the editor. She made turkey Tetrazinni for dinner from the last of the leftovers. She filled up the hours of her day, watched television and went to bed early.

Tuesday morning, she did not call. She drove to the gym. His car was in the parking lot and her heart turned over. When she saw him on the treadmill, she felt torn by different emotions — relief, happiness and anger. She knew she had to control herself. When he saw her, he smiled.

"Good morning, Annie. How was Thanksgiving?"

It was as if nothing had changed for him. She took a deep breath.

"We had a good Thanksgiving, Mark. How was yours?"

"Fine. The usual commotion at dinner. And then, my sister, Helen's car broke down and I drove her and the kids back to Cleveland. We left Saturday and I got back late last night."

"You were in Cleveland?" She needed time for the explanation to sink in. He had been in Cleveland. While she was climbing the walls. Cleveland!

"I had no way to tell you Annie. I couldn't very well call your house."

And then she just blurted it out.

"I had no idea where you, Mark. By Sunday, I began to worry."

"We each have lives, Annie. I would have let you know if I could have."

Annie realized she had gone too far. She didn't own Mark. Or his life. She paused before she responded.

"You're right, Mark. I was off base. You don't have to tell me where you're going, if you go out of town."

"I'm sorry you were worried, Annie."

They walked the treadmills in silence for about half an hour. Annie's mind was in turmoil. She was in much too deep. And she knew it. They had no strings on each other. She was the one who was married. He was a free agent. And if he went to Cleveland to help his sister— or to see another woman, it was his business. She didn't want to think about the latter possibility. But it could happen. She had to face reality.

When they were in the parking lot, she said, "I have to be back home by eleven today, Mark. I'm expecting a call from my editor."

He gave her a long, slow look.

"I've missed you, Annie. Can you call her from my house?"

And then, she told him the truth.

"I feel as if I'm coming apart, Mark. I don't have to be home. I'll follow you to the house."

Their reunion was tumultuous. Once they were inside the front door, Annie started to cry. Great, heaving sobs. He held her until the tears subsided. He kissed her hair and murmured comforting words. She dried her eyes and regained her composure.

"Come into the kitchen, Annie. I'm going to put on the kettle. And we're going to just sit here and talk. Or not talk. Whatever you want."

The sun was coming in through the curtained window and Annie still felt the warmth of his arms about her. She felt a great weight lifted from her heart. He did care for her deeply. There was no other woman.

"Mark, I feel like a fool."

"You're allowed. It makes you human. Remember, I warned you about that — being human."

He was smiling and teasing her. It helped.

"You lift my spirits, Mark."

"Good."

"I felt so alone, not knowing where you were. A feeling of absence and emptiness."

"And now?"

She reached across the table and took his hand. He rose and pulled her to her feet and drew her close to him. He kissed her to seal the bargain.

"I'm going to make sure you don't feel alone anymore, Annie."

Chapter 25

Upstairs in Mark's bedroom, Annie gave herself to him with a fierce abandon. All the anxiety of the weekend was transformed into an intense need to possess him — and be possessed by him. She had wanted him so desperately! And now they were together. He seemed to sense the difference in her need and responded to it with his own passion. He caressed her gently and kissed her breasts. His hands moved slowly down her body. He bent his head and lightly kissed the inside of her thighs. Annie felt a wild urgency rising within her.

"Please, Mark", she begged. "Don't tease me. I want you so!"

He propped himself up on his elbows and looked into her eyes. He kissed her again on the lips.

"It's more than want for me, Annie. I'm in love with you."

They stayed in bed for two hours. Then, Annie fell asleep in his arms. When she awoke, Mark was still sleeping. She lay there reliving the joy she had felt. The exquisite sensations. An excitement and fulfillment that she had rarely experienced before. One part of her mind reminded her that she had never been much of a Freudian. Now, she realized the dimensions of sexual desire and the power it could have over one's life. She was besotted with Mark and with sensual pleasure. Yes, Freud — it was sex, but Mark was also compassionate, interesting, talented, funny and a great cook! She ticked off his other assets in her head.

For the first time, the unthinkable question of whether she might leave David arose in her mind. *Separation — and divorce after 37 years? Destroy David's trust and love for her! Tear the family apart! Her mother!* It was all too awful to even touch!

She lay, watching Mark until she dozed off again. When she awoke, it was after four and Mark was in the bathroom. The shower was running. She came in and opened the shower door. He laughed and welcomed her with a soapy sponge. They had taken a shower together once before. For Annie, it had been a first. She had let go of inhibitions that had lasted for decades. It felt wonderful!

There were two messages on the machine when Annie came home. David, calling to say he would be staying at the hospital. Two women in labor, at different stages. And her mother, whose words and tone sent a cold shock through Annie.

"Annie, it's Mama. I'm not feeling too well. I'm calling the doctor's office. Rachel is going to drive me. I'll talk to you later."

She called her mother's number and there was no answer. She found Rachel's number in her book and there was no answer there either. She called her mother's doctor, but the recording asked that calls be made between regular office hours. It was now 5:30. She left her name on the message recorder and asked that he return her call. She said it was urgent. She felt panic rising, but got herself under control. What next?

She called David on his cell phone. He answered on the second ring.

"Dr. Bertman."

"David, it's me. I came home to find a message from Mama that she didn't feel well. And Rachel was taking her to the doctor's. That was at two thirty this afternoon. She's not home. Rachel's not home. The doctor's office is closed. I left a message for him to call me. She must be in the hospital!"

"Let me check with the Emergency Room here. I'll call you right back."

Annie was still standing with her jacket on, next to the answering machine. She felt numb. And sick to her stomach. While she had been satisfying her lust for Mark Trianos, her mother had needed her. She sat down heavily in one of the kitchen chairs and stared dully ahead. She felt cold and kept her jacket around her shoulders. The phone rang and she grabbed it.

"Yes."

"She's wasn't here, Annie. I know he practices at two hospitals. I'll call over there and find out if she was seen or admitted. Hang on."

Annie's mouth felt dry and she poured a glass of water. Her mind and her emotions were in turmoil. She knew she could have been at the theater or the mall or any number of places and missed her mother's call. But that was not where she had been. She had been having the time of her life in bed with her lover. It became very harsh and clear in her mind. And sordid.

The phone rang again.

"Yes, David."

"She's at Bergen General, Annie. She came in by ambulance. She's still in the ER until they find a room. She's doing okay, according to the nurse I spoke with. Her doctor was there earlier. I'm going to try and reach him now."

"I'm going to the hospital, David. I'll call you from there."

Annie reached the hospital in fifteen minutes. As she drove, she tried to prepare herself for what she would find. Her mother had several close calls in the past ten years with bouts of severe rapid heart beat. The beta blocker she took every morning had brought that under control. But there was always the chance it would reoccur. Or it might be something completely different. Her message had been that she didn't feel well. It could mean anything. She was 87 years old!

Annie parked the car and found the Emergency Room easily. She told the nurse at the desk who she was, and then spied her mother in one of the cubicles. Ruth was hooked up to all the monitors and IV and oxygen tubes. Her eyes were closed and her skin looked ashen.

Oh, Mama, Annie thought. *I wasn't there for you when you needed me.*

She went to the nurses station again and asked if they could tell her what had happened. One of the nurses said the doctor would have to do that. Mrs. Shaeffer was resting and holding her own. That was a good sign.

The phrases 'holding her own' and 'good sign' only raised Annie's anxiety level higher. She asked to talk to the ER doctor in charge. He was seeing one of the other patients and she waited until he returned to the central station. When he did, she introduced herself and asked if he could tell her how her mother was doing. He seemed rushed, but he did take the time to go over to her mother's bed and look at her chart.

"Mrs. Shaeffer was experiencing severe arrhythmia when she was admitted. It took a while to bring it under control. Her doctor, Dr. Stein, saw her and recommended that she stay for observation. We're waiting until a room is available."

"Is she out of danger, Dr.?"

"Her heart beat has returned to normal. We have her on the coronary monitor and that will show any changes. Dr. Stein will see her again, later."

Annie felt a great wave of relief wash over her. She saw that her mother was still sleeping and went out to the waiting room to call David.

"David, I'm in the ER. Mama's okay. She had the rapid heart beat again. Dr. Stein must have told her that he would meet her at the hospital when she called. He'll be back to see her later. I'm going to wait to see him."

"Are you alright, Annie?"

"I am now. She looks very pale, but the ER doctor told me her heart beat was back to normal. Apparently, it took some time to bring it down. It is very scary, David. She looks so frail and helpless."

Annie felt tears welling up in her eyes.

"I have to stay here Annie. Two women are going to pop. One in the next hour, I think. That's the ETA for this baby. And Dr. Stein hasn't called me back yet."

"I'll talk to you later, David."

"Take care, dear. It sounds as if she's going to be fine. She is one tough lady! Don't forget that."

"I know, David. Bye."

Annie went back to see Ruth and her eyes were open. When she saw Annie, she smiled. Annie bent down to kiss her forehead. She sat on the chair next to the bed and held her hand.

"Hello, Mama. Fancy meeting you here! How do you feel?"

"Annie dear, I feel better seeing you. But look at all these contraptions!"

"The doctor said you're going to be fine, Mama. The contraptions are just monitors."

"Did you see Dr. Stein?"

"No, but the ER doctor talked with me."

"And what did he say?"

"He said you had the rapid heart beat, which I am sure you know, and that it is now under control."

"It was very bad, Annie. Worse than I have ever had. It was pounding in my chest, very fast. And I felt dizzy. When I called Dr. Stein, he said to call 911 and he would meet me here. I was going to go with Rachel to his office, but he said to do this. So I did." She stopped to catch her breath and continued. "The ambulance people were very good and kind. And with the siren on, we were here in about five minutes!"

Annie had gone with her mother in the ambulance several times with the siren screaming. It had been a harrowing experience. But, each time, Ruth had snapped back. A strong constitution and iron will power had brought her recovery. Ruth Shaeffer was a fighter in more ways than one.

"Why don't you rest, Mama. Close your eyes. It's the best thing for you. I'm going to stay right here. I talked to David. He's got two women ready to deliver or he would be here. He sent you his love."

"He's wonderful, Annie."

"I know, Mama."

Ruth always said that David was more of a son to her than a son-in-law. He had been very devoted to her over the years and they were very close. He had been there for her with all his medical skills whenever she had needed him. Annie thought about that as she sat by her mother's bedside. It was David she had called instinctively when she heard her mother's message on the answering machine. Not Mark. It was David whose voice had given her comfort and encouragement. As he always did.

The compartments of her life seemed very clear again. She and David at the center. And Mark off to the side in an unfinished area. She would call Jack. And Tessa and Saul later. But for now, she just wanted to sit quietly and be thankful that her mother was doing well.

Chapter 26

Annie was dozing in the chair when Dr. Stein came in after seven to check on her mother. He read her chart first and then stood by her bedside to take her pulse. Ruth opened her eyes and asked,

"How am I, Dr. Stein?"

"How do you feel, Mrs. Shaeffer?"

"I feel okay, but a little weak. And I need to catch my breath when I talk."

"That's to be expected. Your body is adjusting to what happened. But your heart is doing well now and we want to keep it that way."

"Will I have to stay here overnight?"

"I think that would be best. Maybe for a few days to give you a chance to rest up."

"Whatever you think best. You're the doctor."

Annie stood and spoke at that point.

"I'm Annie Bertman, Mrs. Shaeffer's daughter, Dr. Stein. We've met before, of course."

"Yes, I remember your husband too. We see each other in the hospitals from time to time."

"Do you think they will have a room for mother tonight?"

"They are jammed upstairs from what I am told. She may have to stay here until tomorrow."

Then he turned to talk directly to his patient.

"You'll be a good sport, I know, Mrs. Shaeffer, if you have to sleep here tonight?"

Ruth smiled. And some color returned to her face. She always rose to the occasion when asked to.

"I'll be a good sport. You can count on me."

"I'll see you in the morning, Mrs. Shaeffer. If you need anything, push the button and the nurse will be right at your side."

Annie excused herself and followed Dr. Stein to the main station.

"May I talk with you for a moment? This seemed to be a stronger attack than mother has had in the past. Is there any way to prevent these from happening?"

"Her medication, the beta blocker, has been working quite well. If the attacks become more frequent and last longer, we may consider a procedure called catheter ablation. But we would not usually do this with a patient your mother's age."

"And what is that procedure? Is that an operation?"

"No, it's more of a technique. A catheter is inserted, the tip heats up and through precision mapping destroys the point that causes the rapid heart beat. That's the best way I can translate it into layman's terms."

"Well, I can understand why you would be reluctant to use it with an 87 year old patient. It sounds dangerous."

"I wouldn't call it dangerous. There are risks with all medical techniques. Surgical and nonsurgical. But there are also risks from increased episodes of extended arrhythmia."

"Thank you, Dr. Stein." Annie shook his hand. "I appreciate the information and your candor."

After he left, Annie had the same tight feeling in the pit of her stomach. And her hands felt ice cold. She had to call Jack and tell him what had happened. She went back to see her mother and found that a tray had been brought in with a soft diet dinner.

"Chicken soup, Annie! The best medicine." Ruth laughed. "And Jello. I'll lose some weight in here! Why don't you go down to the cafeteria and get a sandwich? Or go home now. I'll be fine."

"I will go get something to eat. But I'll be back and see you before I go home. Enjoy the chicken soup. I bet it's not as good as yours."

Ruth smiled and Annie felt better. She would call David and Jack from the telephones near the cafeteria. She called David first and told him what Dr. Stein had said. He knew about catheter ablation. Then she called her brother Jack in Chicago. His wife, Lois, answered.

"Lois, this is Annie. Is Jack there?"

"Is something wrong, Annie? You sound upset."

"Well, Mama's in the hospital. She had a long bout of the rapid heart beat. They're going to keep her here for a few days for observation."

"I'm sorry, Annie. I'll get Jack. He's in his office. I hope your mother feels better, fast."

Annie and Lois rarely saw each other. When they did, the relationship was cordial. They didn't really know each other that well. But Annie knew that Jack was happy in his marriage and that was all that was important to her about Lois.

"Annie, Lois just told me. How is Mama doing? What happened?"

"She had a severe attack of the rapid heart beat, Jack. She said it felt as if her heart were pounding in her chest. And she got dizzy. I wasn't home when she called me. Dr. Stein told her to call 911, which she did, and she went in by ambulance. He met her at the ER. I talked with him and he felt she was doing okay. He wants her to stay there a few days. And they don't have a room. She'll have to stay in the ER overnight."

"How are her spirits?"

"You know, Mama, Jack. She was eating chicken soup and making jokes!"

"Do you think I should come?"

Jack always put the question to her when their mother was sick. Annie wished he would make his own decision each time.

"I don't know, Jack. If you came, it might frighten her that she is worse than she is. That's always a consideration. But the doctor told me this was a severe attack. And prolonged."

"How about if I tell her, I have a conference in Boston and I'm going to make a stop over to see her?"

"I think that is a great idea. And she would believe it. Stay for one day and visit. It will be a tonic for her, I know. She loves to see you so and you couldn't come for Thanksgiving."

"Why don't you tell her that you talked with me and I'm going to be there tomorrow."

"Whether she believes it or not, she'll be happy when you walk in the door."

"I'll let you know later after I make plane reservations what time I'll be in, Annie."

This time Jack had reacted as she hoped he would. In the past, there too many times when he had not come. There were obstacles that he could not seem to surmount when Annie would call and tell him Ruth was sick. He would send flowers and cards. He would call every day. But he would stay in Chicago.

Annie was relieved that he was coming. She wanted him to talk with Dr.

Stein. Doctors always paid more attention to other doctors when they were discussing a patient. She knew that from long experience as a doctor's wife.

She ate a chef salad in the cafeteria and had a cup of tea and apple pie. She found that she was hungry after all. When she came back to the ER, Ruth was asleep. Annie sat for a while, then asked one of the nurses if she would be sure to tell her mother that she had been there. The nurse promised she would. She was young and earnest and Annie felt she could rely on her.

"And please tell her, I'll see her in the morning."

"I will. Don't worry. She will have the best care here. She's a lovely lady. It's a pleasure to take care of her."

Annie drove home with a heavy heart. She felt her mother was not in any danger. But the events of the day had shocked her to her core. The afternoon with Mark seemed years ago. She pushed it out of her mind. The ecstasy she had felt seemed to have turned to ashes.

Part III

Chapter 27

Tessa had just finished stacking the dinner plates in the dishwasher when the phone rang.

"Tessa, it's Mom. Some not good news. Grandma Ruth is in the hospital. She had an attack of the rapid heart beat this afternoon. But, she's doing okay now. Her heart is back to normal."

Tessa was alarmed. Her feelings for her grandmother ran very deep. There had been a special bond between them since she was a little girl. Ruth had always encouraged Tessa to follow her dreams. And she had helped her through the long painful separation and divorce from Ivan. She gave Tessa loving comfort and sensible advice from her many years of living.

"Is she going to be alright? Why are they keeping her there? Did you take her to the hospital?"

"The doctor said he wanted to keep her there for a few days for observation. She's still feeling weak. She did call me, but I was out — doing errands. Dr. Stein told her to call 911. She went in by ambulance and met him at the Emergency Room."

"Oh, God! She had to go alone in the ambulance! How horrible!"

" Yes. I feel awful that I wasn't home when she needed me."

"How is she now?"

"All I can tell you is that she was eating chicken soup for dinner and laughing."

"Was she telling the nurses and doctors what to do?" Tessa asked. "Trying to take charge? Then we know she is feeling like herself."

"No, she's behaving very properly as a patient and they all love her already."

Tessa felt her grandmother could move mountains because she had seen her do it many times in the past. She thought of Grandma Ruth as indomitable.

It was hard to think of her as 87 years old.

"Can I go see her?"

"Sure. If you can get away. She always loves to see you, dear. It would give her a lift."

"I'll talk to you in the morning. I'll try to get there later in the afternoon."

Tessa put down the telephone and sat at the kitchen table. Through her mind, raced the line, *This is the week that was!'* She was, if her count was correct, and she was sure it was — exactly one week late! And she was always, repeat always, on time.

Coming home on the train, she had done the arithmetic over and over in her head. It always came out the same. Her period had been due the Tuesday before Thanksgiving. It was now seven days late. And she was never late! Ever since she was thirteen, like clockwork, she knew when it would arrive . And, after each of the children, it returned to its regular schedule. She sometimes joked with Robert that they would always know when they could plan a sexy weekend getaway.

She and Robert were very careful with birth control. She used her diaphragm most of the time. But Robert would use a condom, if she wasn't ready. They had talked about the benefits of spontaneity versus safety long ago. And they had found a system that worked for them. When they were ready to have a baby, they had enjoyed the new found freedom. Tessa had conceived Sally within several months.

Now, Tessa knew the system had broken down somewhere. She had heard of defective condoms and women who had forgotten to put in their diaphragms. Was it possible that she had done that one night? Anything was possible in a marriage, she knew from the stories she had heard in the divorce support group years ago. Love and sex and stress all mixed together. Yes, anything was possible.

She had been waiting, each morning, hoping for some sign. But nothing happened. She had not told Robert. He never kept track of their sex life that way. She knew he had no idea. She would buy one of those pregnancy kits before saying anything to him. She knew they weren't foolproof. But they were pretty damn good! The sooner she knew the facts, the sooner she could begin to deal with them. She would buy a kit in the hospital drug store when she went to see Grandma Ruth tomorrow. The irony of that struck her and she almost laughed out loud. An appropriate place to find out if she were going to have a baby!

Tessa couldn't stop her mind from leaping ahead to the distinct possibility of a positive reading. *Another baby!* The thought stunned her. She and Robert hadn't even considered having another baby. They were very happy with the ideal American family, one boy and one girl. Eric and Sally were both growing nicely. Their family was complete. So they thought!

The next morning, as she rode on the train into the city, she did the 'What if?' exercise to help her sort out what she was facing. She had always been staunchly Pro-Choice. And now, she was going to be faced with choices. Now, it would be real — not theoretical. Not some other woman deciding what she was going to do. It would be her body. Her life. And Robert's, of course. She thought of them as one.

What if the test were positive? When would she tell Robert? What would be his reaction? What if she didn't want to have the baby? She had never had to consider that choice before. *What if Robert wanted another baby and she did not?* There was another 'what if' that crept into her mind. *What if she had an abortion and didn't tell Robert?* That was unthinkable based on their marriage. But it couldn't be just pushed under as if it did not exist. *And what if she had another baby?* The big question, would she be able to continue full time at the firm? Maybe, a bigger question — would she want to be full time at the firm with a new baby?

The variables tumbled in her mind. And the choices. Her life had been relatively in place. Home and career, balanced at times precariously, but set on course. Aimed at the partnership. Now, what? She could just imagine Tom Simmons face when she would tell him!

Tessa worked at her desk through the lunch hour. She had brought a sandwich and an apple from home. She didn't want any comments when she left early. By three, she was ready to go. She did not tell either of her bosses. She just went. If there were repercussions, she would deal with them tomorrow. At least, there was no urgent work pending.

She took one of the intercity buses from Port Authority and was at the hospital in Teaneck by four. The woman at Reception told her that Ruth Shaeffer was in room 413. At least she wasn't in the Emergency Room any more. When Tessa found the room, the door was slightly ajar. She peeked in and saw that her grandmother was sitting up and very much awake. She knocked softly so as not to startle her.

"Hi, Grandma. I came to see if you are behaving like a good girl."

"Tessa, darling!"

Tessa went into her grandmother's open arms. She kissed her on the cheek. There were still tubes in place and a monitor behind the bed.

"Grandma, you look like yourself, except for all these attachments. How do you feel?"

"Much better today, Tessa. And being in a private room is a blessing. I did sleep last night, but they brought in some people from an automobile accident after midnight. I heard all the commotion. It was not good."

"When did they move you here?"

"About ten. After breakfast. Your Mom was here to supervise and it all went smoothly. And she brought me my own nightgown. Those impossible gowns they have with the open backs drive me crazy. And my toiletries and slippers. Now, I feel more like myself."

"When does the doctor say you can go home?

"Maybe tomorrow. I hope so. And your Dad was here too. He had talked with Dr. Stein. And guess what — your uncle Jack is going to be here in about an hour. He was on his way to Boston to a conference and he's going to come here and spend the night with your Mom and Dad. I haven't seen him in too many months. That will be so nice."

Tessa was relieved by her grandmother's appearance. And their conversation.

"Robert sends his love, Grandma. I did not tell the children. Mom said you were doing fine and I did not want them to worry.'

"Of course, dear. That makes good sense. They don't even have to know."

"Can I bring you anything?

"I would love to have my needlepoint. But that can wait until I get home. I'm working on something very special."

"What is it, Grandma?"

"Well, Tessa, it's going to be a surprise. So I can't tell you.'

Ruth's eyes took on a sparkle and Tessa only knew that the surprise could wait. What was amazing was that her grandmother had bounced back once more. And was raring to get home and pick up the strands of her life.

Tessa stayed for about half an hour. She knew that it was tiring for a patient to have visitors. In a way, the patient had to entertain the visitor. And Uncle Jack would be there shortly too.

"Grandma, I'm going to go now. Give Uncle Jack my love. Have a nice visit with him. Maybe, I'll bump into him on the way out."

She bent to kiss Ruth once more and said, "I love you, Grandma. I'll talk to you when you're home. Maybe you'll tell me about the needlepoint you're working on."

She did not see her uncle on the way down the hall. She went down in the elevator to the drugstore and found the home pregnancy kits. There were different brands. She remembered when they were anxious to know— when she became pregnant with Sally. She had bought the brand that used colors. And the brand that showed a plus or a minus. She bought both this time too. With very different feelings. The boxes fit into her briefcase easily. Again, the irony struck her. In among her legal papers were two boxes that could send her career completely off the tracks. That brought her back to the 'what if' scenarios. She felt very tired and tried to push it all away until she found out the results of the tests.

Her grandmother often said, when thrown a curve, "Life is not simple." *Indeed,* thought Tessa, remembering John Lennon, — *life is what happens when we are making plans.*

Chapter 28

Tessa was lulled by the swaying of the train and fell asleep on the way home. She awoke suddenly, one station before her stop. A cold wind hit her face as she stepped off the train and made her way to the parking lot. Her shoulder bag and briefcase were heavy. She felt exhausted — physically and mentally.

By the time she reached her house, she was almost in tears. Robert was upstairs with the children. He called down to her, when he heard her come in.

"Tessa. We're up here. Sally is taking her bath."

She put down her bag and briefcase, hung up her coat and went into the kitchen. The dishes were still on the table. The large frying pan was soaking in the sink. The odor of eggs hung in the air. If she had been hungry, she wasn't anymore. She took her brief case and shoulder bag and went upstairs. Robert was in the bathroom with Sally.

"Hi, Mommy. I'm having a great bath. I don't want to come out!"

Tessa leaned over and gave her a kiss on the top of her head. Eric appeared in the hall and she went out to give him a hug. Robert had managed to lure Sally out of the tub and had her wrapped in one of the huge bath sheets. On the surface, Tessa thought, it was one more normal end of the day in their lives. Hectic, but normal.

"How is your grandmother?" Robert asked.

"She's incredible! She looked like herself. The doctor said she can go home tomorrow. She had to go in by herself in the ambulance!"

"Very scary!"

"Yes. But she was smiling and in good spirits. Uncle Jack was stopping to see her. She doesn't see him often and she really misses him."

"Did you have dinner?" Robert said. "Sorry, it is such a mess downstairs.

140

I made the kids cheese omelets. I'll clean it up."

"No, I didn't eat. Just caught the train in time. I fell asleep coming home."

He looked at her searchingly and said, "Are you alright, Tessa? You look all in. Do you want me to make you a tuna sandwich and a cup of tea?"

"Maybe. I'll go down in a little while. First, I'm going to take off these clothes and put on my sweats."

She took her bag and briefcase into their bedroom and closed the door. Then she took out the two boxes and went into the bathroom. Fifteen minutes later, she had the results of both tests. One was blue and one was a plus sign. They were both positive! She was pregnant!

Tessa felt numb. Her anxiety that had building for a week had peaked that afternoon. Now, she felt nothing. Her emotions seemed frozen. Her body went through the motions of changing into her sport clothes. As she was hanging up her suit and blouse, Robert came into the bedroom.

"It will only take me ten minutes to clean up the kitchen. Should I make you a sandwich?"

She turned to look at him. There was no way she could get through the next hour, the next minutes without telling him. They did not hide things from each other. That was bedrock in their marriage.

"Close the door, Robert. And lock it."

"What is it Tessa? What's the matter? You look awful."

He came over and took her in his arms. "Tell me, Baby. What is it? You can tell me."

She stood back from him, walked to the bed and sat down. He came and sat down beside her. She looked at him and said it very simply, "I'm pregnant, Robert."

"You're pregnant?"

He looked as if he couldn't digest the words. She just sat and waited for him to continue.

"You're pregnant! I can't believe it! When did you find out?"

"I'm a week late, Robert. I'm never late. But I kept hoping it was a fluke. But, it's not a fluke. I bought the home pregnancy kits at the hospital drugstore this afternoon. I just took two different tests and the results both came out positive!"

"You've been worrying all week. And you didn't tell me?"

"It was Thanksgiving and I didn't want to ruin it."

"So, you've been walking around each day with a time bomb ticking inside you?"

"Not a time bomb," she said with some irony. "A baby."

At that point, Sally was outside their door.

"Mommy, can I come in?"

Tessa rose and opened the door. Sally was standing there with one of her enormous stuffed animals in tow. "Muffy hurt his foot! Can you help me put a band aid on it?"

"Yes, I will find a band aid for Muffy. Let's take care of him in your room."

Robert went downstairs slowly. When Tessa joined him, the kitchen was in order and he was sitting in his regular chair with a snifter of brandy in front of him. Tessa came over and kissed him. He rarely took a drink after dinner at home. Obviously, he saw the need tonight.

"It's been a long week," she said.

"I guess I need some time to catch up with you, Tessa."

"Yes, you do. I kept doing 'what if' scenarios on the train going into work today. Now, at least the most important 'what if' has been answered. I am pregnant."

"What were the other 'what if' scenarios, Tessa?"

"Robert, why don't we table those for tonight. You just found out what I have been thinking about non-stop for a week. You need time to catch up with this, just as I do, now that we know the answer."

"I'm caught up, Tessa. What were the other 'what if' scenarios?"

His voice had become insistent. Tessa knew the tone. It was rare, but she had heard it before when they were on the verge of an argument. She didn't want any arguments tonight. She couldn't bear that. Not tonight.

"Robert, I can't do this now. I realize you are in some kind of shock. But I can't talk about this anymore tonight. I just can't do it! I'm sorry. I'm have to go to bed."

He looked stricken, but she didn't have the energy to go on any further. She felt completely drained — hollow. Tessa left him with his brandy and walked up the stairs holding on to the bannister.

She said "Good night" to each of the children, went into the bedroom, closed the door and changed into her nightgown. She climbed into bed and was asleep within five minutes.

Chapter 29

Tessa woke before the alarm went off. Robert was in the bathroom. She could hear the shower. Last night came flooding back into her consciousness. She had not heard Robert come to bed. She didn't know how long he sat with his brandy and the news that he was going to be a father again. To say it had not gone well was an understatement.

He came out of the bathroom with a towel wrapped around his waist. She stood up and went to him spontaneously.

"Hold me, Robert. I don't care if you're still half wet!"

He pulled her to him and said, "I love you Tessa Baby. That's all that matters to me."

She reached up to touch his face and raised her mouth for his kiss. It was long and deep.

"I love you too, Robert. You know that."

Tessa felt as if her equilibrium were steady again. She would take this, one day at a time for now. They would discuss the 'what if' scenarios later. But today, she would get dressed, go to work and get used to the idea that she was indeed going to have a baby.

Robert had apparently decided to do the same. He did not bring up his near melt down of the night before. He dressed, woke Sally and Eric and went downstairs to supervise breakfast. Tessa showered, dressed and was in Sally's room within twenty minutes to help her choose an outfit for school.

"Can I wear the pinafore today?" Sally asked. "It's clean now."

"Sure. I know you love it."

Tessa brushed Sally's hair into a pony tail. They went down to breakfast together.

Robert had cereal boxes out, muffins in the toaster and juice poured. Tessa was grateful he had taken the duties. She sat with her muffin and coffee while he took care of the children. He said he would take Sally to pre-school. The day was clear and cold and Eric would walk over to Danny's. Tessa had only to get herself together and make her train.

"Thank you, Robert, for taking charge this morning," she said. "I'm going to try to be home by seven. Although, I may run into trouble with Tom because I left yesterday early without telling him. Wish me luck!"

"Take it easy, Tessa. Don't be too tough on him!"

Later on the train, Tessa settled in her seat and didn't try to do any work. She needed to prepare herself for the transition of walking in the door of the office and assuming her associate's role. It would not be easy today. Most of all, she wanted to avoid any trouble with Tom.

He was not in his office when she came in and she sighed a sigh of relief. She sat down and opened the file she had been working on the day before. Inside the file, she found a note from Tom. It read: "Tessa. See me when you come in. Tom Simmons"

The fact that he had signed it with his full name sent a clear warning. Trouble ahead! She started to work and was making good headway when he appeared in her doorway.

"Tessa. You found my note?"

"Yes, Tom. But you were not in your office."

"Well. I am now." He turned and left. She rose and followed him.

"Close the door, Tessa." She did.

"Sit down." She did.

"I think we have to have a serious talk."

"Okay. Is there a problem?"

"I'm not sure if problem is the right word. There is a growing feeling that you treat your work at the firm in a rather cavalier fashion."

"I'm not sure what you mean, Tom. I thought I was judged by results."

"Yes, results are essential. But you seem to come and go as you please. Your hours are becoming erratic. Yesterday, when I looked for you about four, I discovered that you had left by three. No explanation. Just gone."

"I'm sorry about that Tom. You weren't in your office and I thought I would check in with you this morning and explain."

"Okay. Explain!"

"My grandmother, who is 87, was taken into the Emergency Room the day before. I felt I should go to see her. She is very special to me."

"Well, it seems last week or so, your brother was in the hospital, Tessa. I'm sorry, of course, but it does seem that your personal life is cutting into your work here."

As Tessa sat and talked to her boss, one part of her mind was moving in another direction. She tried to imagine how he would react to the news that she was pregnant. Not well, that she was sure of. For now, she had to fend him off.

"Tom, I can understand your concerns. But you also know how important the firm is to me. During your evaluation last year, you gave me high marks for dedication and performance. I like to believe that I am judged by what I bring to the firm."

"Well, that is the bottom line, Tessa. I can't disagree with you there."

"I will not leave without telling you in the future, Tom."

"I would appreciate that, Tessa."

Back at her desk, she felt good. Crisis averted. For now.

She worked steadily on the research project and skipped going out for lunch. She ordered in a salad and pita bread instead. She would show him that she could put in the hours. She knew that most bosses, not just Tom Simmons, were fixated on the body being at the desk for a set number of hours each day. Flextime was still a relatively new concept in the firm and in the business world in general. She had no idea how he would accommodate to her pregnancy. She was sure he would not be happy about it.

Tessa took a break at three and tried her grandmother's phone. Her mother answered.

"Mom, it's me. Did Grandma come home? How is she?"

"Tessa. She's home and she's fine. I brought her home about noontime."

"I did come to the hospital to see her last night. Did she tell you?"

"Of course, she told me. She was so pleased. And then your Uncle Jack arrived. He doesn't come often enough. When he does, it makes her so happy."

"I'm sorry I missed him. I wanted to catch the five thirty train home."

"Uncle Jack stayed overnight with us and went back today. He told Grandma he was on his way to a conference in Boston, but he really came just to see her."

"Why doesn't he come more often?"

"He's always been very wrapped up in his work. And himself. And he knows I'm here taking care of Mama. It's like that in a lot of families. One child has most of the responsibility for the aging parent. Usually a daughter." She laughed. "Remember that!"

After Tessa talked with her mother, she wondered what her reaction would be to the news of another baby? Tessa was sure she would be thrilled and happy for them. But her mother would also understand any qualms Tessa would have. She knew Tessa's goal to become a partner. She had written articles about the "Mommy Track" and how careers were derailed when women took time off to have babies.

Tessa made a second phone call, to her obstetricians. When she explained why she needed to see one of the team out of her usual check-up schedule, she was given an appointment for early next week. Between now and then, she and Robert would have time to discuss the 'what- if' scenarios. She hoped that they would be in agreement before she went in for the appointment. Too much hung in the balance.

Chapter 30

Thursday morning, Annie awoke with a sore throat spreading across to her ears. Her head felt heavy and her mood was worse. The only good thing about the day was that her mother was back home in her apartment and seemed to be her normal self. Independent and feisty.

Annie found the zinc lozenges and sucked one while she took a hot shower. She hoped the steam would help to clear her head. She knew that she had to call Mark and tell him she would not be coming in to the gym. She would call him about nine.

David had made the coffee before he left, but today she needed very hot tea and honey for her throat. She turned on the tea kettle and waited for the steam to emerge. She wanted the tea to be boiling hot! The newspapers were on the table. She glanced at the headlines in *The Times* and turned to the puzzle. She needed the distraction of being absorbed in the clues and answers, rather than facing what she was going to say to Mark. Having a sore throat made it easier. She would just tell him that she was sick. It was true and it would give her time.

As she sipped her tea, she found she couldn't concentrate on the puzzle. Her mind was too full of what had happened the past two days. The crisis with her mother had caused her to look at her relationship with Mark in a different light. Rushing to the hospital on Tuesday — after being in bed with him all afternoon, had been a form of shock treatment. She saw herself now in a more objective light. And the picture was not pretty. She saw an unfaithful wife. And a liar — to her husband, her mother and her daughter. Sarah was right when she had blurted out, "Are you crazy?"

As she sat at the table, Annie asked herself some hard questions. *What had possessed her to become involved with Mark in the first place? To go to his house when she knew where it might lead? She had known for months*

*that she was attracted to him. And why was she a different woman in bed
with him — free of inhibitions?* That was the core question. She was doing
things with Mark that she had never done with David. And she let him do
things to her that David had wanted to do. But she had stopped him too many
times. And he had stopped trying.

She thought of herself lying on Mark's couch completely naked in the
half light. With him standing and looking down at her. It excited her just to
remember the scene.

That train of thought brought Annie back to square one. She felt aroused
thinking of Mark. She still wanted him desperately — despite her rational
exercise and self flagellation.

What the hell is the matter with me! And what am I going to do?

Her head throbbed. That she was very aware of. She would immerse herself
in the puzzle. Then she would clean up the kitchen, unload the dishwasher
and do other household chores until it was time to call him.

By eight thirty, she could hold out no longer and dialed his number.

"Mark, it's Annie. I woke up with a sore throat and achy head. I won't be
there today."

"I'm sorry Annie. What are you doing for it?"

"Zinc lozenges. They usually work fast for me. And Ibuprophen for my
head. I just feel rotten!"

She did not tell him about her mother's emergency trip to the hospital.
She wanted to have as short a conversation as possible.

"Feel better fast. I'll miss you. In more ways than one."

"Me too, Mark. Bye."

When she hung up, she felt even worse. It was true that she was sick. But,
she had shut him out by not telling him about her mother. She was putting
space between them deliberately. Placing him back in the compartment off
to the side, away from her center.

The phone rang and she grabbed it, thinking it was Mark calling her back.
But it wasn't. It was her editor in New York. It would not be good news.

"Annie. I just got to the piece you sent me, 'Communications Between
Generations'. I'd think it needs some revision. I'll fax it to you with the
notations."

Annie knew this was par for the course with this particular editor. She
never was satisfied with the first draft. In fact, Annie thought sometimes, she
should give her something to criticize right up front. Then, the revision would
be easier.

"What's the problem?"

"Basically, I think it needs more anecdotes. I know you start with one, and it's a good one. But I want more threaded through the research findings. It needs more life. And the quotes always do that. Oh, and it is about two hundred words too long. So, you do have some work to do."

Annie sighed. "What's the deadline?"

"Would you believe, Monday?"

"I'll get started as soon as the fax comes through."

"Thanks."

After she hung up the phone, Annie said the 'F word'! Loud and clear. Just what she needed with her head feeling as if it were filled with cotton batting. And her throat still hurt. She checked the box of the zinc lozenges to see how many she could take in a day. She took another one. She should have expected the call. Now, at least, she would have something to take her mind off her complicated life.

Before she went up to check her fax machine, she called Sarah. They had spoken last Friday. She needed to talk to her again. To bring her up to date.

"Sarah, it's your mixed up friend again."

"Annie, your voice sounds hoarse. Are you alright?"

"Not really. I have a bad sore throat and my head hurts too. Must be the beginning of a cold or something worse."

"So, how are you — other than the show, Mrs. Lincoln?"

"I'm still a mess. And there was excitement with my mother. She was in the hospital after a severe attack of the rapid heartbeat. She's home now, and back to herself. But it was scary when it happened."

" When was that? Were you there when it happened?"

"No, as a matter of fact. I wasn't. When she called me, I was in bed with Mark! And she had to go in the ambulance by herself!"

"Oh, Annie."

"Right. I have never felt so guilty in my entire life. When she called me for help, that is where I was. It was not until I came home and heard her message on the machine two hours later, that I found out. I wanted to die!"

"So what did you do?"

"I called David and he found out what hospital she was in."

"Of course. You called David. Do you hear what you're saying?"

"Yes, I know. I called David. I didn't call Mark. I haven't even told Mark about what happened to Mama."

"Annie, are you beginning to come to your senses?"

"Maybe, I am. I've been sitting here asking myself why this infatuation with Mark started. And how it has reached this point. I'm trying to see if there is one reason or a lot of reasons."

"Well, at least you are asking yourself those questions. I think that is a beginning, dear friend."

"I'm not going to see him today. I just called him and told him I was sick."

"Good. That's a start."

"Thanks a lot. I feel awful! And not just physically."

"You'll get over the cold, Annie. And hopefully, you'll get over him too."

"Well, there's no doubt where you're coming from, is there.?"

"None, whatsoever."

"Bye, Sarah."

Annie went up to check the faxed pages and found them covered with notes, written in heavy black ink. With arrows and stars and circled phrases. Looked like the map of South America! Gave her the 'cold pricklies'. She said the 'F word'. That made her feel better.

Then, she sat down at her desk and started to work. In a perverse way, the revision and the deadline were a blessing. She would have no time to think about anything else. And she would nurse her throat and try to clear her head. She hoped she was not getting the flu.

Chapter 31

Annie stayed at her desk, except for making herself chicken rice soup for lunch. She always kept several cans on hand for days like this. It felt good on her throat and it was comfort food as well. She took a mug of tea and honey back upstairs. She was making good progress with the revision.

She called her mother and found that all was well. It gave her a great sense of relief. The guilt was still there, but at least, there had been no permanent harm. Ruth was busy preparing her Friday night dinner. She sounded like herself, asking how Annie was.

"Your voice sounds like you have a cold, dear."

"I do have a sore throat, Mama. But I'm knocking it out with zinc lozenges and chicken soup."

"Do you have a big weekend planned?"

"No social events. I'm working on a revision of the piece I did on communications. The editor called this morning and faxed enough notes to keep me at the computer for days."

"That's a shame, Annie. And you don't feel well."

"It's not too bad, Mama. Takes my mind off how I feel."

"Don't push yourself, dear."

"I won't, Mama."

The roles were reversed, Annie thought. Her mother taking care of her. What a difference a few days can make.

David called at five to tell her he would be home in about an hour. She brought him up to date on her sore throat and headache.

"I may be getting something. Right now, the zinc lozenges seem to be helping. I don't have that sharp pain I woke up with."

"Do you want me to stop and bring home dinner?"

"That would be wonderful. Italian. Chinese. Whatever you want. I am not very hungry."

"I'll get you won ton soup. And eggplant with garlic. How's that?"

"You're my hero!"

As she said the words she had said so many times before, Annie felt a tremendous wave of remorse. She always called David, her hero. In important situations and in small intimate ways as well. It had just popped out. David — always there. Always caring. Knowing her needs so completely.

They ate in the kitchen and Annie found she was hungry after all. The eggplant was delicious. He asked about her mother and Annie told him that she was fine. Then, he looked at her in a special way and smiled. He said, "First, we'll get you better. And you'll finish the revision of the article. And then, " he paused for emphasis. "And then, how would you like to escape to London for a week?"

Annie was completely caught off guard by the question and the idea.

"London? Now?"

"Well, I have one of those ten days ahead with no deliveries on board. I thought it would be good for both of us to get away."

This was the way they always took their vacations. David could not plan six months in advance. He would find the windows of opportunity, as they called them, and they would make arrangements in twenty four hours. It worked for them. They loved the spontaneity. This time, Annie felt torn. How could she go without resolving her life with Mark. Vacations had always been a romantic time, a time of renewal. How could she do that now?

"I'm not sure if this is a good time, David. I still feel leery of flying, since September 11."

"We have to fly sometime, Annie. I won't let terrorists stop us from living our lives!"

"I agree in theory. But I'm not sure if I'm ready."

"Well, let's think about it over the weekend. It's a great time for theater and we always love going to our favorite places. They've done a major renovation of the British Museum that I read about. And imagine walking in Green Park in the mornings, Annie. That will put you in the mood."

"Okay. We'll think about it David. But, first, I have to feel better. I'm going up and just sit in bed and watch television until I fall asleep."

Over the weekend, in between working on the revision, Annie mulled over the idea of a week in London. Her first reaction had been negative. But, perhaps, it would be the best way to break away from Mark. And try to redirect her newly awakened libido by losing some of her inhibitions with her husband — instead of her lover! The more she thought of that prospect, the more it appealed to her.

By Sunday afternoon, she had knocked out the sore throat and incipient cold. She had also completed the revisions on the manuscript. And she had come to a decision. She would go to London. She told David and he was delighted. He immediately got on the computer with air and hotel reservations. He was trying to set it up for departure on Tuesday.

She drove to the mall and made two important purchases. A navy blue silk nightgown trimmed in ecru lace and a new perfume. She wore two scents, Hermes Caleche or Chanel # 5. She wanted something completely different. For David and mostly for her. She chose Chanel # 19. It had a sophisticated aroma and it was new. She would wear it in London.

By Monday, David had secured the plane and hotel reservations. They would stay at Dukes, one of the small hotels near St. James. It had an intimate clubby feeling and the location was great. Annie could walk to Green Park in five minutes. They had stayed there before.

She put off calling Mark until after lunch. She would not wait until Tuesday morning, when he expected to see her again. She wouldn't do that to him. Her heart was pounding as she called his number. He picked up on the third ring.

"Mark. It's Annie."

"Annie, I was just walking out the door, when I heard the phone. How are you? Are you all better, I hope."

"I'm all better, Mark. But I won't be coming to the gym tomorrow."

There was a long pause until he answered.

"What's the matter, Annie? What's happened?"

"A lot, Mark. First, my mother was in the hospital last week. She had a bad scare with her rapid heart beat. She's alright now and home. But it happened Tuesday, when I was with you. She called me and I wasn't there. It was a sort of a wake-up call to me, Mark."

"I don't understand, Annie. You could have been lots of places when she called. What do you mean, 'wake-up 'call?"

"This is hard to do on the phone." She stopped to get her breath. " But I mean it caused me to stand back and think about what I've been doing. To look at myself. I wasn't too happy with what I saw."

"Why don't you come over so we can sit down and talk about this face to face, Annie. I promise I won't touch you."

"I'm afraid to come, Mark. When I'm with you, something happens to me. You've certainly seen it."

"Yes, I've seen it. And it's been wonderful. You said, you felt alive. And happy. Is that bad, Annie?"

"It's not a matter of good or bad, Mark. We've both said from the beginning that my life is more complicated than yours. I'm married and you're not."

"I know, Annie. I just don't want to lose you!"

"I'm sorry, Mark. I feel this is the right thing to do. David came up with the idea to go to London on Friday night. That's how we do vacations. On the spur of the moment. I thought about it all weekend and decided to go."

"Without giving me a chance to talk with you?"

"It wasn't a decision for the two of us to make, Mark."

There was another long silence. Annie could imagine his face. His eyes. His mouth. Her longing for him was very much alive and intense. She wanted to run to his arms. But she controlled herself. She waited for him to speak. When he did, his voice sounded flat and distant.

"Call me when you get back, Annie."

"I will, Mark. I'm sorry."

Chapter 32

Saturday for Tessa was a day worked around driving Sally to a birthday party and Eric back and forth to his basketball practice. In between, she did food shopping, three loads of laundry and tried to think about what she would say to Robert when they sat down to talk on Sunday morning.

In her own mind, she had been coming to a decision about the pregnancy. She preferred to think about the 'pregnancy' rather than 'the baby'. Pregnancy was more of an abstract term. As soon as she thought of a baby growing inside her, it became very real and personal. She was in a complete state of turmoil.

She and Robert had been ecstatic when Sally was born. Their little girl! And Robert was a loving step-father to Eric. Their family was complete. Or so she had thought.

The very idea of going back to diapers and night feedings was distressing to her. She had been there. Done that. She wanted to move on to the next stage of life. It seemed to her that she would be going in reverse. She felt trapped!

Having an abortion, she knew, could be a traumatic experience. There were women who suffered guilt afterwards. It could be a permanent part of their psyche. She didn't think it would be for her. But who could know the future. And of course, Robert mattered. Would he understand if that was what she wanted to do. And didn't his opinion count? What would he want to do? It was his baby too. Maybe a son. Every man wanted his own son.

All day long, as she went through the motions of daily life, her mind was trying to sort out answers. It boiled down to what she wanted to do. And what he wanted to do. If they agreed, there was no problem. If they disagreed, there would be an enormous problem.

It was all about choices. And consequences. She was not sure of how to tell him what was in her heart and mind. She hoped he would respect the depth of her feelings. She knew he understood that her career as a lawyer was very important to her. He supported her in every way he could. But this was different from giving the kids dinner at night when she was late. This was the rock bottom decision of setting her career off to the side once more. She had done that with Sally willingly and survived at the firm. But it took a toll on her and on her position for promotion. There was no question that it set her back in the eyes of her bosses.

She and Robert had agreed the best time to talk was Sunday morning, when the kids were in Sunday School. It gave them two uninterrupted hours. They sat at the kitchen table.

"I feel like — you first, Gaston." Tessa said. It sounded witty, but she felt very tense.

"Okay," Robert said with a sigh. He was sitting back from the table with his legs outstretched. "I'll go first. I have very mixed feelings, Tessa. That's the truth. When you first told me, I was stunned! And then I was filled with happiness. But, that didn't last too long because I saw the look on your face. I know you well, Tessa. This is not a happy surprise for you. And you had been agonizing over it alone for more than a week."

"I didn't want to tell you until I was sure, Robert."

"I understand. And that's in the past. What we have to talk about now is the present. And the future."

"I know. That's all I've been thinking about every waking moment!"

"And," he said gently, "have you reached any conclusions with your 'what if' scenarios?"

"Almost, Robert. Not quite there. Any conclusions have to be what you want as well as what I want."

"Let's put it on the table, Tessa. Is one of your scenarios, 'What if I have an abortion?"

"Yes."

"Do you think you could live with that?"

"What do you mean, 'live with that'?"

"I mean, would you feel guilty if you had an abortion?"

"I'm not sure. But that is not the central issue for me with an abortion. The central issue is whether it would affect our marriage adversely, Robert. Especially, if you did not want me to have one."

"Do you want me to tell you the truth, Tessa?"

"Yes," she answered, afraid of what he was going to say.

He took his time and said the words slowly and carefully.

"I do not want you to have an abortion. I want us to have the baby."

"I thought you would. And I can understand how you feel, Robert. But it's not your body. And it's not your career that's at stake here."

"Don't you think that's somewhat over dramatic? You stayed at the firm when you were pregnant with Sally. You didn't lose your job."

"They couldn't do anything as obvious as that. It's against the law. But I'm on the Mommy Track. It's going to take me years longer to become a partner."

Robert sighed, stood up and walked around the room. When he came back and sat down, he said, "We have a problem."

"Yes, we do."

Neither one of them had raised their voices, but the depth of their emotions was evident. And they had reached the opposite conclusions for the future. Tessa was dismayed. And she needed time to sort out where they were. She asked him, "This may sound like a naive question. But why is it so important to have another baby? We have Sally. And Eric. They are doing great. Isn't that enough?"

She wanted to take the focus away from the abortion issue. Robert smiled when he answered. "I figure we hit a home run with Sally. Look at all the happiness she gives us. Why not try for another?"

"It's not that simple, Robert."

"You asked me the question and you don't like my answer. I didn't say it was simple."

Tessa didn't want to argue. They were on the verge.

"I made an appointment with my gynecologist for Tuesday. Let me see her and verify that the home tests are correct. Then we'll talk some more."

"Fine. But I've been thinking of nothing else either. For me, it keeps coming down to how wonderful it would be to have another Sally or a little boy. It would add to, not subtract from our lives, Tessa. And you would still be a lawyer. We have money for a full-time Nanny. You know that."

"I know, Robert. I just don't know if I can cope again with being pregnant. And the beginning years. The needs of an infant are very demanding. Even with a Nanny."

"You're going to have the final vote, here, Tessa. You're the one who has to carry the baby. I know that. And I agree that our marriage is the most important thing."

He rose and came over to take her in his arms. He smoothed her hair and kissed her.

"I love you, Tessa baby. We will work this out."

Chapter 33

It started to snow just as the pizza arrived. Half plain and half mushroom. Pizza was a Sunday night tradition. With paper plates and no fuss.

Sally and Eric were at the living room windows, watching the fat flakes drift down.

"Do you think there'll be enough to make a snow man, Eric?"

"There may even be enough to have no school!" he said gleefully.

Tessa called them into the kitchen. "Do you want me to pop it in the oven? Or just take one piece and I'll put the rest in to keep warm."

Robert doled out the slices and said that the weather forecast was only for one or two inches. Eric groaned. "It's December," he said. "Time for a big snow storm."

As it turned out, he got his wish. The snow continued through the night and they woke to four inches on the ground and more coming down. The forecast had changed to ten to twelve inches with wind gusting up to 20 miles per hour.

"It's a mini blizzard," Robert commented. He turned on the radio to find out if the schools would open late or be canceled. Eric let out a whoop when he heard that his school would be closed. And the trains were running at least an hour late. Tessa knew she would not be going in to the office. She dreaded making the call.

Sally was excited. "Can we got out and make a snowman later?"

"We'll have to wait until it stops snowing, Sally. And blowing. This may last all day and tomorrow will be the day to make a snowman." Tessa saw another battle of the wills emerging.

"But, I don't want to wait until tomorrow. I want to do it today!"

Eric jumped in. "Sally, no one makes snowmen during a blizzard!"

"What's a blizzard?"

"When it's snowing and the wind is blowing the snow into big drifts. That's what it looks like out there. That's a blizzard So we just have to wait."

"Oh." Sally sounded resigned to her fate. She took Eric's word as the last word on most subjects.

Robert was putting on his heavy parka and storm boots.

"I'll call you when I get to the office, Tessa. Don't worry if you don't hear from me. The train can be delayed for hours right on the rails, as you know."

She kissed him good bye. "Drive carefully to the station."

They both took it for granted that she would be staying home with the children. As she cleaned up the breakfast dishes, a strange new set of 'what if' scenarios flew into her mind. *What if she didn't have to worry about calling Tom Simmons and telling him that she would not be in? What if that kind of pressure did not exist? What if she were a lawyer with her own practice? And had an office nearby rather than in New York City?*

Tessa had always said that she wanted to become a partner at a law firm in the city. It was like the line from the song, "If you can make it there, you can make it anywhere. New York. New York!" It had been her dream all through law school. When she interviewed, she never considered a firm in any other location. She received a good offer from Ryder and Simmons, and she took it. It seemed to hold the potential she was looking for. She did not want to join one of the huge, prestigious firms where associates were expected to work ten hour days on unrewarding tasks. Ryder and Simmons did not match the starting salaries at the larger firms, but they held out the carrot of a partnership as a possibility in the years ahead. She wanted that carrot.

She stood at the window and looked out at the snow and wind. She really felt relieved that she did not have to be driving to the station and doing the long train commute today. It was a good feeling to be in her warm house. She heard the children upstairs playing in Eric's room. And, for the first time , she thought — *what if there were three children playing up there?*

Being home today would give her time to think about what Robert had told her. He had asked her if she wanted to hear the truth. And she had said, "Yes." Now, that she had the truth, she was faced with the dilemma. He had also said that she had the final vote. But this was not an election. It was their lives and their marriage. She knew that marriage was not always a 50-50 proposition. There were times when each partner gave more than the other. By his understanding and generosity, Robert had made the dilemma even more intense for Tessa. He was putting his love for her ahead of his desire for another child. She felt a wave of tenderness toward her husband well up inside her. And she asked herself if she could she do the same for him.

It was almost time to call the office. Tessa braced herself. Then a wild thought tore across her mind. *What if she told Tom Simmons that she was going to give him two weeks notice!* She could be free of having strings pulled on her every day at work. Free of the knots in her stomach. Free of having to keep her door open when she was trying to concentrate. And she would be free of the three to four hours she spent commuting back and forth to work. It had little to do with the pregnancy. Or maybe it did. Maybe that was acting as a catalyst. Whatever the motivation, she felt a strange sense of empowerment.

Robert would probably be thrilled. And he would help her in every way to establish a private practice. There were many lawyers with their individual shingles in the area. Her mind was racing ahead. This was all out of character. Tessa rarely acted on impulse. She was a planner, with every step mapped out and carefully considered. But today, she felt like a different person.

She called the office and expected to hear the receptionist's voice. Instead, she heard Tom Simmons. Her heart sank.

"Tom. It's Tessa. I won't be able to make it in today. Sorry."

"Well. I'm here Tessa. And I would expect you to be here too."

It was going to be like that, she thought and sighed.

"I have both children here Tom. And we're pretty much snowed in, with blizzard conditions forecast."

"I know the weather forecast, Tessa." His voice was clipped and very unpleasant.

"What do you expect me to do, Tom?"

"It's your life and you have to manage it, Tessa. But, this is another example of your putting your personal life first and the firm second. We talked about that just last week."

Tessa realized that he was not going to give her an inch. And it pushed her over the edge.

"Why don't I just give you two weeks notice, Tom? Then you can find someone who will give a thousand percent to the firm — and the hell with children and family!"

There was a distinct silence at the other end of the telephone line. Tessa was thinking of what his face must look like. When he spoke, it was in a different measured tone.

"I wasn't suggesting that you leave the firm, Tessa."

She knew the work she did was valuable. And that finding a replacement would take much time, effort and money. She had played her trump and she had won. And the truth was that she really meant what she said. She waited a few moments before she answered. She would hang tough.

"What were you suggesting, Tom?"

"I wasn't suggesting anything, Tessa. I was stressing that each of us has to balance our personal lives against the needs of the firm."

"And I have tried to do that. As we discussed last week, my evaluations show that my performance has been more than satisfactory."

Tessa felt as if the same record were being played again. He sang his tune. And she sang hers. There was a pause at his end again.

"Why don't we wrap this up for now, Tessa. Our other line is ringing and Jenny couldn't make it in today either."

"You're lucky you live right in the city, Tom."

Tessa couldn't resist the last word and the extra dig. She smiled. And after she hung up, she realized that she wouldn't have cared if Tom had taken her up on her threat. In fact, she might be throwing her arms up in the air right now and shouting, "Hallelujah! Free at last!"

Chapter 34

Annie and David flew to London Tuesday night and arrived at Heathrow Airport on schedule, Wednesday morning. David always slept on the flights and Annie read books, watched television and tried to doze for an hour or two. She envied his ability to fall sound asleep for three or four hours while she kept checking her watch to see how close they were to landing. She had talked with many other women and discovered the same condition existed. Men slept on planes and women didn't. It was not a systematic survey, she knew, but it sure was a lot of anecdotal evidence.

The day was grey and overcast with a thin rain falling. That was no surprise in December. They traveled with heavy jackets and were prepared with warm hats and gloves. By nine thirty, they were at Dukes Hotel in the small cozy sitting room, drinking hot coffee and eating delicious buttered toast. In a silver toast rack, with the crusts cut off, Annie noted with pleasure. She loved English hotels and the way they served. The jam in a crystal dish. The sugar with silver tongs. The coffee in the large silver pot. It was elegant and she felt relaxed after the cramped hours on the plane.

Their room would not be ready until noon and they decided to walk to St. James Park. They always tried to beat jet lag by going out and doing something when they arrived rather than taking a nap. When the sun was out, it was easier, but they had their umbrellas. The day was not cold, just a typical London day in the winter. They walked to The Mall and crossed into the park, a familiar path for them. They had visited London often over the years. It was the place they went to on their first trip to Europe. Both of them had been fascinated by the city. They agreed with Samuel Johnson's famous tribute, "If a man is tired of London, he is tired of life!"

Annie found it to be a woman's city as well. The British Museum was her all time favorite place. She remembered when she first saw the Rosetta Stone.

She had been so intent on finding the Elgin Marbles, taken from the Parthenon in Greece, that she had almost run right past the Rosetta Stone. It was standing in the center of the wide aisle. She had come to an abrupt halt when she realized it was indeed the Rosetta stone, with the three languages inscribed side by side. The key to deciphering Egyptian hieroglyphics. She was amazed to see it just "sitting there" as she told her mother later.

She loved to visit the Manuscript Rooms with the original authors' works with their notes in the margins. *Alice In Wonderland, David Copperfield, The Wasteland.* As a writer, it was a special thrill every time they went there. Now, she had read that the manuscripts had been transferred to The British Library that had opened within the past year. She was eager to go and see them in their new setting. She had heard it was a treasure house. But, not today. She still felt somewhat raw from the trip. They would save The Library until she recovered from the jet lag.

Instead, they walked through the park and looked at Buckingham Palace in the distance from the bridge over the lake. The weeping willows bending down toward the water were as graceful as ever. Annie couldn't help thinking that Mark would find the scene very beautiful. She had kept him from her mind all during the flight. She was determined to leave him behind when they took off — literally and figuratively. She would do her best to make this a time for her and David to be together. In every sense. She needed to find her center with him again.

As they stood on the bridge, Annie said, "I'm always happy here, David."

"I am too, Annie. It never matters if it is raining. In fact, I'm sort of surprised when the sun comes out in the winter. But, remember the time we came in June, and it was the hottest summer on record. And the air conditioning turned out to be air cooling. We nearly roasted!"

Annie laughed and said, "I took off my shoes and socks when we heard the concert in the park and sat with my bare feet in the grass. It felt wonderful!"

They had many happy memories of London. *It had been a good idea to come,* she thought. They continued to stroll, past Bird Cage Walk to the Houses of Parliament where Big Ben was tolling the hour. People were clustered in groups with their tour leader giving them the history of the historic buildings. Rain did not stop sightseers in London, David observed, or anywhere else. They had always preferred to travel on their own. Annie loved to read travel magazines and kept files of places to go in different countries. Museums, restaurants and out of the way side trips.

Once, in London, they had taken a day trip on The Orient Express from

Victoria Station to York Castle. It had been a wonderful day with lovely food and champagne as they watched the English countryside from their upholstered wing chairs. The Pullman car was perfectly restored with Art Deco paneling and lighting. Annie had written an article about it for a travel magazine.

When they returned to Dukes, their bags were already in their room. They unpacked and decided to skip any more sightseeing. Annie took a long bath in the oversized tub and settled in for a needed catchup nap. She felt virtuous that she had taken her walk first. David read the book he had started on the plane. He loved mysteries and always packed two or three paperbacks when they took a trip. It was a welcome change from the medical journals piled on his desk.

They ate an early dinner and watched the news on the BBC before going to sleep. They both liked to listen to the British announcers, their diction was very different from the news anchors at home. It was part of being in London.

Thursday morning brought more drizzle, but Annie awoke feeling refreshed. She put on her walking clothes, took her umbrella and went out through Green Park toward Buckingham Palace. It was still early enough for people to be crisscrossing the park on their way to work. They looked, she thought, pretty much like the people walking in New York with a few exceptions. Several very distinguished men in tailored overcoats and bowler hats, carrying sleek briefcases. She liked to imagine that they were on their way to deal with important state business. She laughed to herself. They were probably chartered accountants. English bean counters!

She joined David for breakfast about nine.

"Do you want to go to The British Library?" he asked.

"Let's save that for tomorrow and go to the Old Bailey today," Annie said.

They had visited the British courts before and always found the trials to be fascinating to watch. The system of justice was different with the bewigged barristers and judges. And the trials were often sensational crimes. They would sit on the wooden benches in the visitors galleries for hours. And the courts were near St. Paul's Cathedral where they would go down into the Crypt to see what David called, "the history of the British Empire". All the heroes were entombed there, Nelson and Wellington in great splendor, and lesser known men who carried the flag to India, Khartoum and other far flung outposts. They would read the plaques and marvel. Annie was touched by seeing Florence Nightingale in her place of honor among all the men of war.

They did go to The Old Bailey and on Friday to The British Library. In the evenings, they had leisurely dinners at favorite restaurants. And drank lots of good wine. Their bedroom at Dukes was an intimate setting for romance and Annie did her best to forget Mark. But she couldn't help thinking that if she and Mark had been at Dukes, they probably wouldn't have left their room for days.

David noticed the Chanel 19 perfume and did more than notice her new silk nightgown. He looked at her admiringly when she put it on Friday night and said, "You look very beautiful tonight, Annie." Then he turned off all the lights except one of the bed lamps and came to where she was standing. He put both hands on her hips and pulled her to him as he caressed her body through the silk. She lifted her mouth to his, as she had done so many times before, and responded to the intensity of his kiss. He slid the gown over her head and she was standing naked in the dim light. He looked at her and said very quietly, "That's quite a nightgown, but I still love to look at you as you are. We don't do this enough at home."

As they made love, Annie forced Mark out of her mind. She knew if she thought of him at this moment, it would be the ultimate betrayal. She would not do that to David!

Saturday night they went to the Savoy Hotel for dinner and dancing in the River Room . Their table looked out over the Thames and, as she listened to the Cole Porter songs, Annie felt a deep sense of contentment. David smiled and asked her what she was thinking.

"I'm thinking that I'm very happy, David."

He reached over and took her hand.

"I love you Annie. I always will."

Chapter 35

Annie and David flew home on Tuesday. During the flight, she tried to assess where she was in contrast to where she had been a week ago when they left. Had she found her center again with David? That was the big question she asked herself. And the answer was not clear cut.

While they were in London, she and David were good together. He was not distracted by his beeper and urgent calls from patients. He seemed to unwind, as he usually did on vacations, and enjoy the days — as well as the nights. He had been a patient lover over the years, waiting for her to free herself from long held sexual inhibitions. He delighted whenever she moved with him to a new experience. But he never insisted. And they had settled into a certain pattern of lovemaking.

It struck her that Mark, who didn't know the past, treated her as if she had no inhibitions. And that may have been the secret to unlocking her sexuality and giving her the joy she found with him in bed. She became what he wanted her to be. And she loved it!

Now, she had to face coming home and getting on with her life. She had to call Mark. She had told him she would. She was not sure what she would say to him. She did not know whether she was ready to make a final break with him. He was still there in that compartment of her life. And the promise of hearing his voice was excitement in itself. She could not deny that.

Day flights were always easier for Annie and they were home by early afternoon. After they unpacked, David checked his phone messages and found that one of his patients was in labor. He had no time to ease back into the demands of his profession. Expectant mothers had babies when they were ready. He left for the hospital and Annie knew that he would be there through most of the night.

She went to the phone and called Mark. There was no answer. She would call her mother and Tessa and let them know she was home. She would talk with Saul tomorrow.

"Mama, we're home. How are you?"

"Annie, dear, it's wonderful to hear your voice. I've missed you. Did you have a good time?"

"Wonderful, Mama. Have you had a good week?"

"I'm fine. Tessa called almost every day. She's so sweet, taking over for you while you're away."

"I'll come over tomorrow, if you want, and we'll go out to lunch. I'll tell you all the things we did. You would adore the new British Library!"

"Tomorrow's not good, dear. How about Thursday?"

"That's fine, Mama."

As she made the date for Thursday, Annie realized that Thursday would have been the day to go to the gym and see Mark. It was just as well that she would not be able to go.

She called Tessa at the office, but her voice recorder clicked on. She was probably on her way home. She would reach her later.

Annie tried Mark's number again and he answered the phone.

"Mark, it's Annie. We're home."

"How was your trip?"

The impersonal tone of his question caught her off guard. Not, how are you? And not, it's good to hear your voice. She found herself answering him in kind.

"It was a good trip."

"When did you get home?"

"About an hour ago."

There was a pause and Annie waited to hear what he would say next. She felt the coldness in his voice. And who blamed him. Did she expect him to be waiting with open arms for her? She felt a need to explain. Her feelings for him were not dead.

"Mark, I didn't want to hurt you."

"I'm not sure this is a good time to talk, Annie. I'm getting ready to go skiing in Colorado tomorrow and I have all this packing to do."

"How long will you be away, Mark?"

"I'll be there for two weeks and then I'll go to Cleveland for Christmas and New Year's with my sister and her family."

Annie's mind was spinning ahead. He would be gone for more than three weeks. If she wanted to see him — and if he wanted to see her, this evening was the only time. It only took her a split second to decide.

"You sound very angry, Mark."

"I don't think angry is the right word, Annie."

"What is the right word?"

"How about bewildered....hurt...surprised....used. How's that?"

"What do you mean, used?"

"I think you know what I mean, Annie. Used! Woman meets man. Woman finds sexual pleasure. Woman uses man to fulfill her desires. Along the way, man falls in love with woman."

"Oh, Mark. That's a terrible script! Is that how you thought it was?"

"What should I think Annie? All of a sudden, you tell me you're going to London with your husband. You have to sort out your life. And you're sorry. And I'm left here feeling like a damn fool!"

"Now, you are angry."

"I guess I am. I don't like being used as a sex object!"

"Mark, if this were not a real conversation, it would be ridiculous! Don't you know I care for you? Don't you know I respect you? Don't you know I want to be with you right this minute and not only to be in bed with you?"

"No, Annie. I don't know that!"

"Oh, God, Mark— this is not what I wanted."

"Neither did I, Annie. Maybe skiing for a few weeks will help me put our relationship in a different light. I need the cold and the fresh air. Right now, I feel pretty cynical about all of it."

"I don't know what else to say, Mark."

"Neither do I, Annie. Maybe, I'll see you at the gym when I get back."

Annie felt desolate. This was not what she had foreseen. Something made her gamble.

"I'm not usually a risk taker, but should I come over now, Mark?"

He did not answer immediately. And she imagined his face again. It was vivid in her mind.

"I don't think that would be a good idea, Annie. Take care of yourself."

"Goodbye, Mark."

Annie sat holding the phone, after he hung up. All the time that she had been trying to sort out her life and her feelings, he had — of course— been doing exactly the same thing. It was so damned obvious. And she had not been prepared for it. She replaced the phone and tried to deflect the anger she had heard. And the relentless logic of his words. He had said that she had 'used' him to fulfill her sexual desires. Was that true? It sounded so deliberate and hard. No, that was not true. She had found deep sexual satisfaction with him, but she had wanted to give it to him as well. She had feelings of tenderness toward him. She enjoyed just being with him, talking and laughing.

Annie rejected the idea that she had used him. That was not fair! But this was not a matter of being fair. She knew that. She had been very wrong to leave without explaining. She had hurt Mark deeply, only thinking about herself. His words made that very clear. And now, he was going away. He had taken the initiative and she was left to deal with it.

Chapter 36

Tessa had just walked in the door when the phone rang. Robert was going to pick up the children on his way home and she had been looking forward to an hour alone. She let it ring and the answering machine clicked on.

"Tessa, it's Mom. Just wanted to tell you we're home. We had a good time. Hope all is well with you and Robert and the children. Thanks for calling Grandma Ruth while I was away. Talk to you tomorrow."

Tessa hung up her coat and went upstairs to the bedroom. She changed from her business clothes to sweats and sneakers. Her mind was on the appointment she had kept that afternoon with her obstetrician. After the internal examination, Dr. Crawford had confirmed the pregnancy. The baby growing inside her was very real.

Dr. Crawford had listened as Tessa told her they had not planned on having more children. As they talked, Tessa started to cry. She got herself under control and said, "I'm having a hard time with this, as you see. I'm not sure if I could handle a newborn again. Sally is in pre- school. And I'm just getting back in line for promotion at the firm."

Dr. Crawford had children of her own. She and Tessa had talked before about the stresses of raising children and pursuing a career at the same time. Tessa felt she could tell her the truth.

"Robert wants the baby. But he's not pressuring me. He says I have the final vote."

"You're very lucky, Tessa. Some husbands get very insistent. It can ruin a marriage."

"Robert's a very special man. That's a large part of my dilemma. My ex, Ivan, was not. You delivered Eric and you knew that I was pretty much on my own by then in our marriage."

"I'm not going to try to sway you, Tessa. I can only tell you that you are in excellent health and only 36, well within the age range of child-bearing women these days. I have patients in their forties having babies. And I also have women of all ages who cannot conceive and are going with their husbands to the fertility doctors."

"I know that too. I have a close friend who has been trying for years. That makes me feel sort of guilty too."

"It's a very complex decision. You have some time to make it. Why don't you let it be for a week or so. It's still very new to you and you have a lot to consider."

Tessa had said nothing to Dr. Crawford about the frustrations she felt in her job and her growing dissatisfaction with her boss. That important dimension of the problem she would have to deal with herself. It was not at the center of her decision about the baby, but it was a contributing factor. She had been tempted to tell Tom Simmons to go to Hell yesterday on the telephone. It had given her a surge of adrenalin just to think about saying it. Maybe, she needed to remember that feeling and what it meant. She found she was smiling. It felt good.

When Robert came home with the children, she was downstairs in the kitchen preparing dinner. Sally ran in to give her a hug and kiss. Her cheeks were cold and felt wonderful against Tessa's face. Eric greeted her with the traditional question.

"Hi, Mom. What's for dinner?"

"Spaghetti and meatballs. How's that?"

"Perfect!"

The seal of approval. Tessa laughed. She helped Sally take off her snow jacket and boots. The drifts were high from yesterday's storm. Sally told her in great detail how they had built a giant snow person during recess.

"A snow person!" Eric exclaimed. "What happened to a snow man?"

"A snow person can be a girl," Sally replied with new found emphasis.

Tessa laughed again. Gender roles had extended to the next generation and in the context of snow persons! Wonderful!

Robert kissed her and went up to change. They both liked to doff their business clothes at the end of a weekday. He usually wore a tie and jacket to work and ten inches of snow on the ground hadn't altered that. He came down wearing the blue cable pullover she had given him for his birthday. She loved the way he looked in it. She would tease him and say he could be one of the models in the *Sunday Times* ads. Of course, he would need five o'clock shadow on the jaw line to qualify for that intense macho look.

The children were in their rooms and they had some time to talk before dinner. His voice was casual, but the question was not.

"So, how did the appointment go? What did Dr. Crawford say?"

"She said, I am definitely pregnant. No doubt. And she said I am in excellent health."

"I'd say that's wonderful news. But I know you have very mixed feelings, Tessa. I don't really know what to say."

"She also said, I have time to make a decision. She wasn't pushing me one way or the other."

"Well, I would hope not. She is in the business of delivering babies!"

"Don't be angry at her, Robert. I'm just saying that she listened to me when I told her that I wasn't sure I wanted to have another baby. I think she understood. She has small children and a full time career. She advised me to give it some time to think through carefully. I'm trying to do that."

At that point, Sally burst into the kitchen, declaring that she was starving.

"When will the spaghetti be ready, Mommy? I'm so-o-o hungry, my stomach is talking!"

"In about ten minutes. Sit down at the table, and I'll give you a roll to hold you over."

Later, when the children were asleep, Tessa and Robert sat in the den and talked. She had not told him about her conversation with Tom Simmons the day before. She wanted to share it with him.

"When he started that same business of my putting my personal life ahead of the firm, I really flipped out! I let him have it — right between the eyes, which is pretty good considering we were on the telephone!" She laughed at the memory of her declaration of independence.

"What did you say to him?"

"I said, 'Why don't I just give you two weeks notice? Then you can find someone who will give a thousand percent to the firm — and the hell with children and family.'"

"You said that?"

"I certainly did!"

Robert was looking at her in an incredulous way. His mouth was not quite hanging open, but almost.

"And what did he say to that?"

"He completely folded and backed down. Protesting that he was not suggesting that I leave the firm, et cetera, et cetera .... Believe me, the cost of replacing me would be enormous. And he really does need me to do the work I do. He's just become a petty tyrant and I was fed up!"

"And how do you feel about it now?"

"I'm not sure. But it was a moment of truth for me. And after I hung up, I thought that it might have been better if he had taken me up on my offer."

Robert spoke carefully again. It was as if he were walking through new terrain during their entire conversation.

"What do you mean better, Tessa?"

"Better in that I would have been free of his pulling strings on me every day. And free of spending up to four hours every day going back and forth into the city to work. Yes, the operative word of that moment was 'free'. And I'll tell you the truth, my love, it felt wonderful!"

Robert rose and took her hand. He drew her to him.

"Is there any rule against knowing your wife in the biblical sense, the day she finds out she's having your baby?"

Tessa smiled and kissed him. She adored him. That was something she was sure of. And she answered his question, "If there is such a rule, the hell with it!"

Chapter 37

Wednesday morning, Annie awoke with a feeling of emptiness. She had fallen asleep after midnight, the conversation with Mark replaying over and over in her head. She couldn't seem to turn it off. And the more it played, the clearer it all became. She didn't blame him for becoming angry. He had good cause. She would have to face the fact that seeing him again was not going to happen unless he wanted it to happen. He had made the break now — not she.

She had not heard David come in from the hospital during the night. It was almost eight and he had left already. Back to the schedule, she thought. London seemed long ago, already. She took her robe from the closet and went downstairs to the kitchen. Annie usually suffered from jet lag on the trip back home, and today it felt even worse. She needed her coffee desperately.

There was nothing she had to do today. She wished she were working on an article. She needed to concentrate on something other than losing Mark Trianos.

While she drank her coffee, she skimmed the paper and then turned to the puzzle. At least, she would have ten minutes or more of complete concentration. She would call Tessa later at work just to check in and then her mother. She could go to the gym and work out some of her jet lag, but that would be too painful without him. It was a clear, cold day. She would take a three mile walk instead.

As she made desultory plans for her day, the telephone rang. She waited until the machine clicked on and she heard Sarah's voice starting to leave a message.

"Annie, it's me. I called you last week...."

"Sarah. I'm here. We were in London. David found a window of time and we were gone."

"I knew something was up, Annie, when you didn't call back. I just wasn't sure what."

"Well, something is up, as a matter of fact."

"What do you mean? Did something happen on the trip between you and David?"

"No, we had a good time on the trip. A very good time. And I was feeling better about sorting out my life."

"So, what's wrong? Sounds good to me."

"When we returned, I called Mark. I had told him I would before we left."

"Oh, Annie."

"He was cold and angry. And he feels I used him. He left today to go skiing in Colorado and then to spend the holidays with his sister and her family in Cleveland."

"Did you use him, Annie?"

"I don't think so Sarah. I went over that again and again in my mind last night. I truly cared for him. I still do. It wasn't just sex. Even though the sex was wonderful and new for me, I wanted to be with him when we just sat and talked. And he cooked that Greek food for me. I thought about him when we were apart. I wanted to see his face. Yes, it was physical. But it was more than that. Mark fulfilled certain needs in me that I didn't know existed. The word in the books is infatuation. Now, how do I make it go away?"

"I don't have any answers, my friend."

The days that followed were rough for Annie. She stopped going to the gym completely. It would be too hard to be there. She even drove by his house several times, like pressing on a sore tooth. She had trouble thinking about anything else. Mark was always there in her mind. She remembered how she had told him that the decision to go to London was hers alone to make. Well, now he had made his decision — alone. While she had been secure in London, expecting him to be there when she came home. What a disastrous mistake in judgement that had been! Now she had to deal with the consequences.

The only ray of light she found was that she no longer had to lie to David. Or Tessa. Or her mother. When she took Ruth to lunch on Thursday, she told her all the highlights of the trip that she knew would interest her. The British Library, the Sargent exhibit at the Tate, dancing at the Savoy and the shows they had seen in the West End.

"It sounds like a delightful trip, dear. Did David unwind from his hospital routine?"

"He did, Mama. We both had a great time."

Well, that was not a lie, Annie thought. They did enjoy London together. It was coming home that had thrown her life into disarray.

On Friday morning, she called two of the magazine editors for whom she had written recently. She wanted to see if they had any projects in the works that could involve her. Often, she approached them with queries. Today, she was hoping they would take the initiative. She came up dry with the first call. But with the second, she hit the mother lode.

"Annie Bertman! Perfect. I was just going to call you. I need your help."

"What's happening?"

"We've had a huge survey out on Nutrition and Health for women. The returns have just been digested by the computer and I had someone preparing the story for the January issue. She called in this morning with a serious case of complications from the flu. I need a replacement — fast! Can you help me with this?"

"What is it you need? And when's the deadline?"

"I need an analysis and wrap up of the results. About 3500 words. And I also need for succeeding issues, interviews with some of the respondents who said we could use their names. We want to run them as an on-going human interest series. Women in their 20's, 30's, 40's all the way up to their 80's and 90's. Piggybacking on the survey results. Those interviews are part of the package. Each will run about 1500 words. Deadlines will be normal for each issue. But this one is a rush to deadline! You would have only until next Friday. Do you think you can do it for me, Annie?"

Annie was thrilled with the offer. She needed to work and this project was a godsend.

"I don't like working under time pressures, but I'd be happy to take it over. When can you fax me the survey results? I need to start working on it as soon as possible."

"I can't tell you how relieved I am, Annie. The survey and the results will be faxed to you within the hour. And I want you to know that you'll be receiving a bonus on top of your regular rate with us. I know I can count on you to do a first rate job."

"Sounds good."

Annie was reminded of her friend, Lucille, who was on the stage. She often said, when complimented on her acting, "Don't say nice things. Throw money!" Yes, the money was important too. It had taken her a long time to reach her current pay scale.

Through the weekend and into the following week, Annie had a reason to get up in the morning. The assignment was challenging and the deadline was tight. She had done this type of article before. The hardest part was sorting out the survey results and deciding how she would organize the findings. She had to decide what the numbers meant and translate that into coherent and interesting reading. The most obvious way was to take each of the age brackets and discuss them, starting with women in their twenties. Another way would be to take the major health categories and trace each one up through the years. She had to make that strategic decision before she proceeded.

She chose the age bracket approach, banking on women wanting to zero in on their own stage in life, comparing their own statistics with the survey results. Then, they could move up through the coming years and see what was in store for them in each category. The aim of the piece would be not only to inform, but hopefully to offer ways to improve health through proper nutrition.

The more Annie delved into the subject, the more she felt like herself again. She had been devastated after she had talked with Mark on their return. Throwing herself into her work was the best medicine for her. That and being with her family. On Thursday, she had taken her mother to a favorite small restaurant that offered good food and comfortable booths. She had told her about London and her mother had brought her up to date on the University Without Walls course. Her descriptions of the other participants had made Annie laugh out loud. The fun of being together had been a tonic.

She had also talked with Tessa and Saul. He had two more weeks to go with the crutches and sounded impatient to be free of the cast. The children were fine in both households and Annie felt a deep need to see them and hold each one close to her heart. As soon as she met the Friday deadline, she would arrange a visit with each family. She had Hanukkah presents for the children and loved to be with them when they lit the candles in the Menorah.

She would fit the pieces of her life back together like a mosaic. Her marriage. Her children and grandchildren. Her mother. Her work. The compartments and structure of her life. And with the New Year, she hoped that it would not hurt as much when she thought of Mark.

Chapter 38

January was bitter cold and Ruth did not leave the apartment for almost three weeks. She hesitated to go out, with temperature in the teens and harsh winds. The doctor had advised against it and she knew herself that she might become light headed, even going directly to a waiting car. She did her best to plan each day so that she would not feel like a prisoner in her own home. And Annie and Rachel were both wonderful, coming over for visits and doing essential food shopping as well.

The Unicorn tapestry was nearing completion. She was very pleased with the way it had turned out. It was a magnificent design and she felt she had done it justice with her needlepoint. The flaw in the border was not too obvious, but it was definitely there. Ruth had written a note to Tessa, explaining the whole metaphor. It was on her heavy ecru note paper, in a sealed envelope, to be presented with the tapestry. Ruth loved to prepare gifts in a very personal way.

Each day, she spent at least two hours on the needlepoint and several hours in preparation for her University Without Walls course. She had told Annie about the last conference call when 'Mae West' had tangled with 'Big Shot'. And 'William Jennings Bryan' had tried to be the mediator. It had been a riotous conversation and Ruth remembered almost every syllable. When she had stopped laughing, Annie had urged her to write a short story about the class and she would help her get it published. Ruth was considering doing that, but she didn't want to be disloyal to the other participants. She had grown quite fond of most of them. Especially 'Mrs. Miniver', 'Clark Gable' and 'Baby'. It was hard to be fond of 'Big Shot' and 'Fats'.

Every afternoon, she set aside several hours for reading either novels or literary non fiction. Her love of losing herself in a good book never flagged.

She would smile when she recalled the furor about "Mrs. Shaeffer's Reading List" at Ridgewood High School. The command- performance assembly, the irate parents and her triumphal reading of *Hiroshima* were still vivid in her mind. Books would always be at the center of her life.

Annie and David had given a New Year's Eve party and invited her, but she had declined. She knew they did not want her to feel left out, but she had stopped staying up until midnight many years ago. She and Michael would be fast asleep by eleven on most New Year's Eves. They had rarely gone to big parties to celebrate. Paper hats and noise makers were not their style. Annie's party, of course, would not have been like that. It would have been lovely and elegant with their family and close friends. Ruth would have enjoyed seeing Annie and Tessa in their evening attire. That always gave her happiness.

When she saw Tessa during Hannukah, Tessa had looked especially beautiful. Annie and David had taken Ruth with them to visit Tessa, Robert and the children. She had loved seeing Eric and Sally light the candles and open their presents. And she had made potato latkes to contribute to the occasion. Sally was adamant about preferring apple sauce rather than sour cream with the latkes. Ruth was sure Sally would be determined about many things in life. It was a fine characteristic, as long as it did not get carried to extremes. She watched Tessa and Robert rein her in when it was necessary. She saw some of herself in her spunky little great granddaughter and that pleased her.

Since Ruth had not been able to go out to the movies with Rachel and the film group, they rented tapes and watched them on a regular basis at her apartment. She found the movie afternoons to be delightful. Not all of the women came each time, but two or three would sit in her livingroom and have tea and goodies later while they discussed the film. Ruth appreciated their adjusting to meet her needs. Rachel put it very simply, "That's what friends are for."

They watched some of the classics, like *The Philadelphia Story, The Third Man* and *Gone With The Wind.* Ruth never tired of discussing the story lines and the acting in films.

"Have you noticed that today, the women want to be called actors, not actresses? Can you imagine Jean Harlow calling herself an actor? Or Marilyn Monroe!"

"No, I can't," Rachel commented. "But women still don't pull the mega salaries that men do, whatever they're called. Julia Roberts makes 20 million dollars for a picture. But, that doesn't compare with Brad Pitt and Tom Cruise."

"Well, I don't even know the names of some of the top stars today," Ruth added.

The other women laughed and agreed. They saw the current films and enjoyed them . But there was something about the stars of the past that still held their loyalty.

The last week in January brought a break in the cold spell. The arctic air and severe winds receded and the daily temperatures rose into the upper 40's. Ruth was delighted. She would take a taxi to the Mall just to walk around and be back in the outside world. She felt liberated.

On Tuesday, after breakfast, she dressed and called a taxi. She would get off at Macy's. They usually had gorgeous flower displays in the aisles as a harbinger of Spring. When she arrived, she did indeed find the store filled with flowers. Tulips, irises, lilies — the fragrance was lovely. And, as usual, there were sleek saleswomen giving out samples of new perfumes. She always avoided being spritzed, but today she took several of the samples to try out at home. She was having a wonderful time.

After about half an hour, Ruth found that she was tiring. Her legs felt heavy and she needed to sit down. She took the escalator to the restaurant on the second floor and ordered tea and an English muffin. There were a few couples at the other tables. Mostly women in twos and threes. She probably should have not come out alone, but she didn't want to be a burden to Annie or Rachel. She sipped her tea slowly and ate a few bites of the muffin. She did feel a little light headed. It was time to go home. This had been enough of a jaunt into the outside world for one day.

Chapter 39

Tessa reached her decision about the baby before New Year's Eve. In the final analysis, she didn't rely on logic or what-if scripts. Of course, she had weighed the pros and cons over and over in her mind. And she had talked with Dr. Crawford again. But the defining moment for her came one morning on the train, riding into work.

She was thinking once more of Robert saying to her that she had the final vote. It was the enormous gift of his love for her and it touched her deeply. She remembered O. Henry's story , "The Gift of The Magi". The couple sold their most precious possessions, she her hair and he his watch, to buy gifts for each other. She bought him a fob for his treasured watch and he bought her the combs for her beautiful long hair. They had, in essence, given up the one thing they prized most to show their greater love for each other.

Tessa had read that story when she was in high school. At the time, it had brought her to tears. She knew some critics called it contrived or maudlin. "Just another O. Henry trick ending." She disagreed strongly. She saw the irony in the twist, but she also knew that in real life, people did make sacrifices for love. She had learned from her years with Ivan that first love can change. And lasting love means that two people give to each other as well as take.

The day of the blizzard had been a turning point for Tessa. Not only in how she saw her job and her boss. But in the total sense of being free and in control of her destiny. That sense of freedom was an additional factor in her decision. She knew Robert had given her the freedom to decide whether to have the baby or not. And she knew that she could change the direction of her career. There were other ways to practice law than at a city firm. Both decisions had come together for her within a period of several weeks.

When the family had celebrated Hanukkah, she watched Eric and Sally lighting the candles and opening their presents with such excitement. Her parents and grandmother had been with them one night and she thought of how they would all rejoice if they knew that she was pregnant. And what fun it would be for Eric and Sally to have a baby to fuss over. Of course, Sally would have to get used to the idea of not being the baby anymore. But she would probably love to be the big sister and in charge. A new role and a new challenge.

By New Year's Eve, she was ready to tell Robert. They were getting dressed for the party at her parents' house and she asked Robert to do the clasp of her necklace. "It's tricky. Make sure the safety catch is on."

As he maneuvered and clicked the delicate clasp into place, she said to him quite softly,

"I have a surprise for you, Robert." He turned her around and looked at her intently.

"What kind of surprise, Tessa?"

"The best kind, darling man." She kissed him and said, "We're going to have a baby."

"Are you sure, Tessa? I don't want you to do this, if you don't want to."

"I'm sure. And I want to."

He broke into an enormous grin, grabbed her in his arms and held her for several minutes. When he drew back, she saw that his eyes were filled with tears. She reached up and touched his cheek.

"I love you, Robert. And I want us to have this baby. If she or he is as wonderful as Sally, we will be blessed again!"

He enfolded her in his arms and they stood together. Tessa knew she had made the right decision. She felt completely loved.

They did not tell her parents that evening. There would be time to share later. Now, they wanted to savor the happiness they felt. When the champagne toasts were made, Tessa and Robert lifted their glasses together and she knew they were both thinking exactly the same thing. *To our new baby!*

During January, she felt some morning queasiness during the train ride into the city. The motion of the cars was not helpful and she munched crackers to ward off the nausea. Now, she was sure she was pregnant! She stifled a laugh at the circumstances. She would survive — as she had with Sally and Eric. It had only lasted with them until the third month was over.

At work, she found that Tom had pulled back from his badgering. Apparently, her explosion on the phone during the blizzard had come as a shock to him. Of course, she had surprised herself at the time with the vehemence of her threat. He did not refer to it again. And he made no comments when she had to leave early several days. He praised the long and complicated brief she turned in for a particularly acrimonious condominium case. The firm was representing the landlord. Tessa really identified with the apartment owners as she untangled the facts, but that was not how she prepared the brief. As she worked on it for weeks, she thought that it would be very different if she had her own practice. Then, she could choose the cases and whom she would represent. She saw it as a matter of personal integrity.

Tessa raised the idea of leaving the firm one night when the children had gone to bed.

"Remember, during the blizzard, what I threatened Tom with leaving?"

"Of course, I remember."

"Well, he's been behaving like a model boss. But I'm still thinking more and more of what it would be like to be my own boss."

"You mean, set up a private practice?"

"Yes. And not in the city. Somewhere around here. I see other lawyers with their shingles out. I'm sure it would take time to get started. But if others can do it, why can't I?"

Robert's expression showed both interest and approval.

"You can do anything you set your sights on, Tessa. I've learned that."

"I keep thinking I wouldn't be wasting hours every day on the train. And with a new baby, it would make our lives much simpler."

"We would still need a Nanny if you were away in your office."

"Yes, but we might not need a sleep-in Nanny. Neither of us really liked that with Sally."

The more Tessa talked about leaving the firm, the more it appealed to her. She knew starting out could be very slow. Her salary now was solid. But, they had the advantage of Robert's strong income. That gave them the leeway for her to branch out in this new direction. They both saw it as more of a plus than a minus. The dollars were important, but they foresaw her reaching her current pay level within three or four years. They could sustain the initial loss in light of the projected earnings and psychic benefits. The family's health coverage came from Robert's firm.

Tessa began to map out a time line. When to give Tom notice. When to start looking for a site for her office. As she planned, she began to feel more and more excited with the idea. She was prepared to take on all types of clients and cases. She had handled real estate, tax, divorce and other types of law. It seemed to make sense to start with a general practice and then move toward a particular niche as she built her foundation.

At the same time as she was moving ahead on her career track, she was also making lists of what she had to do to prepare for the baby. Find a good Nanny. Or consider day care. Several of her friends had gone that route and were very happy with their choice. She and Robert had to consider that option as well. She knew the drawback of catching the ubiquitous colds and 'bugs' from other babies. But reliability was built in with daycare. She would not have to worry whether the Nanny would show up or not. And the Nanny could get sick too. There was no perfect solution for a mother who worked outside the home.

Robert was in an ongoing state of euphoria since New Year's Eve. Nothing his brother Sam could do at work brought him down from cloud nine. He came home each night from work without the usual stories of power struggles on the front lines of the furniture business. They may still have been going on, but he was not reacting to them as he had in the past. One night, he breezed in with a big grin on his face and announced triumphantly, "I have a new way to deal with Sam. I just ignore him!" Tessa's eyes opened wide with delight.

"I think that's marvelous. And how does he handle that?'

"He doesn't know what to make of it. Today, he was on my back about two of the sales reps and why their numbers didn't match last year's. I just said I'd look into it. Period."

"You used to get defensive and argue with him. Pick up for the sales reps."

"Exactly. He looked surprised when I didn't. He said, 'Okay' and that was that."

The last Saturday in January, Tessa awoke early to find that she was staining. Her heart dropped and her mind went into overdrive. She called Dr. Crawford on the emergency number and left her name and number with the answering service. Then she got back into bed. Robert and the children were still asleep. She shook his shoulder and he turned over and looked at her. When he saw her face, he sat upright.

"What is it, Tessa? What's wrong?"

"I'm staining Robert. I just called Dr. Crawford."

The phone rang and she grabbed it.

"What's happened, Tessa?"

"I'm staining. What should I do?"

"First, of all, don't panic. Is it heavy or light?"

"I'd say light."

"Stay off your feet for the weekend. In bed would be the best idea. Let's see what develops."

"I didn't have this with the other two."

"That doesn't mean anything. Don't worry, Tessa. Some staining is not unusual. You're healthy. And there's every reason you will have a healthy pregnancy."

"I just didn't expect this."

"We never do. I'll be on call if you need me."

"Thank you."

Tessa hung up the phone and looked at Robert. His face mirrored how she felt. Shocked and distressed. After all the what-if scripts and weeks of decision making, life was throwing them a major curve.

Chapter 40

Annie would look back at January, 2002 as one of the toughest times of her life. She used every ounce of self discipline to block Mark Trianos out of her mind. If she could do that — if she did not let herself think about him, she felt her heart might have a chance to heal.

The days were exceptionally cold with strong winds coming out of the North, but she walked her three miles each morning without fail. Only her eyes showed when she finished putting on her parka and wrapping a lacy wool scarf across her nose and mouth. Some days she felt like Amundsen going for the South Pole! When she returned to home base, she felt frozen but virtuous.

She had planned a New Year's Eve party and it had been a success. Tessa and Robert came as did Saul and Diane, along with their close friends. Tessa looked gorgeous in a wine cut- velvet tunic and crepe pants. Annie wore a white silk blouse, black velvet trousers and her amethyst earrings and pendant. She had used the antique Limoge china and Waterford crystal. The dining room had sparkled and her food was praised and devoured. She served honey glazed Cornish hens stuffed with wild rice, new green beans, sauteed Portobello mushrooms and poached pears. David loved being the host and asked each guest to make a toast to the New Year. It was a custom they followed. Annie's toast was, "May the year 2002 bring joy and fulfillment to each of our lives."

She had met the deadline for the Health and Nutrition article and immediately began the related series of interview pieces. She could choose the subjects from the survey responses that had been faxed to her. Some of the women had gone into detail in their answers and reading them gave Annie definite guideposts to making her selection. She would choose one from each age bracket. Instead of starting with the 20's, she thought about doing the reverse. Choose a woman in her 80's for the first interview and article.

She ran the idea by the editor, who pronounced it, " Genius! I love it! We'll begin at the top and work down. Annie, you're wonderful!"

The days passed into weeks and Annie did her best to avoid thinking that Mark may have come home. She steeled herself against going to the gym and she did not drive anywhere near his house.

Her mother needed more attention since the extreme cold had confined her to her apartment. Annie visited more often and called twice a day instead of once. She found reasons to drop in with some special fruits she had found at the food market or a book that she felt would be of high interest to her. Ruth had shown her the exquisite tapestry and the flaw woven into the border. Annie was intrigued with the metaphor and the symbolism. Yes, she thought, life did throw surprises our way. And some of them started out as wonderful, only to turn to heartache.

David had been more affectionate since their return from London. One night, he asked Annie, "Where's that gorgeous sexy nightgown you wore when we were away?"

She had folded it carefully into her lingerie drawer. Now, she realized that she should wear it and the new Chanel 19 perfume too. The silk on her body felt sensual and the perfume brought back how she had felt in London with David. She knew it had not been the same as her passion for Mark. She couldn't lie to herself. But she had felt more free with David in London and they had explored new ways to please each other. He had been thrilled and she had been happy there.

She had shared some of her intimate thoughts with Sarah during one of their long talks.

"It's a terrible struggle, Sarah. I have to keep pushing him out of my mind."

"Is it working, Annie? And is it getting any easier?"

" I think so. When I'm writing, I'm completely engrossed. That's the easiest time. When I'm walking, I try to keep my mind on the elements, the cold and the wind. And making it back to the house without freezing!"

"And, how's David?"

"David seems to be fine. Busy as usual." She paused before adding, "And eager to replay some of the fun we had in bed in London."

Sarah laughed and said, "Fun in bed sounds good to me. I could use more of that."

" It has been good, Sarah. And I'm going to make it even better."

"I know you, Annie. I would say that you are on your way back. You're almost there."

"I'm doing my best."

"You can't do anymore than that, my friend."

That conversation had taken place the day before Annie bumped into Mark at the supermarket. She was pushing a shopping cart and rounded an aisle when she saw him. He was choosing pasta from the shelves. She didn't turn back. She would have to get through it. He looked up when she came nearer. And his face showed little expression when he saw her. She spoke first.

"Hi, Mark. How was the skiing?"

"It was fine. Cleared my head some. How about you, Annie? How are you?"

She looked at him and saw that the meeting was as hard for him as it was for her. She knew how his eyes and mouth looked when he was disturbed.

"I'm doing the best I can, Mark. I have a big assignment, which is a godsend."

He didn't say anything at that point and she knew she should probably just end the conversation and walk away. But, she couldn't do it. He must have seen the distress on her face too. He took a step closer to her and said softly, "I've missed you, Annie."

She looked up at him and the words just tumbled out. "Oh, Mark! I've tried so hard to keep you out of my thoughts!"

Annie felt herself close to tears. She wouldn't let herself lose it in the pasta aisle! The writer in her saw the absurdity of that scene. She started to move her basket past him, but he put his hand on her arm to stop her.

"Annie, come have a cup of coffee with me. At the cafe. We have to talk. Please!"

She knew she should say, 'No', but she couldn't do that to him.

"I'll meet you in about twenty minutes, Mark. I have to check out these groceries. I'm doing the shopping for my mother. She's been housebound for weeks in this cold."

"I'll be there, Annie. Don't disappoint me."

As she stood in the check-out line, she knew she was making a bad mistake. If she sat with him over coffee, the powerful attraction she felt would arise again. She paid for the groceries, and put them in the trunk of her car. Then, she called him on his cell phone.

"Mark. I can't meet you. I'm afraid of what might happen."

"I'm not going to come on to you, Annie. I promise."

"It's not you, Mark. It's me. Just seeing you again has shaken me. When you left for your trip, I was nearly crazy. That's the truth. Now, I'm just getting my life back on course. I can't go back."

"I'm sorry, Annie. I was pretty rough on you the last time we talked."

"Not really, Mark. I had hurt you badly."

There was a pause and Annie added, "There's not much to talk about, Mark. I wish you well always. You know that. I cared for you and I still do. You've changed my life."

"I hope that's for the better, Annie."

"Yes, Mark. For the better." She paused. "I didn't want to hurt you. You know that."

"I know, Annie. I was angry before I left. I'm not anymore."

"Stay well, Mark. I'll look for your paintings in the galleries."

"I'm sorry I never painted you, Annie."

"Good bye, Mark."

"Good bye, Annie."

When she turned off the phone, Annie sat in the car and cried. She knew why she was crying. Certainly it was a release of tension. But, it was more than that. It was the realization that she had ended her affair with Mark Trianos. She had met him by accident and felt the same pull. He was as attractive as ever. But, she had resisted being drawn back into the passion of the past. She would learn to live without him. Just as he would have to learn to live without her.

Her sobbing subsided and she drove home to settle down and wash her face before going to her mother's with the groceries.

Annie thought of her New Year's wish for 'joy and fulfillment' in 2002. January was just the beginning. There was no crystal ball to read the months to come.

Part IV

Chapter 41

Tessa was in a very nervous state the last weekend in January. She stayed in bed as Dr. Crawford had advised. Robert told the children that she had caught the virus that was going around and needed to rest. He brought her meals up on a tray. She was not hungry. And she was very restless. She said more than once, "I can't believe this is happening!"

He tried to reassure her each time. "We don't know yet. Remember what Dr. Crawford said. This is not unusual. And don't panic."

"Well, it is unusual for me!" she countered.

By Sunday evening the staining had tapered off and they were becoming hopeful. They were in the bedroom with the door closed.

"You know, it's really strange, Robert. I have this fierce need now to have the baby. After all those weeks of going back and forth, it would break my heart if I had a miscarriage."

"Stop going down that road, Tessa. You just told me the staining was less."

"I know. But what if it starts up again?"

"Then, we'll worry about it then. Meanwhile, it's stopping."

"I'm going to call Tom Simmons tomorrow and tell him that I'm in bed with the flu. Then I'm going to figure out how to tell him that I'm leaving the firm."

"Isn't that a little premature?"

"Not really. Whatever happens — I'm not staying there. I'm going out on my own."

"You're sure, Tessa?"

"I'm sure!"

Monday morning, Robert brought Tessa breakfast upstairs and got the children ready for school. Even though the staining was slight, she was leery of going the steps. Sally's head appeared at the bedroom door.

"Are you feeling better, Mommy? Can I bring Gorgeous in to say 'Hello'?"

"Come here, baby. I am much better. Bring in Gorgeous and give me a kiss."

Sally's face lit up and she ran to Tessa who reached out for a hug and kiss. Eric soon followed suit. He was more tentative in his approach, as befitted the older brother.

"Are you all better, Mom? Not catching?"

"I'm much better, Eric. Maybe it wasn't the flu, after all. Have a good day in school."

Before he left, Robert cautioned her to take it easy. He brought up juice, fruit, crackers and peanut butter to hold her over in case she decided to stay upstairs. And he asked her several times if he should take the day off and stay home. But she declined. "I'll be fine, Robert. We'll talk later."

At nine, Tessa called Dr. Crawford's office. She was in and came on the line.

"How are you, Tessa? How's it going?"

"I think it's stopping. It's less than Saturday morning. I've stayed in bed except for going to the bathroom. Should I get up and go downstairs?"

"It might not hurt to stay put for another day or two. Until it stops completely. Can you handle that?"

"I'll handle it."

"Call me Wednesday morning. It sounds very promising to me."

A great sense of relief washed over Tessa. She would not lose this baby. It had become so very precious and real to her. The danger of a miscarriage had shaken her sense of control. All the while she had been making her decision, she had never considered this happening. Now, she wanted to feel in control of her body — and her life again. "I will have this baby!" she said aloud.

She called Tom Simmons next. He sounded grim when he answered.

"Tom, I'm sorry to tell you that I'm in bed with the flu. I may not be in for the rest of the week."

A very long silence ensued and he finally replied. "We're swamped here, Tessa."

"People get sick, Tom." She was in no mood to mollify him. Maybe he would fire her! That would bring unemployment insurance, she thought. A new twist on her projected script for leaving.

"I hope you can make it in by Wednesday."

"I'll let you know how I'm doing."

Tight. Abrupt. Unfeeling, she thought. Doesn't give a damn how sick I might be. Only cares about the work load. If she hadn't already made her decision to leave, this would have capped it.

Robert had brought up the local paper as well as *The Times*.. She turned to the Real Estate offerings in the area and read the ads. She could move into one of the professional buildings or perhaps find a small house that could be easily converted to an office. If she were lucky, it might already be offered for rental as office space. She needed two rooms, basically, a waiting room and her office. There was something about the latter idea that attracted her. She felt she could establish an individual practice more easily by being in a separate building. And the shingle out front appealed to her sense of independence.

She called several of the agents to learn more about the properties advertised. Two sounded as if they might be what she was looking for. And the rentals were in the ball park. She set up appointments for the following weekend. She was hoping that she would be back to her normal routine by then.

As far as Tom Simmons was concerned, she had developed a carapace of indifference. She would go back to work when she was ready. And, she would tell him that she was leaving the firm. If he wanted more than four weeks notice, she would stay on. But she had a feeling that he would react in anger and want her to go as soon as possible. That would be just fine with her. He had not lived up to the description of the firm that had been projected when she had been hired. That they were humanistic and caring toward their employees. That was what had attracted Tessa in the beginning, as well as the chance to become a partner. It had not turned out that way. She felt she had given more than a fair measure of work of high quality. She had fulfilled her share of the bargain.

On an impulse, she dialed Saul at his office. He picked up his phone.

"Saul, it's Tessa. Do you have time to talk?"

"Is something wrong, Tessa? Are you okay?"

"I'm okay. I wanted to ask your opinion about something. Is this a bad time to talk?"

"I can talk. Shoot."

"I've been thinking of leaving the firm. Going into private practice out here on the Island."

"A big move, Tessa. Is the commute getting to you?"

"Not just the commute, but that is part of it. Three or four hours every day. No, it's more of wanting to be in control of the work I do. And not having my boss constantly jerking the strings."

"But, isn't that the only way to make partner? To put in the required years at their beck and call?"

"Yes, that's the drill. But, I don't want to do that anymore. And if I made partner at the firm, I'm not sure I would be happy there. The atmosphere has turned out to be far from nurturing."

"Lawyers rarely nurture, from what I have heard, Tessa."

"I agree. But I thought I found a place where that would happen. And it hasn't."

"So, what's your plan?"

"I'm looking for a place to rent and hang out my shingle. Do you think I'm crazy?"

"Smart. Beautiful. Accomplished. Yes. Crazy — No! Sounds like you have it all sorted out."

Tessa laughed. When she needed him he was always there for her with encouragement.

"I love you, big brother!"

"Me too. Let me know how it goes."

She knew what his reaction would probably be if she told him about the baby. He would be happy for her and tell her, full steam ahead. Saul had always had complete confidence in her abilities since they were children, better known as the 'Bertman twins". There was nothing, he would tell others, that his sister, Tessa, could not do if she wanted to do it.

Chapter 42

Tessa called Dr. Crawford Wednesday morning to tell her the staining had stopped completely. She felt wonderful — as if tight iron bands had been lifted from around her heart.

"Should I stay home for the rest of the week?" she asked.

"That might be a good idea, Tessa. Take it gradually. And by next Monday, you should be able to pick up your normal schedule."

"I want to share something with you. I'm planning to leave the firm in the city and open a private practice in the area."

"Is it because of the baby?"

"Not really. Although that may have been the catalyst. I hate all the hours I spend on the train. And the firm has not turned out to be the place I would be happy in — even as a partner."

"Well, I wish you well. And with a new baby, it probably will be much easier to plan your lives if you have an office nearby."

"That is part of my thinking."

"Let me know if the staining should start again. Although I think you're going to be fine."

"Thank you Dr. Crawford, for your concern and attention. I really appreciate it."

Tessa called Robert immediately. He was not at his desk and she left him the good news on his voice mail. She felt a surge of energy. She was eager to move on with her plans. But, first, she had to call into the office and tell them she would not be in until Monday. That would not be a pleasant conversation. She was in luck when she called. Tom was not in and she gave the message to Jenny.

"Please tell Tom, the doctor said I would be able to go back to work on

Monday."

That was, at least, partly true.

She was impatient to see the two rental properties on Saturday. She would go by herself and then Robert would return with her if either or both were promising. She began making lists of furniture she would need. Robert could get wholesale prices for her desk and files. The couches and chairs would come from his own inventory at the warehouse. She envisioned a simple waiting room. Leather couches and chairs. Carpeting. Comfortable and substantial. If there was enough light, a ficus tree in the corner. And one white phaleanopsis orchid on an end table.

By Saturday morning, Tessa was raring to go. The staining had not reoccurred and she felt her normal energetic self. The children were watching television and Robert wished her, 'Good luck' as she left to meet the rental agent at the first property. It turned out to be poorly located on a side street and the rooms were dark as well. But the second was what she called, "a definite possible." It had originally been a small house and now held two office suites. One was rented to a dentist whose sign read "Family Practice". The other was vacant. The location was excellent, on one of the main streets. There was traffic and it was clearly visible.

The rooms were good size and there was plenty of light. Tessa could visualize them furnished. She could see her sign, "Law Offices. Tessa Bertman" on the shingle. She mused that the men and women who were patients of the dentist might need legal help as well. Her mind took a bizarre twist — maybe they were in need of a divorce! She laughed out loud. It was new. It was exciting! She had told Saul about the impending career switch. Now, she would tell the children and her parents. And Grandma Ruth. Tessa remembered their last conversation about her career. She felt her grandmother would be very pleased with her decision. It was all becoming very real.

Robert gave the final stamp of approval that afternoon and Tessa prepared herself for Monday, when she would tell Tom Simmons. She would be ready for almost any response he would make. No matter how nasty he became, the bottom line was that she was leaving.

Monday turned out to be a grey rainy day. *The perfect setting for this melodrama,* Tessa thought as she rode in on the train. Jenny greeted her with a warning look of raised eyebrows and a gesture toward Tom's office. Tessa had expected that. She hung up her coat, took a look at the pile of files on her desk and walked to Tom's office. He did not raise his head when she came in.

"Good morning, Tom."

At that, he looked up and his expression was far from friendly.

"There's enough work on your desk, Tessa, to keep you busy. You may have to put in extra hours to catch up." He then turned his attention back to the work on his desk.

If she hadn't been getting ready to leave, his frosty edict would have triggered an explosion. As it was, she remained calm and sat down in one of the chairs opposite his desk. He looked up.

"I have something to tell you, Tom. I'm going to be leaving the firm."

Now, he stared at her intently. If he was surprised, it did not show in his face. What did show was rising color. He was apparently becoming furious. When he did speak, he sputtered.

"You're what! You're going to leave the firm?"

"It's not something I decided overnight, Tom. There are many factors I've considered."

"And what may those factors be? It seems to me that you have been given all sorts of leeway to fit your work load into your private life!"

Tessa wanted to avoid a blow by blow argument. It would be a no-win. She would tell him about the baby.

"It seems that I'm pregnant, Tom. That's one of the major factors."

"We do have maternity leave, Tessa. You know that." His lips were tight as he said it.

"It's not just the baby, Tom. The four hours on the train each day are another reason."

She would not get into her desire for an independent practice. To choose her own cases and the clients she wanted to represent. And she would certainly avoid discussing the atmosphere in the firm that she had found to be far from humanistic. Those reasons were too private.

The color in Tom's face subsided. He looked sullen.

"Well, I can't stop you if you want to go."

"I won't leave you in the lurch, Tom. I can continue to work for some months while you look for a replacement."

"That won't be necessary, Tessa. We can manage. Why don't you wrap up what's on your desk. That should be two weeks, I would think. It shouldn't be too hard to replace you."

Tessa realized that he thought he was insulting her. In reality, she was thrilled!

"That's sounds fair, Tom."

That evening, after Sally and Eric were upstairs, she related the conversation to Robert verbatim. "He was apoplectic at first! Red as a beet. Furious! Then he calmed down and turned mean. As I thought he might. It's perfect. I'll be through in two weeks." Tessa was jubilant!

Robert hugged her. "I'm proud of you, baby. You did it! And in style. You always do."

Chapter 43

Once she had told Tom Simmons about the baby, Tessa knew she had to tell her family as well. In the world of six degrees of separation, she didn't want them to learn second hand. And news traveled fast along the gossip grapevine. Even in a city as large as New York into suburban Long Island and New Jersey.

She and Robert told the children on Tuesday morning before they went to school. They were all sitting at the breakfast table and Tessa began. She was most concerned about how Sally would receive the news.

"Sally. Eric. We have something important to tell you. We think it's very exciting news. What would you say if I told you that there were going to be three children in our family?"

Eric spoke first. "Three children? Are you going to adopt another kid?"

Eric was very literal. She had said 'children'.

"Not adopt, Eric. I'm going to have a baby."

Sally, who had remained silent, let out a shriek, "I'm the baby!" She started to cry in large gulps. "I don't want another baby!"

Tessa went to Sally and gathered her into her arms.

"You will always be my baby, Sally." She waited until the tears stopped and continued. "And you will be even more than that. You will also be a big sister. That will be special fun."

"Why will that be fun?" The large blue eyes were very skeptical but Tessa knew she was making progress.

"It will mean that you will be in charge. You love to be in charge. Like when you are with your cousin Emily. Don't you like to be the big cousin? And tell her what to do?"

She had definitely caught Sally's attention. As the child pondered that thought, Tessa turned back to Eric, who was continuing to eat his cereal.

"So, Eric, what do you think?"

"I think it's cool, Mom."

Thus, spake the pre-teenager! 'Cool' — the quintessential compliment. Tessa sighed. And Robert reached over to muss Eric's hair. They had crossed the first hurdle. Then Sally asked if she could go up to her room and "tell Gorgeous about the baby" and that she was going to be the "big sister". Tessa laughed with pure happiness. They were home free.

When she reached the office, she closed the door and called her mother. She didn't think Tom would intrude and open it as he had in the past.

"Mom, it's Tessa."

"Are you at work, Tessa. Do you feel fine?"

Annie had been told the same story of the past week in bed with the flu.

"I'm fine Mom. And I have some wonderful news to tell you. Are you sitting down?"

"No, I'm standing up. But what's the news? I can always take good news."

"You're going to be a grandmother again. How's that?"

She waited for a response and then her mother said in an incredulous voice, "I like that very much, Tessa. Are you telling me that you are having a baby?"

"I am. And that Robert and I are wildly happy about it!"

"Tessa. I'm stunned. And happy for you, dear child. It's come as something of a surprise."

"If you promise not to tell anyone else, except Dad, it came as something of a surprise to us, too."

"Tessa, my head is all a whirl— but my heart is full. I have tears in my eyes.. This is the most wonderful news. Your father will be thrilled. May I tell him, or do you want to?"

"You can tell him, Mom. And I'll talk with him tonight when I'm home. And I want you to tell Grandma Ruth too. Can you see her today? Tell her I'll call her tomorrow. I'll tell Saul, myself."

Tessa paused before she added, "Oh, and the other good news is that I'm leaving the firm. I'm going to set up a private practice near home."

"Tessa, as it says in the *Times* puzzle, my mind is 'a reel' with all this news. You are turning your life around. I need time to absorb all this. And I'll stop to see Grandma Ruth this afternoon. She will be so happy. She loves you so."

"Let me call you tonight, after the kids are asleep."

"Dad should be home then. I love you, dear. I am very happy for you and

Robert."

"Me too, Mom."

Tessa called Saul next. His reaction was similar to her mother's. A combination of amazement and happiness. And, as always, positive and upbeat.

"You've knocked me for the proverbial loop! I give you a lot of credit. A new baby. And starting your own practice at the same time. Wow!"

"The timing seems right, Saul. I'm thirty six and counting."

"Aren't we both!"

Tessa laughed. His biological clock was somewhat different from hers.

It took her about ten minutes to settle down to her work after talking with her mother and Saul. She was on a natural high and it felt great. She ordered lunch in and stayed at her desk until five thirty. She could hardly wait to see Robert and the children.

When Tessa opened the front door, Sally came hurtling out of the den to greet her. She was in a state of excitement. Her pony tail was bouncing as she ran.

"Mommy, I told Mrs. Ross that I'm going to be a big sister!"

"And what did she say?"

"She said, I would be the best big sister in the world!"

Hooray for Mrs. Ross, Tessa noted, placing her on her to-thank list.

"And you will be, Sally. The way you take care of Gorgeous and love her. That's how you can take care of the baby."

"Will the baby be a girl like Gorgeous?"

"We don't know, yet. But as soon as we do, we'll tell you and Eric."

"How will you find out?"

"They can take a special kind of picture in a few months. And then we'll know."

Sally seemed satisfied with that explanation. Tessa felt enormous relief.

Eric was up in his room and came out on the landing to say "Hi." Whether he had shared the news with his friends or had played it 'cool' himself, she didn't know. When he was ready, he would. Tessa had seen Eric make major adjustments after the divorce to the joint custody arrangement. A new baby would not alter his life as it would Sally's.

She told Robert about her mother's reaction to the news and Saul's.

"They were both very surprised. My mother was in tears. And they are so happy for us. That made me feel wonderful. You should call your mother tonight and tell her. I'm going to talk to my Dad later."

It was all playing out well Tessa thought as she went upstairs to change. She was most thankful that the big sister idea had caught Sally's imagination. And Eric was a trooper. He was used to all kinds of change. A new baby did not faze him.

After nine, she called her parents and her Dad answered.

"Tessa. I am delighted, darling! How do you feel?"

"Well, I had a scare last week, Dad. I didn't really have the flu. I started to stain and Dr. Crawford put me to bed. I didn't tell Mom that happened. I didn't want her to worry."

"And, has it stopped completely?"

"It's stopped. Dr. Crawford said staining occurs sometimes. Of course, I knew that. But, it didn't happen with Eric or Sally. Robert and I were so worried about losing the baby, Dad."

"It's not unusual, Tessa. Dr. Crawford has a fine reputation. You know that I think very highly of her. You can trust her judgement, dear."

"I didn't want to worry you and Mom. You understand, Dad?"

"I do, Tessa. You're a big girl and you and Robert have to be in charge of your lives."

"I love you, Dad."

"We're very happy for you, Tessa."

"And what do you think about the career move? The shingle with Tessa Bertman?"

"I think it's the right move at the right time. Whatever we can do to steer clients your way, we'll be working on it, you can be sure."

"I can hardly wait to get started. I've already found a suite to rent twenty minutes away."

"Once you decide to do something, Tessa, you move at laser speed."

"Not quite. But it is all falling into place. I'll leave the firm a week from Friday."

Tessa talked next with her mother. She wanted to hear about Grandma Ruth's reaction.

"Well, of course, she was completely surprised. And then she started to cry. Her emotions are always near the surface these days, Tessa."

"Was she okay?"

"She's fine. Just very happy. And then, she said something very poignant."

"What did she say?"

"That you might name the baby after Grandpa Michael."

"I haven't even thought of naming the baby, Mom. But that would be very fitting. And it would give her great happiness. I'll talk with Robert about it when the time is right."

Tessa felt good after talking with her parents. But tired, as well. She would go to bed early. Dr. Crawford had told her to pace herself. She didn't want to push her luck. She needed rest and so did the baby!

Chapter 44

Annie was filled with a sense of well being. Tessa's news about the baby had caught her completely by surprise and it carried her up on waves of pure happiness. She had worked steadily throughout January to bring herself to an even keel. And she had not gone back to Mark after their chance meeting. She was no longer parceling out each day, fighting her way back to a normal equilibrium. Now, she woke each morning thinking of the future and the new baby. She felt alive again and it was a wonderful feeling.

Her mother's birthday was February 28 and she thought that would be a perfect time for a family celebration. She would run it by her first, of course. Ruth had told her that her friends were taking her to the Russian Tea Room for luncheon on her birthday. It had been a favorite place for her and Michael in years past. Now, with the renovations, it was quite spectacular and Rachel suggested it as "divine for a birthday luncheon". The 28th was a Thursday. Annie would plan the family party for the following weekend, on Sunday afternoon. She knew that Ruth tired in the evenings.

When she dropped in, several days after telling her about Tessa having the baby, Annie brought up the idea of a party.

"Mama, you've always said that if you had been born one day later, you would be a Leap Year baby. And only have parties every four years. Well, you're a February 28 birthday lady. And I know you're being taken to The Russian Tea Room, which sounds lovely. But, how about a family get together at our house on the Sunday afternoon after your birthday?"

"I don't want you to fuss, Annie."

"Why not? I can't think of a better reason for a party. And it will be fun for everybody."

"It would be wonderful to see everyone. I can hardly wait to talk more with Tessa. She called me. She sounded on cloud nine. And she also told me that she is leaving the law firm in the city. I think that is a smart move. She wasn't really happy there. She was just marking her time until she became a partner."

"So, we're on, Mama — Sunday, March 3, for your birthday party. And you have to pick out something special to wear. You'll be the guest of honor."

"Well, I'm not going out to look for a new outfit, if that's what you mean. You know how I hate shopping for clothes!"

Annie smiled and kissed her on the cheek. She did not argue when her mother was adamant. "You always look elegant, Mama. And I'd say you have the right to wear whatever you want to your own birthday party."

Ruth smiled back. Annie knew she enjoyed the sharing and bantering back and forth.

"Does one o'clock sound right? I'll make a buffet lunch. Then the children can run around more , rather than trying to get them to sit still at the dining room table. We can feed them first in the breakfast room."

"That sounds perfect, dear. I love to see the little ones, but sitting quietly with all the adults would be a treat for me."

Annie laughed and declared, "So be it, says the caterer!"

She found in the weeks ahead that her days were full. She was doing the interviews for the Nutrition and Health series and had started with a woman in her mid 80's, as had been agreed upon with the editor. She had created a fine set of questions and the woman she chose turned out to be a winner. Not only were her answers informative, they were witty and wise as well. Annie loved writing the article about her as the first in the series. She thought that it would be a tough act to follow.

Annie was also engrossed in two other pleasurable tasks. The preparations for her mother's party and taking Tessa up on a request to help with choosing furnishings for her new office. Life was spinning on a normal course and Annie felt herself again. The compartments were back where they belonged. She and David in the center. The children and grandchildren next to them. Her mother nearby. And Mark Trianos no longer a part of the picture.

The phrase, "If winter comes...." kept running through her head. She called Jack and told him about the party.

"Do you think you and Lois could come? It would be so wonderful if you could, Jack."

"I'm going to do my best to be there, Annie."

"She was so happy when you came to see her in the hospital. You have no idea. Eighty eight years, Jack. She's still a dynamo in so many ways!"

" I'll check with Lois and call you back, Annie. I'd love to be there."

Jack called her the next day and said they were coming. Tessa and Saul were enthusiastic about the party and promised to bring appropriate gifts. It would be a lovely afternoon. David planned a champagne punch to set a festive tone.

Annie had worn the navy silk nightgown several times since David had asked her about it. She also found that the scent of Chanel 19 put her in the mood for adventures in her own bedroom. And David certainly noticed the changes in their lovemaking. She wanted him to touch her in more intimate ways than he had in the past. She guided his hands over her body and whispered what she wanted him to do. He followed her lead and she found herself responding to his caresses. It took time for her to reach a climax, but the increasing tension was exciting to her. She had learned how to let go of her inhibitions with Mark. She sensed the irony, but she no longer felt the guilt. The affair was over and she could give herself completely to her husband. He had waited a long time for that to happen.

David said one night, after the silk night gown had fallen to the carpet and she stood naked in his arms, that London had been the best vacation they had ever taken. He said that the week was a turning point in their sexual life. And in a way, Annie thought, he was right. David was the same attractive man he had always been. But she had changed profoundly. She felt free with him as she had never felt before. She was whole again — and then some. They were finding new tenderness and joy in each other. After 37 years, Annie thought, that was quite an accomplishment!

She met Tessa one Saturday afternoon to see the suite of offices. First, she hugged her and stood back to admire what she saw. Tessa was wearing her dark green shearling coat over camel slacks and sweater. Her hair was lustrous, loose about her face.

"You look so beautiful, dear. Pregnancy always agrees with you."

" I feel fine, Mom. Just some morning sickness, but it's almost all gone."

They walked about the rooms and Tessa had a sketch of where the furniture would go in the waiting room and in her office.

"Robert has beautiful leather pieces right in the warehouse. And, believe, me," she added, "the price is right. His Dad is so happy about the baby, and that I'm going to stop the long train commute, that the furniture is their present to us."

"That's quite a present! I'm impressed."

"They've always been supportive. But I think they are thrilled that I will have more time to spend with the children. And with Robert, of course. They never quite understood his making dinner and assuming some of the Mommy role. They're pretty traditional, as you know, but they never put pressure on me. And I've appreciated that."

"I'd say they've been terrific in-laws. And they really love Eric."

"If only Sam wouldn't drive Robert crazy. But Robert has a new way to deal with it. He just ignores him."

"And is it working?"

"It seems to be. Sam doesn't know what to make of it. If there's no argument, there's no fun, apparently. He's been doing less of it lately."

Annie treasured the times she had alone with Tessa. Mother-daughter excursions had been part of their family life for years. After Tessa married, there were fewer times that they could meet, but they did plan afternoons in the city at least twice a year. They would have lunch in the theater district and see a Saturday matinee or walk on Fifth Avenue or Madison and succumb to temptation in the shops.

Being with Tessa as she planned her new office was very gratifying to Annie. She had been on her own for years as a freelance writer. She knew the downside of building relationships with editors, but she also knew that being your own boss meant freedom. Tessa had talked of her boss pulling the strings on her. She wouldn't have that anymore. She would have an upward climb of creating her client base, but Annie had supreme confidence in Tessa's abilities. She had seen her tackle many a challenge. And succeed.

When they stopped at a cafe in the nearby mall to have a light lunch, Annie told Tessa how she felt.

"I am so very proud of you, dear. Dad and I are thrilled about the baby. And we think you have made the best decision to set up your own practice."

"I know it will take time, Mom. I'm not expecting to take off like gang busters."

"You have time, Tessa. And I've never seen you give up when you want something."

"I'm spreading the word and I have some friends and contacts who have already approached me. One woman, is just about to leave her husband and wants to explore divorce proceedings . I'm starting to do preliminary work with her next week. The office should be set up by the end of the month if all the pieces fall into place. I have the sign maker delivering the shingle Wednesday. And I've drafted the ad for the newspaper — 'Tessa Bertman is pleased to announce the opening of her office for the practice of law."

"I'll drink to that!" said Annie, as she smiled and lifted her glass of iced tea.

"Thanks, Mom. I can hardly wait to get started. It's beginning to feel real."

Chapter 45

Ruth Shaeffer enjoyed every minute of her 88th birthday. Beautiful cards had been arriving all week and she had them arrayed on the dining room table. At nine, the doorbell rang and she accepted a long florist's box. It was filled with a glory of Spring flowers. Mauve and peach French tulips, white and yellow freesia, lilacs, iris and several branches of flowering quince with their tiny pink blossoms. All set against long stems of pussy willows and fragrant blue green eucalyptus leaves and ferns. Annie knew she loved to arrange her own flowers. Ruth was in heaven!

She spent over an hour dividing up the flowers into separate vases. Her prized Baccarat vase looked spectacular in the center of the dining room table with the tall quince branches, tulips, pussy willows, eucalyptus and lilacs. She set smaller groupings of iris and freesia in more casual ceramic and crystal vases in the bedroom and kitchen. The entire apartment was filled with the colors and fragrance of Spring. She adored the eucalyptus aroma that would linger on for weeks.

By ten, the phone was ringing with 'Happy Birthday' calls. Annie, David, Jack from Chicago, Tessa and then Saul. She was touched by their warm wishes and thanked them for their cards. She described the flower arrangements to Annie. She would see all of them before the family party on Sunday. It was going to be quite a week. And today was just the beginning. She felt elated.

Ruth took a long bath, dressed and was ready when Rachel picked her up at noon to keep their lunch reservation at The Russian Tea Room. There were four women and she sat in the front with Rachel. The car was good size and comfortable. While they drove into the city, Ruth thought that she would love to have the buckwheat blinis with caviar, if that was not too extravagant. She would wait until the others ordered to see.

They arrived on time and were seated at a good table. Ruth was pleased. Rachel ordered a bottle of champagne and the party started out on a high note. They drank a toast to "the birthday girl". She felt wonderful! But she would only drink a small part of her champagne. She did not want to become light headed, today of all days.

They all studied the menus and when two of the others said they were having the blinis and caviar, Ruth joined in as well. It was a special treat that she and Michael had splurged on years ago. She never forgot how the waiter had swirled each blini in melted butter, then added a dollop of sour creme and a small portion of caviar. He used the tiny horn spoon for the caviar. Then he rolled it up and presented it on the plate with a flourish. Ruth had been as enchanted by the ritual and showmanship as she was delighted by the taste of the food. It was a gourmet treat.

They drank very hot sweet tea, served in tall glasses with silver handles, at the end of their meal. And Rachel had chosen a lovely apple tartin for dessert, complete with a candle for Ruth to wish on. It was a time to remember, she thought, surrounded by loving friends and sharing a memorable luncheon in a glamorous setting. She had worn her black wool crepe suit, grey satin blouse and the double strand pearl necklace. She felt sophisticated — the right choice for New York. In fact, she felt like one of the "ladies who lunch" , who were often described in the fashion columns. Ruth laughed out loud at that thought.

"What is tickling you," Rachel asked?

"I was thinking that we are the 'ladies who lunch' today. All decked out and drinking champagne and eating caviar. As if we do this every day."

"Maybe we should do this more often," Rachel responded.

"Here! Here!" A chorus arose from around the table.

It was after four when Ruth arrived home, feeling wonderfully fed and feted. There was a telephone message from Diane of birthday wishes and that pleased her. She had been more attentive the last time they were together. It was as if Diane finally realized that her generation had not invented women who worked outside the home.

She would take a rest and then call Annie and tell her about the luncheon. She was feeling quite tired after all the excitement. She didn't seem to have the energy to hang up her clothes and she lay them carefully on the chair instead. She put on her favorite challis nightgown and slipped between the welcoming sheets. Her eyes closed and Ruth slept.

When she awoke, it was dark outside and for a few moments, she felt disoriented. A glance at the bedside clock showed that it was past seven. Her nap had lasted over two hours. She would try to reach Annie.

"Annie, are you having dinner?"

"Not yet. David's going to be late. How was the birthday luncheon?"

"It was marvelous! We had champagne. And the blinis and caviar. We had the most fun!"

"It sounds wonderful, Mama."

"Rachel even had a birthday candle in the dessert, which was a delicious apple tartin."

"And did you make a wish and blow it out?"

"I certainly did. And I won't tell you what it was."

Ruth heard Annie laughing. "You'll never change, Mama. You are an original!"

"I'll take that as a compliment."

"I love you. And now you have to rest up for Sunday. Everyone is looking forward to it."

"I can hardly wait for Act II of this on-going birthday party."

"Jack and Lois are coming on Saturday. They'll stay with us."

"I'm planning a smashing outfit, Annie."

"You'll be the belle of the ball, Mama."

Ruth spent Friday and Saturday in low gear. She needed to recoup after the excursion to New York. She found that emotional excitement could deplete her energy level for days. What the psychologists called eu-stress, rather than distress. Highs as well as lows sapped her strength. She knew her body and when it needed to rest. She had talked this over at great length years ago with her doctor. He told her to be her own monitor. And she had followed his advice.

By Sunday morning, she was feeling stronger and ready for the party. David was coming to pick her up at 12:30. She had her usual breakfast, attacked the Sunday puzzle in *The Times* and had it half done by ten o'clock. She would compare notes with Tessa on some of the clues that had her stumped.

She had decided to wear the long paisley skirt and creme silk blouse. It was a perfect outfit for an at home afternoon party and she loved the swish of the skirt about her ankles. She chose her gold rope necklace and Mabe pearl and gold earrings. Michael had bought them for her 70th birthday. She treasured them and wore them only on high occasions. *This certainly was the right time.*

When Ruth arrived at the house with David, she felt excited, but somewhat tense. She didn't know if she could handle being the center of attention all afternoon. And when the children came running to greet her, she realized that she needed to sit down. Annie sensed what was happening and took over.

"Mama, come sit in the living room in your favorite chair. Children, give Grandma Ruth a chance to catch her breath. Then you'll give her a kiss and say, 'Happy Birthday'."

She led Ruth into the living room and helped her settle in the wing chair. Then she asked,

"Are you ready for the children?"

"I'm fine now, dear. Tell them to come in."

All the great grandchildren were assembled. Eric and Sally. Beth and Emily. And Ted who had flown in with Jack and Lois. They were a bit subdued and came one by one to give Ruth a kiss and to offer their birthday wishes.

Sally, as usual, was more exuberant in her greeting. She came with outstretched arms and reached around Ruth as far as she could go to deliver her best hug.

"Are you really 88 years old, Great Grandma?" she asked.

"I really am, Sally. Isn't that a lot of years?"

"Will there be 88 candles on your cake?"

"I don't think I could blow out that many. Would you help me?"

"We would all help you. That would be fun!"

Ruth's eyes were bright with emotion. She felt better than when she had walked in. The afternoon would be fine.

As it turned out, everyone took turns for one-on-one talks and that gave her a chance to be with each one for real sharing. Tessa brought her a plate of Annie's delicacies from the buffet and they sat at the dining room table. While they talked about the baby and opening the new office, Ruth thought of the Unicorn tapestry that was now finished and waiting for Tessa and Robert's anniversary to arrive. It was a precious secret for her. Tessa seemed confident and very happy with her new course in life. To Ruth, that was all that mattered. She had faced many challenges in her own life and had felt all the stronger when she had seen them through. She was sure Tessa would do the same.

After lunch, she had a chance to sit with Jack and Lois and hear about their lives in Chicago. She could sense from the way they finished each other's sentences that they complemented each other in their dispositions as well as their ideas. They shared glances and smiles as they talked. It had taken Jack a long time to find a woman who was truly compatible, Ruth knew. He was not the easiest man to live with, but Lois seemed to be very loving. And at the same time, she appeared to be her own woman. Ruth, of course, admired that quality in her — independence of spirit.

Diane came to sit with her and admired her earrings.

"They were a present from my husband on my 70th birthday."

"They're very beautiful. And your whole outfit. I would love to have that skirt myself!"

Annie had complimented her on her choice of clothing for the day as well.

"You look very chic, Mama. Like a Park Avenue hostess, I would say. That's a Brooke Astor outfit," Annie had said.

"Well, she has a few years on me, dear."

"And still going strong, from what I read. But then, so are you."

David served the champagne punch and Ruth sipped hers very slowly. At three thirty, he called all the adults and children into the living room and raised his glass to Ruth.

"To our dear mother, grandmother and great grandmother. You are brilliant, wise and generous of your spirit and your energy. You are a remarkable woman. We will always love , respect and treasure you. Happy Birthday!"

There was no way that Ruth could speak at that moment. Her eyes were filled with tears. David kissed her cheek softly and Annie came to her and sat on the ottoman, holding her hand. Everyone who was there that afternoon would remember Ruth Shaeffer's 88th birthday party and the toast that David had made to her. It was to become part of their family history.

Chapter 46

Annie called Ruth about ten on Monday morning to talk about the party. There was no answer. *She must be taking her bath,* she thought. When she tried again after eleven, and her mother did not pick up the phone, Annie felt a stab of alarm.

She would drive over and check to see that everything was fine. She would see the flower arrangements and they would sit and have a wonderful time going over all the details of her birthday party.

She rang the bell and waited. She rang it again and then took out the duplicate key she had to the apartment. Her heart was thudding as she walked in and called out, "Mama. It's Annie." There was no response. "Mama, are you alright?"

She walked through the dining room, past the exquisite Spring flowers her mother had arranged, to find Ruth lying on her side in her bed. Her head was propped on two pillows and she appeared to be sound asleep. Next to her bed on the end table was a white vase filled with eucalyptus. The spicy aroma filled the room. Annie bent down to kiss her cheek and her heart froze. Her mother's cheek was cold.

It was hard for Annie to remember later, exactly what happened next. She knew she had called 911. And David on his cell phone. Then, she just sat on the bed and held her mother's hand and wept.

She told David, when he met her in the Emergency Room, that the attendants had been very kind and very capable. She had gone in the ambulance and held her mother's hand. She realized later that they had not turned on the siren.

David spoke with the doctors who told him, "Mrs. Shaeffer had died before the ambulance arrived at her home." This had been verified at the hospital. Annie said that she didn't really want to know what had been the cause.

"It doesn't matter now, David — if it was a stroke. Or a heart attack. She's gone." She broke down into sobs. "My dear Mama is gone. I can't believe it!"

"I'm taking you home, Annie. I'll try to reach Jack at the airport. They have a one o'clock flight."

David drove Annie home and went up to his office to call the airport. Annie sat in the kitchen, huddled in one of the chairs. She still had her coat on. She couldn't move or think. Her mind and body were filled with lead. She felt very cold. David came downstairs and said, "I have a call into Jack at the airline counter. When they check in, I should be able to catch him."

Annie looked up. "It doesn't seem possible, David. She had such a wonderful time yesterday. We were all so happy together. She was so alive!"

He knelt next to her and put his arms about her. Then he took a deep breath and said,

"Can you think of a better way to go, Annie? She went out at the top of her game. You know she would never have wanted to be infirm or an invalid. She had the Living Will to make sure that no one kept her alive with "those contraptions", as she called them."

"I know all that is true. But right now, this moment, I can't even think that way. I only know she was here, laughing and having fun yesterday. Wearing the earrings my father gave her and teasing Sally about the 88 candles. It's too fast for me, David — I can't bear it!"

David went back up to make the necessary calls to the family. Annie sat and thought about her mother. She knew plans had to be made. But, not now. Not yet. A line from Auden, one of her mother's favorite poets flew into her mind. *"I thought that love would last forever: I was wrong."* It was from 'Funeral Blues'. Annie started to weep again.

She whispered, "Oh, Mama. My heart is breaking. I miss you so!"

Chapter 47

Ruth Shaeffer's funeral service took place on Wednesday morning, March 5, in the synagogue that she and Michael had joined when they moved to Teaneck. The day was clear with temperature in the 40's. Annie was grateful for the sun. She recalled vividly that it had rained the day of her father's funeral.

She did not wear black. She wore a dove grey suit her mother had always admired. It gave her a feeling of closeness. Everything was taken care of at home. Two of her friends would set out the food for when they would return to the house from the cemetery.

The rabbi had known her mother for almost twenty years. When he had visited with Annie and Jack and David on Tuesday in preparation for the service, he spoke of her with great respect and affection.

"Your mother was a remarkable woman. She never lost her intellectual curiosity. I guess that was the teacher in her. I enjoyed our conversations on so many subjects." Then he added, "Confidentially, she gave me ideas for more than one sermon."

"Did she ever tell you about 'Mrs. Shaeffer's Reading List', rabbi, and the furor it caused at Ridgewood High School?" Annie asked.

She wanted the rabbi to know what a fighter her mother had been. Not afraid to stand up for her principles. And usually victorious, as she had been at the highschool.

When the rabbi delivered his eulogy on Wednesday, he included that story. He called her a 'woman of valor'. Then, Tessa spoke on behalf of the family. She had insisted that she would be fine . She wanted to say how she felt about her grandmother. She told of the inspiration she had been as a woman ahead of her time. "Grandma Ruth never seemed to be afraid of doing something new. In fact, she loved a challenge. She helped me find my way this past year when I wasn't sure which direction to take." Tessa spoke simply and eloquently.

She ended with the soaring lines spoken by Juliet about Romeo. Tessa prefaced them by saying, "I have to speak about a woman rather than a man. I hope Grandma Ruth would have approved of my taking liberties with Shakespeare." Tessa looked directly at her mother as she began.

"When she shall die,
Take her and cut her out in little stars,
And she will make the face of heaven so fine
That all the world will be in love with night,
And pay no worship to the garish sun."

Annie was deeply moved. Yes, she thought, her mother would have approved. And she would have been very proud of Tessa at that moment. She looked at David and he had tears in his eyes too.

The service at the cemetery was brief. The immediate family sat under a green canopy as the rabbi recited the traditional prayers. They rose as he led the family in the mourners Kaddish. When the beautiful sandalwood casket was slowly lowered into the ground , Annie felt as if her heart was going with it. David had his arm about her shoulders and she could feel his strength — and his love supporting her. It was customary to take the shovel and throw some of the earth upon the casket. Jack went first and then handed the shovel to Annie. But she was not able to bring herself to do it. *I can't, Mama,* she thought. She passed the shovel to David, turned away and walked through the path formed by the other mourners. Tessa came with her and held her arm.

Annie sat on an ottoman in the living room. She would observe 'Shiva', the seven day period of mourning. Everyone had come back to the house from the cemetery and they had been greeted by her three little granddaughters. Eric and Ted had attended the funeral, but it was agreed that Sally, Beth and Emily were too young. It warmed Annie when Sally ran over and hugged her.

"Grandma, do you see I'm wearing the pinafore you gave me?"

"It's so pretty on you, Sally. And I love your hair in the two bunches."

They had talked about her being a big sister at the party on Sunday. Annie found it almost impossible to believe that it was only four days ago. The world had turned over for her since then.

She watched as small groups of people sat and talked as they balanced their plates. Her mother's close friends were there. Rachel and the other two women who had taken her to The Russian Tea Room were sitting near the windows. Rachel had been devastated when David called her. He didn't want her to find out by reading the obituary in the paper.

Tessa came and sat next to Annie.

"I brought the registry book and was just looking at the names, Mom. There are several I don't recognize. And there were people at the service I didn't know. Maybe, they are friends of yours or Dad's colleagues."

"I didn't really see all the people, Tessa. Just those who came up front before the service."

"One of the men handed me a note. I have it. Do you want to see it?"

"Later, dear. I'll read the notes and cards later. There'll be time for that all week. There'll be time."

Chapter 48

Annie moved through the week like a sleepwalker. Each day, the house was filled with family and friends. Bringing dinners. Special delicacies. Cakes. Fruit baskets arrived. And two beautiful vases of flowers. Letters and cards. An outpouring of affection and concern.

Annie and Jack, who was staying until Sunday, sat and talked about their childhood and their parents. She took out her photograph albums and they spent hours looking at the pictures. Annie sitting in the pear tree. Jack with the Victory Garden, holding up a bunch of scrawny carrots. The family, in bathing suits, on one of the outings to Cold Spring Lake. Their father in front of the pharmacy.

Tessa stayed overnight. It was easier than driving back and forth to Long Island. Robert, Saul and Diane came for several hours in the late afternoon, often with the children. Friends made condolence calls. Annie found all the company quite tiring and would excuse herself and go up to her bedroom to rest. David would insist at times that she did not have to "entertain". But, she wanted to talk about her mother. That was the purpose of the seven days, she said. To remember and to share the stories. She would take up the threads of her life again. But, not yet.

"It keeps Mama alive for me, David."

"I know, dear."

Annie read the sympathy cards and letters each day. Several were from her mother's former students at Ridgewood High School. She was particularly touched by what they wrote. "Your mother was my favorite teacher."

"Mrs. Shaeffer taught me how to think, as well as how to write."

"I loved the books on her reading list." She found the note that Tessa had given her from one of the men who had attended the funeral service. He was also a former student and what he wrote was very powerful. She shared it with Tessa.

Dear Mrs. Bertman,

I am greatly saddened by your mother's death. It is a fair statement to say that she changed my life. I was a very bored kid in highschool. And something of a troublemaker too. But, my grades were good enough, or I would not have been placed in her English class.

From the first day I walked through her door, I felt that I wanted to be in school.

She treated us as if we mattered. And our ideas mattered. She wanted us to do our best and held us to high standards. I would have to revise an essay over and over, with her notations as the guidelines. I began to understand what clear writing was. And clear thinking.

And the books she had us read were completely new to me. My mind was opened for the first time to literature. Those books were like gifts and I loved reading them!

People often say that one teacher changed their lives. Your mother did that for me.

I will never forget her.

With my deepest sympathy,
Richard L. Evans
Associate Professor of English
New York University

"He came to the funeral, Mom. He must have seen the obituary in The Bergen Record."

"I'm sorry I didn't have a chance to meet him, Tessa. I wonder if Mama ever knew how he felt and if she followed his career. I'll write him when I start sending out the thank you cards."

Tessa sorted the mail each day and opened the letters and cards for Annie. She looked up on Friday and asked, "Do you know a Mark Trianos?" Annie felt a stab of sweetness. She would not deny knowing him. "He's a man I met when I used to go to the gym. An artist." Tessa replied, "I'm not surprised.

This is one of those beautiful cards with a Marc Chagall painting on the front."

As Annie took the card, she remembered how she had told Mark about her mother's family coming from Poland. The Chagall painting captured the icons of the old country with exuberance and bright primary colors. Annie and Mark had talked about those qualities in Chagall's work. He had signed the card, "With deepest sympathy, Mark Trianos." He had kept it impersonal. Just signing it 'Mark' would have raised questions. She was very grateful for that. And she was moved that he had found a way to reach her. To tell her he knew she was grieving. And that he was thinking of her.

Jack flew home on Sunday and Annie insisted that Tessa go home to her family.

"I'll be fine, dear. You need to be home with Robert and the children. This has been a hard week for them as well without you there."

"I'll go with you to Grandma Ruth's apartment whenever you are ready, Mom. It can wait until next month, you know. There's no law saying you have to go right away."

"I know, Tessa. Dad and I have already agreed that we'll just pay the rent until I'm ready to tackle closing the apartment."

There was only one thing Annie wanted to find sooner in the apartment — the needlepoint of The Unicorn Tapestry. The gift for Tessa and Robert's anniversary. She knew her mother had finished it several weeks ago. And that she would not have taken it to be framed. She would have left that as a matter of choice for Tessa, depending upon where she planned to hang it. Annie was pretty sure she knew where her mother would have put it for safe keeping. Their anniversary was in May, but Annie wanted to give it to Tessa before then. It would take away some of the sharp sense of loss. She would go with David next week and look for the tapestry.

Chapter 49

After the Shiva week was over, Annie said Kaddish every morning when she was alone in the bedroom. She would also read one of the prayers that expressed grief and some days she cried. She felt a deep well of emptiness in her heart. She knew it would heal, but the pain of missing her mother was terrible. She missed hearing her voice. And seeing her face. Her presence.

"I miss you so — Mama," she would say aloud in the empty room.

In trying to comfort her, some of the visitors last week had emphasized the many years her mother had lived. And that "it was a blessing that she did not suffer". At times, Annie wanted to shout in anger. "Just tell me you're sorry. Don't try to rationalize her death for me! None of that changes the fact that she is gone!"

But, she had controlled herself and had not lashed out. She knew they were well meaning. She had learned that after her father had died. And she had never offered those words to mourners since that time. Her close friends spoke of the relationship Annie had with her mother. "You were a wonderful daughter, Annie. You brought her great happiness." And Sarah had written, "You enriched her life for all those years, Annie. Don't ever forget that!" These were the words that brought her comfort.

She turned to her writing again to try to regain her emotional footing. The next interview in the series would be a woman in her seventies. She skimmed the group of respondents and found someone who sounded promising. She was a breast cancer survivor and lived an active life in New Orleans. Annie felt the background of the city would add zest to the story. She would weave in Dixieland jazz and Preservation Hall. She called her and introduced the idea of the article.

David resumed his normal schedule of office hours and deliveries in the middle of the night. Annie went back to taking her three mile walks in the morning. March turned out to be mild, and she saw the daffodils blooming in sheltered places along the way. Her own garden needed some attention, and she spent time each day doing clean-up. Picking up the branches and twigs that had fallen from the oak trees and pruning the dead growth on the azalea bushes. She loved Spring and especially this year, it gave her a needed sense of rebirth.

She was most thankful that Tessa's pregnancy was going smoothly. Since she had left her job in New York, she was free to concentrate on opening her new office. Tessa had been the dearest of daughters after her grandmother's death. And Annie had written her a special letter to express her appreciation. She said that Tessa's eulogy at the funeral and her devotion during Shiva were " the loving links between the generations".

Annie asked David to go with her to her mother's apartment one Saturday when she felt she could handle it. The birthday cards were still set out on the dining room table. The flowers were dead in the vases and a sour odor hung in the air from them. Annie felt sick to her stomach.

"I'm not sure I can do this, David."

"Where do you think she would have put the tapestry? I'll look for it. You go back outside and get some air."

"I'll be alright. My guess is here in the big drawer of the server. She kept her best tablecloths there."

Annie opened the drawer and on the top was the tapestry, rolled and wrapped in beautiful floral paper. The note, addressed to Tessa lay beside it. Annie lifted it gently and left the apartment. David said he would follow in about five minutes. He wanted to throw away the flowers and air out the dining room.

Annie sat in the car, holding the tapestry. She thought of the many colors her mother had woven into the needlepoint. The intricate design and beauty — her metaphor for life. And the flaw. Yes, the flaw in the tapestry. Life was not perfect! Her mother had foreseen everything.

She would give it to Tessa on Passover at the end of the month. The first Seder was always held at their house with the entire family. It was a time of hope and renewal. The celebration of the Exodus and of Springtime. That would be a wonderful time to present the tapestry. Annie felt her mother would have agreed.

Before Passover, there was another family event that lifted Annie's spirits. Tessa had the ultrasound test and they discovered that the baby was a girl. She had told her mother that Sally, in particular, had been fascinated by the picture. Then Sally came to the telephone and announced, "Grandma, I just saw the baby and she's very little. I'm the big sister already!" Annie laughed out loud for the first time since her mother's death.

Annie found that preparing for Passover was good for her. Making the matzoh balls and chicken soup. Chopping up the nuts and apples for the charoseth. All the traditional foods took time and they were a form of therapy, she thought. We go through the motions and we begin to feel better. She set the table as always with her best china, crystal and sterling silver. The Haggadahs, the booklets that told the story of the Exodus, were at each place. The children would all sit at the big table. It was really their night to take part and ask questions. To taste the bitter herbs that symbolized being slaves in Egypt. And the charoseth that looked like the bricks in the pyramids that the Israelites built for Pharaoh.

David conducted the Seder and everyone took part, reading passages from the Haggadah. As they took turns around the table, Annie felt the absence of her mother very sharply. She had loved the Seder and had read certain psalms each year. It was a highlight of their family tradition. Annie could almost hear her clear voice reading the words. David had asked Annie if she wanted to read the psalms, but she found, when the time came, that she wasn't able to do it. She asked Tessa to read the first psalm and Saul, the other. Perhaps, next year, she would read them. Not tonight.

After dinner, which was deemed delicious and proven by the large quantities of food that were consumed, Tessa said that she and Robert wanted to make an announcement.

"We thought this would be the perfect time to tell you that the baby girl who will be born into our family this summer will be named Ruth, in honor of our beloved grandmother."

Annie's eyes were moist as she rose to go to Tessa and embrace her. And she decided that she would wait to give her the tapestry. This was too wonderful a moment. It needed to be savored.

David raised his glass of wine. "Please join me in a toast to Ruth Shaeffer and to her great granddaughter — who will carry on her name."

Chapter 50

May 5 was the date Tessa set for the official opening of her new law office. The newspaper ads would run weekly during April. She and Robert had met at a furniture showroom to choose her desk and file cabinets. They were a dark burnished cherry and very expensive. Robert's reaction was, "You are going to have the best there is. When clients walk in, I want them to be impressed!" And he added with a sly smile, "Besides, I get an industry discount." Tessa was very pleased. She wasn't going to argue with him.

The following week, they had gone to his warehouse together and she had selected the leather couches and chairs for the waiting room.

"I don't want black, Robert. Every law office I see has black leather."

"That's fine. Why not navy blue for the couches and camel on the armchairs? Elegant!"

"I like it. It's a classic combination. You know your business, sir."

"I should hope so. I've been in it long enough. And Dad wanted you to have the top of the line."

The painter was hired and the nubby twist carpet she had selected would be laid as soon as he was finished. The pieces were falling into place.

Tessa felt fine physically. And every Monday, when she awoke and realized that she didn't have to take the train into the city to wrestle with Tom Simmons, she was elated. She had come out of the shock of her grandmother's sudden death. Now, she would work through the grieving for her. That would take time. Tessa felt saddened that Grandma Ruth would never see her office. That was a milestone they would not share. But naming the baby for her was a wonderful tribute. And it gave Tessa comfort.

The ultrasound picture had been a big event for the children. They had each reacted, of course, in their own way. Sally was dazzled that it was really a picture of the baby inside her mother. And proof that she would indeed be the big sister. Eric, gave his approval again with another "That's cool!" pronouncement. Cryptic but significant words in his world.

Tessa was beginning to line up clients even before she opened her doors officially. She was working on the divorce case, And she had been approached by another woman who felt she needed a restraining order to protect herself and her children from an abusive husband. A third call had related to reviewing and updating a will. She would begin with the cases that came her way. Later, as her practice evolved, she might concentrate on a particular niche. She had studied other legal ads. Some offered a laundry list: 'Wills. Estate Planning. Powers of Attorney. Medicare and Medicaid. Elder Care. Tax. Business. Real Estate. Litigation." She had kept hers simple with six areas. "Real Estate. Tax. Business. Divorce. Wills. Litigation."

She knew from her work with Ryder &Simmons which kinds of law could bring in the big fees. She wanted some of that work. But she definitely wanted to practice the kinds of law that affected women's lives directly. And she knew that the catch-all of 'Litigation' would also include civil rights issues, a subject dear to her heart. Tessa felt excited with the wide open prospects ahead of her.

In mid April, she felt the baby move for the first time. She was in bed, getting ready to go to sleep. She sat up and called loudly to Robert, who was brushing his teeth in the bathroom.

"Robert! Come here! She's moving around!"

He rushed in with some toothpaste still in his mouth.

"Feel!" she declared triumphantly.

He did and grabbed her in a huge embrace. Then he ran back, rinsed out his mouth and returned to feel the baby again. Tessa was beaming. She had her hand on her abdomen.

"It was just a little kick. But I felt it."

"She's on her way!"

"Wait till Sally feels her moving around. She will completely flip out!"

"I'm not sure Eric will want to take part in this. We'll let him take his time."

Tessa laughed. "It's all wonderful, my love. I feel great! I'm so happy. And you're happy. What could be better?"

Robert reached over to turn off the bed lamp and answered her question, "Better would be if I showed you just how happy I am." Tessa reached up to pull him down next to her. They had enjoyed making love these past months with new found freedom and passion.

"You are more beautiful than ever, Tessa baby. I do adore you."

"I love you, Robert. Being married to you has brought me so much happiness."

He kissed her the way she loved to be kissed and there was no need to say anything else.

Chapter 51

Annie was getting dressed to meet Tessa for lunch in New York. Tessa wanted to go to the art galleries in Soho to look for paintings for her office. Annie felt it would also be a perfect day to bring the tapestry and give it to her. She had chosen one of her favorite restaurants in the East 60's. She wanted a beautiful formal atmosphere for the presentation. This was not the time for one of the trendy 'in' places. They were usually too stark and too crowded. They would take a cab downtown after lunch and browse the galleries.

Annie arrived first and went to their table. The tapestry was in a Saks shopping bag. She would wait until after lunch to give it to her. Tessa arrived, wearing a gorgeous smile and a black pants suit. She kissed her mother and sat down in the comfortable arm chair. The waiter hovered just enough to make sure she was settled.

"Guess what, Mom? The baby moved!"

Annie beamed. "I want to jump up and run around the table to feel!"

"Control yourself," Tessa said. "You'll have plenty of feels."

"You know I'm a demonstrative grandmother."

They both laughed in agreement. Tessa said, "Let's order. I'm ravenous."

Their lunch choices turned out to be marvelous. Tessa had wild mushroom ravioli with a sauce that she said, was "to die for". Annie tried 'intoxicated salmon' with a bourbon glaze. She described it in superlative terms. They both had decaffeinated coffee and skipped dessert.

"I have to keep my weight down, Mom. Even though I adore sweets, as you know."

As they sipped their coffee, Annie felt the time was right to present the tapestry.

"Tessa, I have a surprise for you. It's something Grandma Ruth made for you. She was going to give it to you and Robert on your anniversary."

Tessa had paled when Annie spoke and Annie became concerned.

"I didn't want to upset you dear. Get your breath. Let's just sit a while. If you want me to wait for another time. I will. I don't have to do this today."

"It's all right, Mom. It just came a little fast, when you said that. I feel fine."

"You know that Grandma Ruth was a whiz with her hands. She crocheted the beautiful carriage robe and hat that the new baby will wear. And she did her needlepoint, of course. Well, she did a very beautiful needlepoint for you. Are you ready?"

"I'm ready, Mom."

Annie took out the tapestry and handed it across the table to Tessa. She watched as she untied the ribbon and tore open the floral paper. Then, Tessa slowly unrolled the tapestry and held it up with both hands. It was large — 36 x 24. People at the adjacent tables looked over. Tessa appeared to be overwhelmed.

"It's the Unicorn Tapestry! The one at the Cloisters Museum. We saw it together when I was a little girl."

"Yes. She knew how you had loved it. And she wanted you to have it— to see and enjoy every day."

"It is so very beautiful. The colors! The greens and the blues and the cremes. And the work she did! The fine stitches. I can't get over it. Mom."

Tessa rolled it up and started to cry. Annie took it from her and waited until the tears eased.

"It was a true labor of love, dear. And there's something else special about it, besides its remarkable beauty. She explained that for you in a note she wrote."

Annie handed Tessa the ecru envelope to open. As she read it, Tessa's eyes filled with tears again. When she had finished, she gave it back to Annie to read. Annie felt a sharp pang when she saw her mother's familiar handwriting.

My darling Tessa,

I remembered so well that you loved The Unicorn Tapestry when we visited The Cloisters years ago. You were enchanted by the figures and the colors. I told you the story behind it and you thought it was wonderful. It held mystery and magic for you as it has for generations.

As I have been working on it, I have seen something special in the intricacy and beauty of the design and the colors. You know how I love metaphors. I guess that is part of all the years that I was an English teacher. Well, I believe the tapestry is a metaphor for life in its intrinsic beauty, complexity and aura of mystery. It's all there, when you study it, as I have these months of doing the needlepoint. I've loved doing it, Tessa. Every minute. Every stitch!

And I carried the metaphor one step further. If you look very carefully at the border, you will find a place where I reversed the green and blue threads. The design goes the other way. That's the flaw in the tapestry. I learned that years ago when a weaver of oriental carpets told me that, "A carpet cannot be perfect. Only God is perfect!" They deliberately weave a error or flaw into the design of a handwoven carpet. I love that concept. And I saw a further interpretation of my metaphor of the tapestry as life. The flaw represents the surprises that occur, some good and some bad, and the mistakes, choices and consequences that we face. Life, I have learned these many years, is not perfect. Thus, the tapestry cannot be perfect.

I hope you and Robert enjoy The Unicorn tapestry for many years to come. It is my gift to you, dear granddaughter. It is also a symbol of the love we share for each other.

Always, Grandma Ruth

Annie reached across the table to hold Tessa's hand. Neither one of them spoke. She felt her mother's loving presence very deeply. And she knew Tessa would keep the letter forever. It was part of the legacy that her grandmother had left her. Someday Tessa would share it with the baby who was to be named for her — little Ruth who was starting to make herself felt in the world.

Annie smiled at Tessa. The circle was complete. The metaphor was true.

Epilogue

On the Sunday after Tessa's open house for her new law office, Annie arranged to meet her in SoHo for lunch and an afternoon of browsing in the shops and art galleries. It was mid May and Spring had arrived with a flourish. The white dogwoods were in full flower and the deep blue bearded Iris stood tall against the base of the oak trees.

As Annie drove into the city, she thought of how happy Tessa had been and how impressive the office had looked. There had been a good mix of friends and family at the open house, as well as several clients Tessa was working with already.

On the large wall facing her desk, Tessa had hung The Unicorn Tapestry — set off with a cream linen mat and a heavy, burnished gold frame. She said that she wanted it to be where she could look up and see it every day. "I love the beauty of it. And I remember Grandma Ruth whenever I see it. But I also know where the flaw is in the border, for days when things are not perfect!"

Annie and Tessa met in a cafe with a tolerable noise level. They ate salads and spent an hour talking about the open house and Tessa's plans for the future. After lunch, they began their stroll at a leisurely pace. The day was balmy. The streets were busy. They would stop at times and go into a shop or gallery.

Tessa saw the card first, propped up on an easel in one of the gallery windows. It announced the work of "Mark Trianos. Oils and Pastels" . When she saw it, she called her mother's attention to it. "Mark Trianos. That must be the man who sent you the condolence note. Your friend from the gym. You said he was an artist."

Annie felt her heart drop. She hadn't really thought of Mark in the weeks since her mother's death. She had closed that chapter of her life and moved on. Her emotions had been centered on coming through the grief and loss she felt. David had been there for her as he had in the past and she deeply appreciated his love and support.

"Let's go in," Tessa said. She turned to Annie. "Are you coming. Mom?"

"Yes, I'm coming," Annie answered.

The gallery was mid-size and the walls were lined with paintings. Annie recognized most of them. The series of nudes that Mark had done of his wife, the paintings that had caused such a furor with her relatives. And the large abstract oils. There were several new ones that Annie did not remember. Mark was standing with his back to the door, talking with a couple looking at one of the abstract paintings.

Just beyond him on an easel was an oil of a nude woman reclining on a couch. Sunlight was filtered through gauzy curtains and her face was in shadows. Her body, painted in lush shades of soft pinks and amber, was rounded and seductive. Her pose was relaxed, as if she were waiting for her lover. The title of the work was 'Autumn Afternoon'.

Annie felt a shock wave when she saw the picture. Tessa saw it at the same time, and exclaimed, "What a gorgeous painting!" As she walked over to it, Mark turned and saw them. He excused himself from the couple and came to greet them, extending his hand to Annie as he approached.

"Annie. So good to see you here. Thank you for coming."

Annie, feeling numb, introduced Tessa to Mark. "This is my daughter, Tessa Bertman. She spotted your card in the window."

"I love this painting, Mr. Trianos," Tessa said. "The mood, the colors. It is very beautiful."

"Thank you. It's one of my latest works."

Annie found that words would not come. She stood looking at the painting, seeing the the afternoon as it was, the light coming through the windows. Mark was watching her quietly.

He addressed Tessa, "May I show you the rest of the paintings?"

"I would like that."

They moved off and Annie stood in front of 'Autumn Afternoon', fighting with her emotions. Part of her was angry that he had done this. Part of her was thrilled that he had painted her with such exquisite tenderness. Only they knew who the woman was. Her face was completely hidden in the shadows.

When Tessa returned, Mark had moved back to the couple and the large abstract oil.

"He really is talented, Mom. I don't understand the abstract paintings but the pastels are marvelous. That series of nudes is really something. And I love 'Autumn Afternoon'. It has an air of mystery and romance."

Annie smiled. "Yes, it does. It's very lovely."

"Would you consider buying it?" Tessa asked. "I don't see a price tag on it."

"No, dear I'm not thinking of buying it."

"Well, I'm going to ask him the price. I'm curious."

Tessa went over to Mark while Annie waited. When she returned, there was a somewhat surprised look on her face. "Do you know what he said, Mom? He said he was sorry, but that painting was not for sale." Annie smiled and gave a small shrug. "Artists do that, sometimes."

Printed in the United States
32555LVS00007B/1-63

9 781413 764871